SHATTERED DREAMS
by Laura Landon

PRAIRIE MUSE PLATINUM
www.prairiemuse.com

Brentan Montgomery, Earl of Charfield is convinced he'll never fall in love – until he meets Lady Elyssa Prescott. Now, his greatest fear is that Elly will discover the lie that brought him into her life and his deceit will shatter their dreams for happiness.

Lady Elyssa Prescott has accepted her future...a solitary woman living on the remote fringes of society. When her muzzled heart is captivated by a man who refuses to see her deformity, she nearly begins to trust that she, too, might be allowed to dream.

Harrison Prescott, Marquess of Fellingsdown, finds himself in the precarious predicament of having to rectify a foibled escapade conceived by his twin siblings. But in so doing, he places his crippled sister's heart in harm's way. And midst it all, his own crippled heart comes face to face with **Lady Cassandra Waverley**, whose betrayal cost him his own first love.

Four vibrant souls...four shattered dreams. Four lives masterfully interwoven into a tale you've come to expect from Laura Landon.

———

For my dear friend *Mary Schwaner*
because without her help, none of this would be possible.

Also by Laura Landon
MORE THAN WILLING
SHATTERED DREAMS
and coming December 2010
WHEN LOVE IS ENOUGH

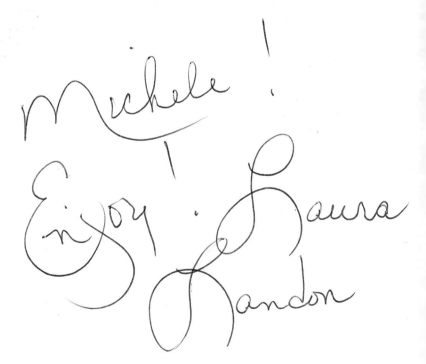

SHATTERED DREAMS
Copyright © 2010 by Laura Landon
First print edition
ISBN 978-0-9830741-0-6

CHAPTER 1

Fellings Down, England
April 6, 1858

Brentan James Montgomery, Earl of Charfield, brought his prized chestnut Arabian, Danza, to a halt at the top of the ridge overlooking the Duke of Sheridan's country manor, Fellings Down. He sat for several long seconds, unable to breathe. The view before him was magnificent.

Fellings Down wasn't Sheridan's family seat and Brent wasn't sure why he'd assumed The Down, as everyone referred to it, would be smaller and less significant. Nothing further from the truth. The question was why neither the duke nor any of his children had entertained here before. It wasn't that The Down was inferior in any way.

A beautiful, four-story stone mansion sat atop the rise in front of him. The structure exemplified the strength and elegance for which the Duke of Sheridan and his family were known. Breathtaking lawns and gardens flanked the U-shaped manor house. The lush expanse of vivid color was the most spectacular display Brent had ever seen.

But the blooming flowers and perfectly manicured bushes weren't what interested him most.

Somewhere concealed within The Down, Harrison Prescott, Marquess of Fellingsdown, heir to the Sheridan dukedom, kept his prize possessions – his stable of magnificent Arabian horses.

Brent's heart raced at the thought of seeing them close up. His heart thundered even faster when he thought of the payment that would be forthcoming when the next two weeks concluded.

Brent still couldn't believe Fellingsdown had made such an offer. Although the two had attended school together and competed with each other academically, they'd never been what either of them considered close friends. Nor had they been rivals. They'd simply been paired together because of their above-average intelligence.

Which was why he was still surprised that Fellingsdown had made him such a spectacular offer - breeding rights to Fellingsdown's prize Arabian, El Solidar. All that was required of him was to shower Fellingsdown's reclusive sister with enough attention during their two week house party that she would forget a man with whom her family refused to allow her to become involved.

At first, Brent thought Fellingsdown intended to offer him a colt from El Solidar if he'd *marry* the sister. He'd broken out in a cold sweat knowing how close he was to realizing his dream of owning a colt sired by one of Fellingsdown's prized Arabians only to give it up.

But give it up he would - if being forced to marry was the

only means to get the one thing he'd always dreamed of having.

For an offspring from one of Fellingsdown's magnificent Arabians, Brent would have walked through hell and back. But he refused to marry, especially a woman he didn't love.

To his surprise, Fellingsdown had offered him a prize Arabian colt if he'd simply entertain his sister for the next two weeks.

Brent thought he'd met all of Fellingsdown's siblings at one time or another and considered each of them quite handsome by even the strictest standards. This one must not have inherited the others' good looks. Or their sharp wit.

Well, he didn't care if she had three chins and a dozen hairy moles on her face. All he had to do was be her devoted companion for the next two weeks and the next colt Danza gave him would be sired by El Solidar.

Brent relaxed in his saddle and looked again at his destination. He might as well go down and join the festivities. Welsley, his valet, should be there already, and the sooner Brent met his host and was introduced to the sister he'd been hired to woo away from an unsavory suitor, the sooner he could get this over.

His horse had only taken a few steps toward The Down when a movement to the left caught his eye.

At first he thought one of Fellingsdown's horses had gotten loose and was running through the countryside. But the horse wasn't alone. A small rider sat atop the mammoth bay, her head and body hunched over the horse while her skirts flapped in her wake. The female must have lost control of her mount because the horse was traveling at a speed far faster than any woman he knew would dare to ride.

"Bloody hell," he murmured as he nudged Danza to a run.

If he didn't race toward her, but aimed for a point in front of her, he should be able to cut her off before her horse reached the open meadow. After that, nothing would slow the horse down until it reached a low thicket over which he'd have to leap. But Brent doubted if the huge Arabian would have a rider on his back by then.

He let Danza race at full speed, knowing that if any horse could catch the bay, it was this one. But as he neared the runaway horse, a niggling of something he couldn't explain clawed at his insides.

The rider didn't seem in danger of losing her seat. In fact, the slender form seemed at one with her mount. And there was something strange about the position of her hands. She wasn't clutching the horse's neck in order to stay upright, but sat secure in the saddle, as if she rode with a natural balance honed to perfection over the years.

Something deep inside him wanted to doubt that what he was seeing could be real. He'd seen many expert horsewomen ride through Hyde Park on spirited horses, many of them sitting a saddle as well as any man. But never had he seen anyone ride this expertly. Or this confidently.

He kept his gaze locked on her slender form. She'd lost her riding hat long ago, or she'd never had one, and her long auburn hair blew free in the breeze. The sight was as intoxicatingly ethereal as anything he'd ever seen. A greater sense of protectiveness, as well as wonder, clutched his gut and refused to let go.

He pushed Danza harder, convinced he had to catch up with her before she reached the hedge. A part of him still couldn't believe any female would dare ride at this speed toward a hedge the horse would have to jump. Surely no sane person would take such a chance. Especially one so delicate and feminine.

He lowered his head and closed the distance between them. He was almost near enough to reach out for her if it was necessary to snatch her from her horse. That was clearly his intent – until she turned her head.

Their horses raced neck and neck. Brent moved Danza closer, determined to do whatever it took to protect her.

He focused his gaze on the vision beside him and she looked at him.

Their gazes locked and he was struck by the most remarkable sensation he'd ever experienced.

Her face was more perfect than that of an angel. Her features more delicate. Her cheeks a rosy-hued pink, flushed from the excitement of the race.

She pursed her lips to evidence her determination. But it was the color and shape of her eyes that speared through him. His breath caught and for just a fraction of a second, his heart skipped a beat.

Her eyes were huge, big and round and colored a brown so dark they seemed black. Brent knew the excitement of the race had turned them dark and a certainty flashed through his mind that they would be this same color at the height of passion.

Except, it wasn't the size of her eyes or the rich color that caused him such hesitation, but the expression in them when she looked at him. She spoke to him with only a look. But she wasn't sending him a message. Or a plea for help.

She was daring him to race her.

She issued her challenge with a gleam in her eyes. Her confident expression defied him to ignore her.

"Bloody hell," he may or may not have said out loud. He wasn't sure. All he knew was that she seemed to know the instant he accepted her challenge because...

...she smiled.

The sun had been shining but not as brightly as now.

The air had been clean and fresh but not as clear and refreshing as now.

The grass in the meadow had been verdant and green, but not as lush as now.

And all because of a smile.

For the briefest of seconds he lost his concentration. As if the chit knew her effect on him, she took advantage of his hesitation and seized the lead.

He raced to catch up with her. Their horses matched stride for stride, each long reach of their muscular legs eating the distance between where they'd started and the hedge he knew had been her goal from the beginning.

They raced forward, the sound of the horses' thundering hooves hitting the ground in unison. The huffing from their sturdy lungs exploding in the air.

Arabians were known for their courage and endurance. They were, without a doubt, the most powerful breed of horse known to man. Yet this small, fragile wisp of a woman showed no fear. She rode with the confidence of master to servant, in complete control of the mighty beast. An overwhelming sense of admiration and respect engulfed him, battling with a strange emotion he couldn't explain.

Together they raced toward the hedge that blocked their path. Brent had never felt this great a sense of exhilaration in his entire life. He didn't think his blood had ever rushed through his veins as fast or furiously as it was doing right now.

Together, as one, the riders and their horses neared the hedge. Without hesitation, they took the initial leap that lifted their front legs from the ground. At the same instant their powerful rear legs gave a mighty push that propelled them through the air.

As one, they cleared the hedge.

Time stood still. It was as if he, the beautiful woman beside him, and the two magnificent horses beneath them were suspended in midair. As if time halted and every exhilarating emotion he'd ever experienced came back to revisit, only this time a hundred times more intensely. And still he soared through the air, the height of excitement continuing to build within him.

Together their horses reached the apex of their jump, then held. For what seemed a thousand remarkable seconds, time froze. Then, with a euphoric rush, they began their descent.

Their landing was smooth, almost as perfect a conclusion as the journey. Nothing could compare with what he'd just experienced.

The hedge was behind them now and ahead of them a thick grove of trees formed a barrier to the meadow clearing. He sensed the woman slow her horse and followed suit.

They both galloped a short distance farther, giving their horses a chance to recover their wind, then she stopped and he pulled alongside her.

She turned to him, her huge, dark eyes shining with excitement, her cheeks colored even deeper, her full lips open to give him the most exuberant smile he'd ever received. And she spoke, her voice so deep and rich he knew if he ever fell under her spell he'd be lost forever.

"That was marvelous!" she said with more unbridled

enthusiasm than he'd heard from a woman in his whole life. "*You* were marvelous! Your *horse* was marvelous! Oh, I haven't enjoyed anything so much in...forever!"

Brent stared at her in wide-eyed wonder as a rush of molten heat surged to every part of his body. He felt as if he'd been struck by something more powerful than lightning. She was, without a doubt, the most beautiful woman he'd ever seen. Being near her, listening to her voice, seeing the excitement in her eyes, drowning in such a wide, inviting smile, affected him like he'd never been affected before.

"*I* was marvelous?" he asked, unable to believe she'd complimented him. "You matched me stride for stride. You took that hedge as if it were nothing more than a bump across the road."

He leaned back in his saddle and looked into her face. Never before had he met anyone who possessed such grace, such beauty. It was as if she were an extension of the horse beneath her. "That was the most expert horsemanship I've ever witnessed. Where did you learn to ride like that?"

She blessed him with another open smile. The laugh that followed sent him soaring through the heavens.

"It's not hard when you have such a magnificent horse to help you. You just give him his lead and let him have his way."

"We both know it's more than that."

"Perhaps, but I was fortunate enough to grow up around them." She patted her Arabian's neck lovingly. "Most of my youth was spent in the stables. It doesn't take long for each one of these magnificent creatures to turn into your best friend and you theirs. The bond between you is something people who aren't fortunate enough to own an Arabian don't understand."

He was alive! For the first time in his life he'd met someone who valued the same things that were important to him. Someone who had the same love he had.

"Are you a guest of Fellingsdown's?" Brent asked, knowing from her inexpensive attire she wasn't, but not wanting to imply that being part of the staff who cared for Fellingsdown's Arabian's was demeaning in any way. If the duties that went with his title weren't so demanding, there would be nothing he'd like better than to spend every hour of every day with his horses.

She laughed. "No, I'm hardly a guest."

"And Fellingsdown allows you to ride his prized horses?"

There was a gleam of mischief in her eyes that made him want to laugh.

"You might say it's my job."

"Then I envy you."

Her perfectly shaped eyebrows arched in the most expressive manner. "Why?"

"Because your time is your own. For as much as I'm certain I'll enjoy my stay here, there's nothing I'd rather do than have time every day for riding."

"Hopefully, then, Lord Fellingsdown won't occupy so much of your time that you won't find time to ride. It would be a shame to ignore such a magnificent horse."

"Yes, it would."

She moved her reins as if she intended to leave and he was desperate not to let her go without setting a time to meet her again. "Do you go to the stables often?" he asked.

"Yes. Every day. About this time."

"Perhaps we will meet again."

"Perhaps."

"And perhaps I can challenge you to another race."

She smiled and his blood turned hot.

"I look forward to it."

"May I escort you back?" He wanted an excuse to spend a few more moments with her.

She shook her head, but there was nothing shy or demure in her look. "I have an errand to run before I return."

"Very well." Reluctantly, he turned his mount toward the house. "Until next time."

She didn't say more and he left her, thinking of the one stipulation the Marquess of Fellingsdown had made – that Brent woo their recluse sister away from her knight in shining armor without breaking her heart.

He wanted to laugh. There wasn't a chance in hell he could possibly be attracted to Fellingsdown's sister. Or that he would allow her to become attracted to him.

Not when he'd just met the most perfect woman on earth.

CHAPTER 2

"Is everything ready?"

Harrison Prescott, Marquess of Fellingsdown, looked at the three people in the room: his twin sisters, Patience and Lillian, the youngest of the Prescott brood, and George, his closest brother both in age and all else that mattered. His remaining brothers, Jules and Spence, were handling the arrival of the guests while he covered the last-minute details for the upcoming two-week house party.

Harrison studied the serious expressions on the faces of his twin sisters and for the first time in his life he wasn't moved by their remarkable beauty or their endearing innocence. His having to host the two-week event at The Down was their fault. They deserved his terse tone and ill temper.

Patience spoke first. "Yes. The guests have begun to arrive and are being shown to their rooms. Jules and Spence are playing hosts until we return."

Harrison studied the list on the top of his desk. Dear God,

but he prayed this went well. If it didn't...

"Is Elly ready?"

Patience and Lillian slowly turned their heads and looked at one another.

A wave of concern washed over him. "What?"

"She isn't here," Patience said.

"She must be out riding," Lillian added.

"Damn! You were supposed to keep an eye on her today. You were supposed to make sure she stayed close."

Patience and Lillian both blanched at his rare use of profanity and his reprimand but he didn't care. This was their fault. If they hadn't...

"She'll be back soon," Patience said. "She promised she'd be ready when it was time to go down to meet the guests."

Harrison raked his fingers through his hair in frustration. "You know how she loses track of time when she's riding. We'll be lucky if she returns by dark."

"Don't worry, Harrison," Lillian added. "Elly knows how important this is to you."

"To me! We're doing this for *her*! Which we wouldn't have to do if you two hadn't been so irresponsible!"

"Harrison," George warned.

Tears pooled in his sisters' eyes but he ignored them.

"We've already told you how sorry we are," Patience said boldly. "We only wanted Elly to be happy."

Harrison shoved back his chair and bolted to his feet. He braced his palms on the top of the desk and leaned toward them. "Just because the two of you have fallen in love and have married doesn't mean Elly has the same dream."

"Every woman does," Lillian cried out. "We simply wanted her to know what it was like to have someone remarkable pay attention to her. We wanted her to feel special. And wanted."

"How could you think creating an admirer who doesn't exist would make her happy?"

"We had to do something," Lilly said in a rare show of bravery. "She's never even had a beau. She only hides away here at The Down."

He slammed his fist on the top of his desk. "You make it sound like Elly's starved for attention, that she's been locked away in the country because we don't want her around us." Harrison stepped around the corner of the desk. "Plenty of people pay attention to her. She receives more love and attention than any other woman in England. *Male* attention, I might add."

"But the four of you are her brothers!" Lillian cried out. "That's not the same!"

Harrison gave his sister a hostile look that made her shrink back, no doubt wanting to run into her husband's comforting arms. But the Earl of Berkingham wasn't here. Only he and George and the two females who'd caused this travesty. "For the life of me," he continued, "I can't imagine what in *hell* possessed you to do something so irresponsible."

"We wanted Elly to have a romance," Patience repeated for the hundredth time. "We wanted her to know someone thought she was special."

"By allowing her to give her heart to someone who doesn't exist?" Harrison waved the letters that were the cause of their problem.

"We never imagined it would go this far," Patience, always the braver of the two, answered.

"Just where did you imagine a correspondence like this would end? Didn't you think for one second that Elly would eventually want to meet this—" Harrison crushed the love letters in his fist and threw them into the fire. "—this...paragon of virtue and masculinity?"

"No," they answered together.

"Elly's never shown any interest in men," Patience continued. "Not that it would have been possible the way the four of you stand guard over her."

"Just what do you mean by that?"

Harrison thought of their two brothers who were downstairs, Jules and Spence. They were both tall and broad-shouldered, the same as George and he were. United, they presented an impressive front in their determination to protect Elly from any harm – which they would each do to the death. Partly because she was special. Partly because they were responsible for what had happened to her.

"You know as well as anyone that the few times we've convinced Elly to travel to London, the four of you surrounded her like an armed guard. There wasn't a man in all of England who was brave enough to face such an invincible force to even carry on a conversation with her."

"It was *Elly* who always shied away from going out in public. Or have you forgotten the reason she might hesitate to be put on display?"

"It's *you* who can't forget, Harrison. You and George and Jules and Spence. You're the ones who won't let her risk hearing something that might offend her. You who are afraid she might be stared at when she's in public. It's the four of you who are overprotective of her because you can't stop punishing yourselves for what happened. Lilly and I just wanted to let her glimpse the world she was missing."

"So you thought giving her some nameless fantasy was

what she needed."

"We just wanted Elly to think someone wonderful admired her," Lillian said.

"Every woman needs to be loved just once in her life," Patience added, recklessly treading into deeper waters. "She's seven and twenty already. Everyone knows she's far past the age when any man will—"

"Enough! What you did was implement a half-witted scheme with the potential to cause irreparable damage."

George had been very quiet so far, but at Harrison's outburst he sat forward in his chair. "Have you written Mother and Father to tell them we're hosting a two-week house party?"

"Yes."

Patience and Lillian's eyes opened wide. "Do you think that was wise?" Lillian asked after sharing a concerned look with Patience. "They'll know something's wrong when they hear."

"Something *is* wrong," Harrison fired back. "*Very* wrong!"

"But maybe Mama and Papa wouldn't have found out," Lillian offered tentatively.

"Do you think there's a chance in hell we could have a gathering of this magnitude without one of Mama's friends writing her as soon as the first invitation went out? Have you forgotten who your parents are?"

Patience's gaze lowered to the floor. Lillian's followed.

"Nothing happens the Duke and Duchess of Sheridan don't know about. Usually *before* it happens." His last statement almost contained a rare hint of something that anyone who didn't know him might mistake for humor. "But if everything goes as planned, and the party accomplishes our goal of making Elly forget the secret admirer you two so aptly invented, Mother and Father will agree this was necessary."

Harrison turned on his heel and paced from one side of the room to the other. He had to make Elly forget the secret admirer Patience and Lillian had introduced her to in a series of love letters. And she could never discover what they'd done. If she did, it would kill her.

Harrison would rather have a stake thrust through his heart than have her suffer any more than she already had.

"So," he said, filling his lungs with air, then releasing it. "It's time to begin this fiasco. George, go down and assist Jules and Spence." He looked at the twins. "Find Elly and make sure she's ready on time."

Patience and Lilly nodded then turned to the door. Patience stopped with her hand on the knob and turned.

"We know who you've invited as guests for the house party, and who Jules and Spence and George have invited. But as yet we don't know who you've invited for Elly. Or for yourself."

Harrison lifted his gaze. It was time to reveal the man he'd chosen to play the role as the perfect partner for Elly, the person he'd chosen to make her forget the imaginary admirer Patience and Lillian had invented. It was too late for them to do anything but accept his decision.

"As for myself, I've invited Aunt Esther as my guest. I'm sure Aunt Gussie will appreciate her company and we could hardly host an event without inviting Aunt Gussie and Uncle Bertram."

"But wouldn't you rather invite—"

Harrison stopped Lilly's words with the same glare Elly had often teased him was cold enough to freeze the Thames. "Don't think there will be a chance for you to play matchmaker. The object of this affair is to keep *Elly* from getting hurt, which wouldn't be necessary if the two of you hadn't put us in this predicament."

Harrison took a small amount of satisfaction in seeing his sisters' cheeks turn scarlet.

"Whom have you selected for Elly?" George asked.

"Yes," Lilly asked, chewing her bottom lip. "We all know she won't make this easy on him."

"That's probably the most understated remark anyone could make," George said on a laugh.

"It can't be just anyone," Patience added.

"No," Lilly said, turning back into the room. "He has to be someone Society considers an outstanding catch."

"Yes," George added. "And he can't be a milquetoast. Elly will shred him to pieces before he's been here a day."

"And he can't be dim-witted," Patience spouted, focusing her gaze on Harrison. "You're the only one of us who can hold his own against Elly."

Harrison fought the reservations eating at him. "I know. And even I'm not always successful."

"But most of all," George said on a heavy sigh, "he has to be someone so perfect he can topple Elly's suitor from his pedestal. Who did you invite that has all those qualifications?"

Harrison straightened to his full height and faced three of his six siblings. They looked at him with expectant expressions as if they were confident that he'd chosen the perfect suitor for Elly. This is the way it had always been. He was the one they always came to when they needed help. And he'd always been successful. He'd always taken care of them - except for once. The day he'd almost let Elly die.

"Let me first explain that you are correct in the qualifications Elly's guest needs to possess."

"You've found someone who has all of these attributes?"

Lillian asked.

"In my opinion, there is only one person whose reputation is widely known when it comes to charming the fairer sex."

"Who?"

Harrison didn't answer George right away. He couldn't. Once he revealed the man he'd chosen he wouldn't be able to stop the uproar.

"Why do I have a feeling we're not going to like this?" George said with a frown on his forehead.

"Probably because you aren't."

"Who is it?" Patience asked stepping closer to George so the three of them formed an indefensible line of attack.

Harrison stood a little taller. "Think of the most irresistible male in all of England. Someone who's reputed to be as rich as Croesus and possesses an unbelievable amount of luck, both with cards and...and with women. Someone whose comings and goings are noted by everyone in Society, and whose opinion, both personal and professional, is constantly sought."

"I can't believe there is such a paragon," George said on a guffaw.

"Neither can I," Patience and Lillian added.

"Then put a name to the man every eligible female has tried to leg-shackle for years. Someone whose presence at any function guarantees its success."

Patience's eyes grew wide as recognition dawned. Lillian's expression changed moments later.

"You can't be serious," Patience said barely above a whisper.

"Tell me you didn't," Lillian demanded with a horrified look on her face.

George's frown deepened. "Who? Who is it?"

"The scoundrel is said to break some poor woman's heart

on a daily basis."

"And he's said to have had more mistresses than even *he* can keep count of."

"Who?" George said loud enough to finally draw his sisters' attention.

"The Earl of Charfield!" they cried out in unison.

George's jaw dropped. He finally closed it and took a step forward. "Bloody hell, Harrison. You can't be serious."

"He's not at all appropriate for Elly," Lillian said firmly.

"He's not the sort of person Elly should even be introduced to," Patience said with force.

Harrison lifted his brows. "Really? Every woman still drawing breath thinks he's the most handsome man alive. And every father with a daughter to marry off considers him the catch of the century."

George slammed his fist on the corner of a nearby table. "But this is Elly! Exposing her to Charfield is like handing a lamb over to a hungry wolf."

"Not if the wolf knows up front that his role is to be the perfect partner to Elly, and that his *only* task is to make her forget an admirer her family considers an inferior choice for her."

Harrison placed his palms flat on the top of the desk and leaned forward. "Not if he knows that each one of her brothers will stand in line to tear him limb from limb if he breaks her heart."

"How did you get him to agree to this?"

Harrison shrugged. "Charfield's reputed to own the finest Arabian horses in the world – next to ours. He'll do anything for the opportunity to cross their bloodlines with ours."

Patience and Lillian dropped onto the nearest settee as if

they didn't have the strength to stand. "But he's a womanizer," Lilly said. "A rake. He could break Elly's heart."

"You should have thought of that before you pretended to be Elly's secret admirer!"

His sisters' shoulders dropped in defeat. He regretted his sharp words the moment they left his mouth. "Enough recriminations. The time for assigning blame is over."

He went around the desk and held out a hand to each sister. "Come now. Put smiles on your faces. The Down is hosting the first party we've had in years. That alone will guarantee its success."

The twins rose to their feet and gave him bright smiles. "Of course it will," Patience said. "We'll make sure of it. For Elly."

"Yes, for Elly."

CHAPTER 3

Elly recalled the stranger she'd met that afternoon and breathed a deep sigh. For the first time in her life, emotions she'd never realized she possessed stirred deep inside her.

There was no doubt he was one of the guests and she'd probably see him countless times during the next two weeks, but for a few unbelievably idyllic moments, someone special had treated her as if she weren't different. For the first time ever someone thought she was the same as any other woman.

Of course, that wouldn't last. In a matter of hours she'd meet him again and everything would change. But for a few special moments, while they'd raced toward the hedge, then jumped it together, she'd been normal in a handsome man's eyes.

She'd never experienced such a euphoric feeling in her life.

A small part of her wished she could stay in her room for the next two weeks so that feeling wouldn't change.

But that wasn't possible.

Elly gave her hair a final glance and took a deep breath. The sooner she went down, the sooner she could meet their guests. Except for the man she'd met earlier, the reaction of the other guests didn't matter. The house party wasn't being held for her. No one would probably even notice her.

She swiped her damp hands against her skirt. It wasn't as if she'd be paired with anyone. The twins wouldn't be that thoughtless, and one of her brothers would always be at hand to escort her when needed. When they weren't, she'd rely on Uncle Barclay to partner her. He was her paternal uncle and a joy to be around. If Harrison intended to force her to suffer through the next two weeks, she intended to have someone whose company she enjoyed.

She couldn't believe the reason they were hosting a party. According to Harrison, one of her brothers had fallen in love. Either George, or Jules, or Spence, or Harri—

She stopped. No, it wasn't Harrison. Even though he was the one she wished could find love again, she knew it wasn't him. Perhaps it was George.

Elly sighed. No, it wasn't George, either. She and George were twins and from the time they'd been able to speak they'd told each other everything. George would have told her if he'd fallen in love. He wouldn't use a house party to introduce his family to the woman of his dreams.

It had to be either Jules or Spencer. They were both younger, five and twenty, and three and twenty respectively, but that wasn't too young to give your heart to someone. Look at Patience and Lillian. They'd only been twenty when they'd fallen in love and married.

Oh, she wished Harrison had told her which brother had invited someone special but he said he didn't want to give her any clues because nothing was finalized yet. Besides, he said it would be fun to have her guess.

She released a heavy sigh then slowly pushed herself to her feet. She stopped when the door opened.

"Oh, Elly," Patience said, pausing just inside the doorway. Lillian followed her in. "You look lovely."

Elly turned, then sat back onto the chair and watched the twins cross the room. They were not only exact replicas of each other, but they resembled their mother so much it was like seeing her face every time she looked at one of them.

Elly, however, took after her father, with dark hair and dark eyes and a bronzed complexion that wasn't at all fashionable. The hours she spent riding only deepened her coloring.

"That shade of scarlet is perfect on you," Lilly exclaimed, giving Elly a gentle hug so she wouldn't cause any wrinkles. "I'm so jealous. With our coloring, Patience and I couldn't be caught dead in a color that bold."

"I've been waiting for an excuse to wear it. Mother had it made for me the last time she was in London."

"It's lovely."

Patience stepped back to where Lilly stood so Elly wouldn't have to crane her neck to look at them.

"Have any of the guests come down yet?"

"No. We informed everyone that dinner wasn't until seven. It's not yet six."

Elly nodded.

"It's going to be a wonderful two weeks," Lilly exclaimed. "You wouldn't believe the plans George and the boys have made."

Lilly looked as if she could barely contain her excitement. Patience wore the same expression. Elly wished she could share their enthusiasm.

"Even Harrison is contributing to the festivities."

Elly lifted her brows. "Harrison?"

"Yes. He came up with the most brilliant ideas of them all."

The girls gave her the daily itinerary and Elly let them ramble.

Each day would include an outing of some sort. There'd be the expected picnic by the lake, boat rides down the stream, and carriage rides through the arbor for which The Down was known. They'd also scheduled trips to the village, especially to shop in Mr. Devon's crystal palace where they made the most marvelous crystal pieces. And of course, they'd planned a variety of lawn games on the afternoons when the weather was sunny and warm.

For the men there'd be hunting and fishing opportunities while the ladies stayed indoors and read or went outdoors to stroll through the gardens. Then, every evening they'd entertain each other with parlor games. And music.

Since music had always been an important part of the Duke and Duchess of Sheridan's home, Harrison had arranged for a number of smaller ensembles to be brought in several times during the two weeks to entertain their guests. There would be a variety of groups, including a chamber orchestra, a brass quintet, and a concert pianist.

The most lavish and formal affair of the two weeks, though, would be the ball The Down would host the night before the guests departed. Invitations had already gone out to all their neighbors and the whole countryside was abuzz with enthusiasm.

The twins assured her that this was going to be the event of the decade.

"You're excited about the party, aren't you?" Lilly asked fussing with her gloves. "I mean, you don't hate the idea, do you?"

"Of course I don't. I know how important this is to Harrison and the boys. And to both of you, too."

"Perhaps in the future we can convince you to come to London with us." Lilly's tone was hopeful. "We'd all be with you. We'd make sure you had a wonderful time."

The short, uncomfortable silence that engulfed the room indicated Lilly had entered forbidden territory.

"We'll see," Elly said as if she were considering the possibility of going.

A knot tightened in her stomach, the uncomfortable memories gnawing at her insides.

They didn't understand. The twins had been too young to remember what it had been like for her.

"There are some very handsome gentlemen among the friends the boys invited," Patience said with a glimmer in her eyes.

"I know." Elly answered before she could stop her words from escaping.

Both her sisters gaped at her, their dainty eyebrows arched high. "You do?"

Elly hoped her cheeks weren't as red as they felt. "Actually, I met one of our guests when I was riding."

"Which one?"

"I'm not sure. I didn't get his name."

"He didn't introduce himself?" Patience asked.

"No. I don't think he considered I might be a relation. I wasn't dressed as I'm sure he thought one of the Duke of Sheridan's offspring would be attired when out of the house."

"What did he look like?" Lilly asked.

Elly's cheeks turned a degree warmer. "Oh, I can't honestly say." She tried to pretend the laughter in his midnight-blue eyes hadn't haunted her since he'd ridden away from her. Or that she hadn't studied every item of furniture in her bedroom trying to find just the right piece to match his dark, sable-brown hair. Or that she could stop the strange swirling in her chest every time she remembered the laugh lines at the corners of his eyes or the deep creases on either side of his mouth when he smiled. And oh, how easily he'd smiled.

"Was he tall?" Lilly asked.

"I don't know. But he was riding the most magnificent Arabian I've ever seen. He must have nearly as fine a stable as Harrison."

"Leave it to you to notice the horse instead of the rider," Lilly said on a laugh, but she was the only sister who found any humor in Elly's answer. The serious expression on Patience's face gave Elly pause.

"What?"

"I think you made the acquaintance of the Earl of Charfield," Patience said. Her hushed tone contained more than a hint of both awe and warning.

"Charfield?" Elly said, trying to remember if she knew the name. She wasn't sure. "Which one of our brothers invited him?"

"Harrison. But I really wish he hadn't."

"What do you mean by that?" Elly's sisters shared a glance she couldn't interpret. "Is there something wrong with Charfield's character?"

"Not his character...exactly," Patience started to explain.

"We really should warn her," Lilly said, making eye contact

with Patience.

"Warn me about what?"

"About Lord Charfield," Patience added. "He's a...a...a rake!"

"Oh," Elly laughed. "Is that all?"

"Is that all!" both sisters squeaked at the same time.

"You have no idea the hearts he's broken," Patience started.

"Or the scandals in which he's been involved," Lilly added.

"Is he shunned by Society?" Elly suddenly wanted to know.

"Shunned?" Patience said in a mocking tone.

"Shunned?" Lilly echoed in the same tone. "Not only is he *not* shunned, but every matchmaking mama is doing everything in her power to trap Charfield into marrying her daughter."

"If he's such a horrible choice, why is everyone trying to push their daughter off onto him?"

"Because he's one of the richest, most eligible men in London, of course."

"Yes," Lilly added, "and one of the luckiest. None of the gentlemen at his clubs stand a chance of winning if he's at the table."

"Does he cheat?"

"Of course not," Patience said. "Someone would have called him out by now if he did. He just never loses!"

"Oh, how inconsiderate," Elly said, desperately trying to hide her laughter.

Patience propped her fists on her hips in obvious frustration. "There's not a social affair held where his name isn't at the top of the guest list. Even Lady Pomeroy, who only invites a select few to her annual ball, is rumored to have changed the scheduled date because Lord Charfield was unable to make her first choice."

"Well, if Lady Pomeroy went to such lengths to include him I can hardly see why the two of you are concerned that he's attending our small country party."

Lilly wrung her dainty hands. "We just don't want you to be hurt."

"Hurt? I don't see how I can be hurt."

Patience stepped closer. "He's broken countless hearts, Elly. It's rumored that once he turns on his charm, women fall at his feet."

Elly laughed. "Are you afraid I'm going to make a fool of myself over someone who will probably not even notice that I'm there?"

"Of course not," Patience said. "It's just that you haven't had all that much experience with men."

"I see," Elly said, trying not to show her emotions.

"I mean," Patience continued, using her words as a shovel to dig a hole even deeper, "we know you're far too sensible to lose your heart to such a scoundrel."

"Thank you for that." Elly placed her hand over her heart. She tried to pretend she agreed with them even though she wasn't sure the twins were complimenting her. "I'm glad you have such confidence in me."

"We do," Lillian said. "We both know that when you fall in love it will be to someone with a stellar reputation."

Elly laughed. "Can you see that in your crystal ball?"

Lillian giggled. "Of course. It's perfectly clear."

"And Harrison? What do you see in his future?"

Sad expressions covered their faces.

"You know Harrison will never risk falling in love again," Lilly said. "Not after he was hurt so badly before."

"I doubt he'll ever marry," Patience added. "It's been nearly five years and he's never once shown interest in another woman."

"It's not Harrison we're concerned for," Lilly said. "It's you."

Elly smiled. "Well, don't be. You have nothing to worry about. You forget. I've already met the man of my dreams. I'm sure Lord Charfield can't hold a candle to my secret admirer."

Patience and Lilly's faces paled.

"But you've never met the man you've corresponded with," Patience said. "Perhaps he's exactly like Lord Charfield. Or worse."

Elly laughed. "Don't concern yourselves. Lord Charfield won't give me a second glance."

Lilly flapped her arms in the air in a graceful sign of frustration. "Don't be so confident, Elly. No one is safe from his charms. Not even you."

The temperature of the air in the room dropped and Elly struggled to keep the smile on her face from faltering.

After an uncomfortable silence, Lilly stepped closer and put her arm around Elly's shoulder. "Oh, Elly. I didn't mean that like it sounded." Her rosy cheeks turned a blazing scarlet.

"Of course you didn't. And I didn't take it that way."

Elly put on a brave face and gave her hair a final pat. She knew the twins had nothing to worry about. Charfield wouldn't pay her a moment's attention once he saw her make her way across a room.

"Have you come to escort me down?" Elly asked, scooting to the edge of her chair.

Both sisters moved closer to assist her, Patience on her left and Lilly on her right.

Elly slowly stood then steadied herself before taking the

cane Patience held out to her. With an uneven gait, she walked across the room. Her limp was pronounced and forced her hip to swing to the left. Her left arm had a tendency to move outward, making her appear clumsy.

She hated how her body shifted unnaturally with each step, how even her shoulder dipped, but at least most of those present at the party were familiar with her awkwardness. Her inelegance wouldn't be too uncomfortable for them to be around. At least for one night.

She stepped out the door and hobbled down the steps.

Tonight would be the worst. After he saw her and...knew, she could go back to being an invisible part of the gathering. It was only two weeks, after all. Surely she could survive that.

And there was one positive aspect to Harrison's party. Even though she wouldn't be the female on whom the very handsome Earl of Charfield chose to shower his attention, she'd at least be able to look at him and...dream.

CHAPTER 4

Brent gave his shirt sleeves a firm tug beneath his black evening jacket, then left his guest room to make his way to the drawing room where everyone would meet to socialize before dinner was served. His part in this two-week play was about to begin. And if there was anything Brent knew how to do, it was play a part.

In fact, he'd played the role of the rake and carefree rogue so long he wasn't sure he knew the real Brentan Montgomery, Earl of Charfield, any longer.

Even though no one in Society would ever believe it, his dream had always been to settle down with a woman he loved and raise a houseful of happy children. But after years of unsuccessful searching, he'd given up all hope of finding any such woman. And he refused to marry a woman he didn't love and be miserable for the rest of his life.

Oh, his name was still at the top of every matchmaking mama's list, and he was considered one of the most sought-after bachelors in London. But when not one of the hoards of beautiful young ladies he'd met over the years roused even a hint of desire, he'd turned his attention to adding to his stable of Arabians instead of finding someone with whom he could be happy.

His role at Fellingsdown's party was just another part he had to play to add another treasure to his collection. And for such a magnificent prize, Brent was willing to endure anything. It was only two weeks, after all. He'd survived years of courting the dullest, most dim-witted females Society had to offer. Fellingsdown's sister couldn't be any worse.

Could she?

He bolstered his resolve and stepped confidently down the right side of the winding double staircase with a long-perfected smile on his face. Even if she were the most hideous creature imaginable, the prize at the end of two weeks was worth any amount of boredom he'd have to endure. He couldn't wait until next spring for Danza to present him a colt sired by the magnificent El Solidar.

His smile broadened and he stepped down the stairs with a jaunty air. The closer he got to the bottom, the louder the laughter and the buzz of conversation grew. By the time he reached the drawing room door, he was prepared to play his part.

Armed with the ease for which he was known, he stepped inside the room and looked around. There was laughter and conversation aplenty and Brent felt a momentary sense of relief that the two-week party hosted by Fellingsdown seemed to be on its way to becoming a pleasant affair.

He stepped into the room and to the side, thankful no one noticed his arrival. His obscurity would give him an opportunity to observe the guests and hopefully spot the woman he'd been hired to entertain for the next fourteen days. She would no doubt be easy to find.

From the number already gathered, he assumed most of the guests had already arrived. But he didn't see a female so lacking in physical attributes that Fellingsdown had to bribe someone to escort her.

He stepped further inside and scanned the perimeter of the room a second time. Fellingsdown stood by an open window with his brother George. There were two very striking women in their small circle that he recognized from several of the balls he'd attended. Neither was the sister he'd been hired to accompany.

Fellingsdown's other brothers, Jules and Spencer, stood on the opposite side of the room talking to another group. One of Fellingsdown's twin sisters, Lady Parkridge, he assumed, moved from one small cluster of guests to the next, but no one she stopped to talk with looked like he imagined Fellingsdown's on-the-shelf sister would.

Brent reached out to take a glass of brandy a footman held out to him and lifted the glass. His arm stopped midway to his mouth and his breath caught in his throat.

The magnificent rider he'd met as he'd arrived sat on a velvet sofa in the center of the room looking as elegantly regal as if she were holding court. A younger woman sat beside her, the Countess of Berkingham, he thought. But how could one be sure when one twin looked so much like the other? It didn't matter. The dark-haired beauty was the one from whom he couldn't take his gaze.

Her rich auburn hair was pulled loosely from her face in a seductively becoming style and fastened with tiny pearl pins. Delicate wisps framed the perfectly shaped face he remembered from this afternoon. She wore an inviting smile as if that expression was a part of her.

Her gown was of dark scarlet, the bodice revealing enough to hint at the perfection hidden beneath. He couldn't imagine a shade that would compliment her coloring more perfectly or a style that flattered her more.

This afternoon she'd been beguiling and beautiful. Tonight she was breathtaking.

He stared at her for another long moment but wasn't content just watching her. He had to talk to her. For a few minutes before he began his charade of pretending to be enamored of Fellingsdown's ugly sister, he had to spend just a few glorious seconds in her company.

He took a sip of Fellingsdown's excellent brandy and noticed Lady Berkingham rise to greet two new guests who'd entered the room. Before anyone could occupy the empty seat beside her, he moved toward the sofa as if a magnet pulled him in that direction.

"Good evening, my fearless horsewoman," he said when he reached her.

She hadn't been looking in his direction. When he spoke she snapped her head toward him and looked up.

Time ceased to move forward. A warm blanket settled inside his chest.

Her eyes opened wide and sparkled with recognition. At the same time the corners of her mouth tipped upward in a slight smile, then broadened to a wide, welcoming grin.

"Oh, it's you." Her voice was as deep and rich as he remembered from earlier.

His heart took another tumble in his chest.

"May I?" He pointed to the chair beside her.

"Of course. Please, sit down."

Brent lowered himself to the chair opposite her. "Have you recovered from your excitement this afternoon?"

She gave a sideways glance in both directions then leaned forward. "I can't ever remember enjoying myself so."

Brent laughed. "Neither can I."

"I'm afraid, however, most of the people in this room would be shocked at our behavior."

"Including our host?"

She smiled broader. "Oh, *especially* our host."

Suddenly, Brent remembered the purpose for this party. Was it possible that this elegant creature was the Marquess of Fellingsdown's special guest? She was, after all, the most fascinating woman Brent had ever met. The thought that she was linked to Fellingsdown disturbed him more than he cared to admit.

"Does our host's opinion matter to you?"

The exquisite beauty's gaze traveled to where Fellingsdown stood among a circle of a half-dozen males and females.

"Of course," she answered and the warmth Brent heard in her voice sent an uncomfortable niggling he couldn't explain. It wasn't jealousy. Of course it wasn't jealousy. He hadn't known her long enough to have formed any feelings for her.

But when she looked back at him, the blood in his veins heated several degrees.

"So, unless *you* intend to tell him about our adventure," she said with a gleam in her eyes, "I can almost guarantee he'll never find out."

Brent laughed again. Only this time the laughter came from deeper inside him. A place that hadn't felt any laughter in a long time. "You really are a little minx."

"Oh, I assure you I'm not."

She batted her long, dark lashes, and donned the most innocent expression he'd ever seen.

"But..." She leaned closer and lowered her voice. "If you feel inclined to accept another invitation, I happen to know another jump that is not nearly as...elementary as the one we took this afternoon."

"Are you issuing another challenge?"

She leaned back and studied him with an appraising eye. "You look like a man who is always ready to accept a dare."

"And you, my minx, look like a woman who enjoys issuing a challenge."

She laughed. "Oh, I am."

"Then I accept."

"Good. Tomorrow, perhaps?"

Brent nodded. "Will you be racing the same horse?"

Her delicate brows lifted. "Regalia? Of course. It would hardly be fair, otherwise."

Brent took two glasses from the tray a footman held out to him and handed her one.

She took it with a smile and a word of thanks, then held it to her lips and took a sip.

The knot in the pit of his stomach dropped even lower and he wondered what it would be like to feel those lips against his own.

"Are you sure Fellingsdown won't mind you riding his Arabians?"

"No, he won't mind. He's given me permission to ride any horse I choose."

"You and the marquess must be on very good terms. I

can't imagine him permitting just anyone to ride one of his magnificent Arabians."

"Oh, we are. On very good terms. And he trusts me to take excellent care of them. I love and appreciate them as much as he does."

Another disturbing wave rushed through him and this time he could no longer avoid putting a name to it. He was *jealous* of Fellingsdown.

For years Brent had been convinced there wasn't a woman alive who shared his passion for horses. Yet sitting within his reach was a woman who not only shared his same passion, but was more beautiful than any female he'd ever seen.

And Fellingsdown had found her first.

"You must also have a fine stable of Arabians, if the horse you rode belongs to you."

Brent couldn't help but smile. "It does and I do. I have a dozen more beautiful Arabians at Charfield Manor."

"A dozen?" she said with raised eyebrows. "I'm impressed. That's nearly as many as Harrison has at The Down."

Harrison.

The knot tightened in his stomach. If there was any question that the emotion he experienced when she spoke of their host was a form of jealousy, that doubt evaporated with the ease in which she'd used Fellingsdown's given name.

"We reached that number when Danza presented us with a beautiful filly foal last March. Her name is Xenna."

"Does she have any of her mother's markings?"

He couldn't help but smile. Her interest was refreshing. "Yes. She even has the white cross on her forehead. I'm afraid she's everyone's favorite and will be too spoiled before she's old enough to ride to get any good out of her."

She shook her head. "You can't spoil a horse too much. Especially an Arabian. The more you pamper them the more devoted they become. A loved horse will race her heart out for you."

He sat back in his chair and another surge of admiration for her exploded inside him. How on earth could he pay court to Fellingsdown's reclusive sister for the next fourteen days when the woman of his dreams sat not two feet away from him? How on earth could he pretend a fascination for someone else when his every thought would be focused on the beautiful woman beside him? "How did you ever become so wise about horses?"

"I told you I spent most of my youth around them."

"Yes, you little minx. Which led me to assume that your father perhaps was employed at The Down."

She laughed.

Ah, hell. Even her laugh was mesmerizing.

Endearing.

Captivating.

"I admit that my attire was a little misleading. Harrison always tells me I look like a castoff when I go out riding. But it's much easier to ride when you're dressed for comfort rather than style."

"I take it you and Fellingsdown have been acquainted for a number of years."

"Oh yes, forever."

A spike rammed through his heart. If Fellingsdown had known this delightful woman forever, why on earth hadn't he married her? Surely she wasn't his mistress. He'd never heard Fellingsdown's name linked with anyone except Lady Cassandra Waverley before she jilted him for the Marquess of

Lathamton, but that didn't mean it wasn't possible. Especially if he kept a mistress in the country and never took her to Town.

Brent experienced an undeniable rush of anger. If there weren't so much riding on the bargain he'd struck with Fellingsdown, he'd demand the blackguard make an honest woman of her. Or he'd offer for her himself.

The air caught in his chest. What the bloody hell was he thinking? He didn't even know her name. How could he consider trying to rescue her when he knew nothing about her?

He mentally shook his head and studied her. He found her looking at him with an equally serious expression.

"What?" A curious little frown changed her features.

He relaxed in his chair and smiled. "I just realized I don't even know your name."

She laughed. "Most people would consider it highly improper for me to carry on a conversation with you when we haven't even been properly introduced."

"Then perhaps we'd better take care of that small matter. I am Brentan Montgomery, the Marquess of Charfield. And you are?"

She hesitated as if she wasn't sure she wanted him to discover her identity. Or perhaps she wasn't sure how to explain her illicit relationship with their host.

Brent made a promise that he wouldn't show the slightest reaction when she imparted that she was an intimate friend of Fellingsdown's.

She gave a sigh that spoke a thousand regrets before she opened her mouth to speak. "I am—"

"Ah, Charfield," Fellingsdown's deep voice said from behind him. "I see you've already discovered the most beautiful woman in the room. Have you been introduced?"

"No, we were just taking care of that detail."

"Please, allow me to do the honors."

The beautiful lady tipped her head back and gave Fellingsdown a warm, generous smile. Brent wanted to slap away his host's possessive hand as it rested on her shoulder. Instead, he smiled as he waited to hear how the marquess would introduce her.

"Elly, allow me to present Brentan Montgomery, Marquess of Charfield. Charfield, this lovely young woman is the Lady Ellyssa Prescott...

"...my sister."

The floor dropped beneath him and he reached out to steady himself against the chair where he'd been sitting only moments ago.

Sister?

Fellingsdown had called her his sister.

Brent wanted to cry out for joy. He wanted to offer a prayer to Heaven. He wanted to thank Fellingsdown for giving him this opportunity.

But most of all, he wanted to wrap his arms around Lady Ellyssa Prescott and tell her how happy he was that she wasn't who and what he'd feared she was. Except—

The terms of his agreement with Fellingsdown came back with glaring clarity. For the next two weeks he was to shower Lady Elyssa with his complete attention.

He smiled. Oh, that wouldn't be hard to do.

And he couldn't in any way threaten her reputation.

His smile faded. He looked at those full, lush lips and thought he'd die if he couldn't kiss her. And not just once.

And of the utmost importance, he couldn't allow her to fall

in love with him.

What little remained of his smile died. There wasn't a chance in hell he could comply with that term.

Not even for a colt sired by El Solidar.

CHAPTER 5

He knew.

Elly tried not to stare at his face after Harrison introduced her but she couldn't pull her gaze away. His broad smile faded in slow, agonizing degrees as both the shock and surprise of who she was registered.

She wasn't sure what he expected. Perhaps someone ugly beyond description with warts and hairy moles to mar her complexion. Perhaps a screaming lunatic the Prescott family hid away in the country because she wasn't fit for polite company. Or...

...perhaps he'd simply heard the truth about her.

Elly swallowed hard. The Marquess of Charfield wouldn't be the first nobility she'd met who couldn't abide being in the company of someone who wasn't perfect. He wouldn't be the first person who used the excuse that there was someone across the room with whom they needed to talk as their reason to escape her.

And he hadn't even seen her deformity yet.

The familiar painful weight pressed against her chest and she steeled her defenses. She knew what to do to protect herself from hurt. She'd done it often enough.

She lifted her chin that telltale notch and waited to see which line of escape he'd use.

"It's...it's very nice to meet you, Lady Elyssa," he stammered more awkwardly than she was sure he'd been the first time he was introduced to a young lady.

"Please, excuse me," he said, recovering a little more quickly than most people did. "I didn't expect Fellingsdown to have such a beautiful sister."

Charfield turned to give Fellingsdown his full attention. The look they shared seemed to indicate there'd been a misunderstanding between them.

"The world is indebted to you, Fellingsdown, for inheriting all the family imperfections and gifting your sister with such remarkable beauty."

Harrison laughed with an appropriate amount of good humor. "I see you haven't changed since we were together at school." He looked down at her and winked. "Be careful what you believe, Elly. Charfield has always had a remarkable way with words. Our last year at school he almost convinced the head master that the goat they found eating his way through the kitchen had not only found its way there on its own, but had the ability to close and lock the door behind it. Luckily for him, it was so near the end of the term they let him finish just to be rid of him."

"I wasn't the only one in on that minor debacle, Fellingsdown." Elly shot her brother a look of disbelief. "You, Harrison?"

"Of course not. I would never take part in anything so

reckless."

"I'm afraid he's telling the truth, Lady Elyssa. In fact, several of the lads, myself included, owe your brother a great debt. He spent several hours in the headmaster's office speaking in our defense."

"You proved the goat guilty?"

"No. I convinced the headmaster that expelling Charfield and the others might remove them for the remainder of the current term, which would be finished in a few short weeks, but that they would most certainly return for the following term, during which time the school would have to put up with any number of additional shenanigans. It didn't take a great deal of talking to convince the head schoolmaster to allow them to finish out the term and be done with them."

"Oh, so you were only an accomplice. I'm ever so relieved. I feared you might have actually been involved with a crime of sorts."

"She's got you there, old man," Charfield said on a laugh that caused a look of exasperation to cross Harrison's face.

"You will soon learn that Elly seldom allows anyone to get the better of her."

"Is that true?" Charfield lifted his eyebrows.

"I've had a hard life, Lord Charfield." She raised a limp hand to her forehead in a pose of faintness. "I've had to hold my own against the badgering of four domineering brothers. I must admit, such a hardship sharpened certain skills."

"You have my sympathies, my lady. And my admiration."

Harrison threw up his hands. "I've taken enough abuse for one evening." He took a step away from them then stopped and gave Charfield a serious glance. "May I rely on you to see Elly in to dinner?"

"Of course. It would be my pleasure."

Elly experienced a jolt of shock, followed by a stabbing of panic. She couldn't believe Harrison was handing her over to someone else. Especially someone who made her heart race every time she was near him. Which was exactly why she had to stay as far away from him as possible. She couldn't imagine anything worse than seeing the look of pity and disgust in his eyes when she took her first step with him.

"That won't be necessary, Harrison. George will see me in to dinner."

He nodded his head to where George stood on the other side of the room deep in conversation with a lovely blonde. "I think George has intentions of partnering Lady Brianna Thornton in to dinner. He seems quite captured by her."

Elly followed his gaze. "Then I'm sure Jules will—"

"As you see, Jules is deep in conversation with Miss Amelia Hastings. I'd hate to interrupt them. She's a lovely young lady. And Spence," he said, holding up his hand to stop her next words, "has promised to see Lady Hannah Brammwell in to dinner. Have you met her?"

Elly shook her head.

"You really must. She's charming."

Elly was incapable of saying anything. Why was Harrison doing this? He must know she was counting on one of them to keep her company tonight. But if Charfield escorted her, there'd be no hiding from him or from the other guests. He drew attention like fireworks at a celebration.

How could she remain hidden when she was beside the most handsome man in the room? And how would she survive sitting beside him without being obligated to carry on a conversation with him for endless hours?

She clutched her hands together in her lap. Sitting next to him didn't bother her; talking to him didn't either. He was as easy to talk with as any of her family. In fact, she looked forward to finding out as much about him as she could.

She clenched her hands tighter. What she wasn't sure she'd survive was the long journey from the drawing room to the formal dining room. Walking at Charfield's side, having him feel every uneven step she took would be an unbearable torture. She wasn't sure she could hide the embarrassment and humiliation she always felt when she was beside someone so perfect.

And no one was physically more perfect than the Marquess of Charfield.

She darted a desperate glance at Harrison as she scrambled to think of another excuse to keep from having to expose herself so completely. But she couldn't. Nor did she have the opportunity.

Before she could say more, Fitzhugh, the butler, appeared in the doorway to announce dinner. An uncontrollable jolt of panic raced through her and even though she tried to hide it, she knew Harrison could see the fear in her eyes.

"Allow me to help you up, Elly," Harrison said, stepping to the side of the sofa to retrieve the cane Lilly had placed out of sight.

She had no choice but to slide forward like she had to before she could rise. When she'd reached the edge of the cushion she lifted both hands to grip the arm Harrison held in front of her and pulled herself onto her good foot. When she was steady, Harrison handed her her cane.

A part of the self confidence she harbored died. She knew her cheeks were fire red and she kept her gaze focused on the familiar pattern of the carpet beneath her.

"If you'll see Elly in to dinner," Harrison said, transferring her hand from his arm to Charfield's, "I'll escort our other guests into the dining room."

"Of course," she heard Charfield say, but she wasn't brave enough to look at him.

Her heart thundered in her chest. She'd known it would come to this. She'd known that eventually he'd see the unsightly way she moved, the ungainly manner in which she rose from a chair, her awkward movement as she walked from one place to another. But she'd thought perhaps it wouldn't be just yet. She thought she might be able to observe him throughout the night without him getting such a close-up view of how clumsy she was.

She looked up to give Harrison a final pleading glance, praying he'd realize how uncomfortable she was and change his mind. But when she focused on Harrison's features, every word she'd readied herself to speak escaped her mind.

Harrison stood ramrod straight, his hands balled into tight fists, his teeth clenched so tightly the muscles on either side of his jaw jumped in agitation. Every hint of color drained from his face.

Elly noted the fury in his expression and followed his gaze to the other side of the room. The object of his hardened glare stood in the open doorway looking as magnificently beautiful as Elly had ever seen her.

All thoughts of her own discomfort faded as a frigid tension filled the room.

She glanced at Harrison, hoping to find the right words to make the situation easier. His voice stopped her.

"Who the bloody hell invited her?"

———

It took more courage for Cassandra Waverley, Marchioness of Lathamton to stand in Harrison Prescott's home than she thought she possessed. Not because she was afraid of Harrison or cared about his reaction - she was far past caring what he thought or what he'd do, but because being under the same roof with him was the last place she wanted to be.

All that made the coming scene the least bit tolerable was knowing he didn't want her here any more than she wanted to be here. And if his look of shock and barely concealed fury was any indication of his feelings, her unexpected appearance had at least achieved the goal of putting him at a disadvantage. That small victory gave her an immeasurable sense of pleasure.

For a long time neither of them moved. She held a relaxed pose as the guests looked first at her, then at Harrison. Her heart picked up speed as one second stretched into another without his making a move to greet her.

Then his lips moved.

Cassandra nearly laughed aloud when she realized what he said. Even if no one else in the room heard his words, she'd read them with blatant clarity.

"Who the bloody hell invited her?"

Elation welled within her.

She smiled and stood her ground, forcing him to make the first move. Oh, she'd give anything if she had the option of turning on her heel and giving him the cut direct. But she didn't.

Shortly after receiving her invitation, she'd received a note. The contents of the message left her with no choice but to attend Fellingsdown's summer party.

Somehow she had to survive the next two weeks or she'd lose everything.

For several seconds longer she kept her gaze locked with his, then she broadened her gloating smile. Propriety would force him to greet her. Even if he'd refused to come to her aid before, that had been a private matter. This was public and she knew he wouldn't dare commit such a breach of etiquette before his family and several of his peers.

She slowly lifted her brows and tilted her head, her gesture a dare to ignore her any longer.

Elly placed her hand on Harrison's arm and said something Cassie couldn't make out. Whatever it was caused the muscles in his jaw to clench tight. He gave her a final lethal glare, then put a smile on his face as he turned to his guests.

"Please, everyone. Dinner is ready. George, would you lead our guests in to dine?"

Cassie took a step to the side to let the dinner guests walk past her. Each guest greeted her with a smile or a nod or a word of welcome. She paid special attention to both Patience and Lilly as they walked in to dinner on their husbands' arms. But she couldn't see anything out of the ordinary in their expressions.

Elly was the last to exit the room, but that wasn't unusual. She was always embarrassed because of her uneven gait and chose to hang back rather than walk at the front of a crowd. Her expression didn't indicate if she were the one who'd sent the invitation. The only look Cassie recognized was embarrassment.

Cassie knew her friend's discomfort was because she was on the arm of the very handsome Earl of Charfield.

Under any other circumstance, Cassie would feel enough

compassion for Elly she'd rush to her rescue, but not tonight. Not when it would take every ounce of her fortitude to match wits with Harrison. She'd waited four long years to repay him for abandoning her and she might not get a better chance.

When the last guest exited the room she returned her gaze to where Harrison stood. He stiffened his shoulders and took one angry step after another toward her.

"What are you doing here?"

There was nothing welcoming in his voice. She was glad. The harder he found it to tolerate her presence, the easier it would be to stick her barbs where they would hurt most. Perhaps he'd make a point to avoid her after tonight.

There was nothing she wanted more for the next two weeks than for him to stay as far away from her as possible.

"Good evening, Harrison," she said as cordially as her icy tone would allow.

"Why are you here?"

"Because I was invited."

"By whom?"

She gave him what she prayed was a smile dripping with mockery. "I assumed by you."

"You know better than that."

His tone contained a sharpness that revealed the depth of his anger. "Yes, I suppose I should have. Regardless, I was invited and so I've come."

"Then please make this easier on both of us and leave."

"And if I don't? Would you remove me from your home, Harrison?"

He hesitated then answered her with, "I'm hoping you won't make me."

She held his formidable glare for several agonizing seconds

and fought the urge to storm past him and out the front door. Nothing would relieve her more than to show Harrison Prescott her back and never see him again. But she couldn't. In this, she didn't have a choice.

She took a deep breath and braced her shoulders. "I was invited to this gathering and have the invitation to prove it. Whether you approve of my presence or not doesn't matter. You have no hold over me. I won't allow you to intimidate me or force me to leave."

Harrison's eyes had always been a brown so deep and rich they were almost black. Their warmth had always been one of the endearing qualities she'd loved most about him. Tonight there was no tenderness in them. Nor did they glisten with hospitality or kindness.

Tonight they blazed with a fury so intense it almost bordered on—

No, not *almost*. His gaze blazed with a fury so intense it sparked with blatant hatred. But he had no more right to ownership of that emotion than she did. The memory of how he'd rejected her when she'd needed him most stiffened her resolve. She raised her chin a haughty inch and lifted her shoulders in defiance.

"Then stay, *Lady Lathamton*. It matters not to me."

With that he spun on his heel and walked toward the door.

"You would leave me to see myself in to dinner?"

He halted at the doorway. His shoulders stiffened even more, if that were possible, and the loud, angry huff of his breathing sent a shiver down her spine.

He turned and took a step back to her. "No," he said, gracing her with a smile that lacked the warmth she'd once seen. The lift of his lips sent icy chills spiraling through every part of her body. His fake smile contained only bitterness and resentment. And another emotion Cassie refused to consider.

"Although *leaving* you is no more than you deserve, I refuse to stoop so low as to do so. Especially since I know I could never compete with the master of deceit."

His words were like a slap to her face and caused the intended pain. "No," she managed with a haughty air that gave him pause. "*Abandonment* is more your style."

"Do you blame me?"

She wanted to laugh. "No, one can hardly expect the righteous Marquess of Fellingsdown to defend someone the gossipmongers accused so thoroughly. After all, how could anyone expect the future Duke of Sheridan to accept anything less than perfection?"

"I never expected you to be perfect," he said with sharp, clipped words. "All that mattered was your love. Your faithfulness. But you could give me neither, could you, Lady Lathamton?"

Cassie wanted to slap the condescending expression from his face. She wanted to storm from the room and leave the man she'd once loved with all her heart far behind. She wanted to go back to the home she'd made for herself with her son and never have to look at Harrison Prescott, Marquess of Fellingsdown again. But she couldn't.

When he held out his arm, she had no choice but to place her hand atop his jacket sleeve. And pray he didn't notice how much his words had affected her.

Or how close to tears he'd brought her.

CHAPTER 6

Elly's heart pounded so hard inside her chest she was certain Charfield could hear it. If he did, though, he didn't show it. Neither had he seemed overly surprised when Harrison helped her to her feet then handed her the cane.

Most surprising of all, he hadn't shown any embarrassment when he realized he'd been saddled with someone who was deformed.

She worried her bottom lip, not knowing exactly how to handle this. Wasn't it enough that she had to worry about Harrison and Cassie? Elly wasn't sure she'd survive this evening. Or the next two weeks.

She knew it was highly unlikely a minute would go by when at least one of her siblings wouldn't check on her. Even the twins' expressions told her they'd come to her rescue at a moment's notice.

She could imagine the dread Charfield was experiencing. No doubt he was cringing at the thought that Harrison's actions tonight were a prelude to what would be expected of him the next two weeks. He may even think her brothers and sisters had tricked him into attending because they were trying to force a marriage.

Her face warmed. She had to reassure him that after this first dinner, he wouldn't be expected to escort her again. She couldn't bear to have him think her family intended to foist their lame sister on him. She wanted him to know this before they went in to dinner. It would make the evening so much more bearable.

Elly looked over her shoulder to the room where they'd left Harrison and Cassandra. She was glad they weren't coming yet. It would give her time to say what she must.

"Are you going to force me to initiate a conversation all night or is your silence just a temporary condition?"

Elly swallowed a startled gasp and stopped in the middle of the long hallway that led to the formal dining room. She blinked once then looked up at him.

He was smiling.

"What?"

"I'd like to know what's churning through that pretty little head of yours. You're terribly quiet and I'm sure silence is not one of your virtues."

She breathed a deep sigh. "You're right. I'm hardly ever quiet."

"Then why don't you tell me what has you so worried. Is it Lady Lathamton?"

"Lady Lathamton?"

"I couldn't help but notice your brother's reaction to her appearance."

"That's because seeing her here was such a shock."

"Why a shock? Lathamton estates borders The Down to the east doesn't it? Surely she visits often."

When Elly didn't respond right away Charfield leaned against the door frame and crossed his arms in a relaxed pose. "Are you saying this is the first time Lady Lathamton has visited since her marriage?"

"Yes," Elly said softly. "Lady Lathamton has been in mourning for the last year."

"I heard about Lathamton's illness and death."

"Yes."

"That doesn't, however, explain your brother's almost violent reaction to seeing her." The furrows deepened across his brow.

Elly gave up trying to hide anything from Charfield. "We all thought there might be a marriage between Cassie and Harrison. But when that didn't happen..."

"Of course. I seem to recall your brother's name being linked to Lady Lathamton's before she married. And the suddenness of her marriage to another man."

"Yes, but—"

"I'm surprised her name was included on the guest list."

Elly swallowed hard. Before she could come up with an excuse Charfield would believe, his lips curved upward and he laughed.

"He didn't know, did he?"

Elly stiffened her spine. "We could hardly have a gathering at The Down and not invite Lady Lathamton."

Elly leaned heavier on her cane. She wasn't sure why she felt the need to try to explain why Cassie had been invited, or why there was so much animosity between her brother and her best friend. But she did. "I'm not sure what happened, but

Cassie and Harrison didn't part on good terms. They seemed so happy when they were together, then..."

"There was the hint of scandal and her sudden marriage to Lathamton."

Elly nodded. "It happened so fast. One minute she and Harrison were planning a future together. The next Cassie was married to another man."

Charfield pushed himself away from the wall. "And you think you can get them back together again."

"I want my best friend to be able to visit me whether Harrison is here or not."

"You saw your brother's reaction when Lady Lathamton arrived. Do you think that's possible?"

Elly hoped her expression didn't reveal how hopeless she feared the results would be. "I have two weeks. A lot can happen in two weeks."

Charfield smiled. "That's true. Ever so much can happen in two weeks."

Elly's heart skipped a beat. Charfield didn't know how right he was. *Ever so much could happen in two weeks.* That was another reason she had to disassociate herself from him as soon as possible. The pull she felt toward him spelled nothing but trouble.

Yes, ever so much could happen in two weeks. Even heartache was a distinct possibility if she were foolish enough to let it go so far.

She looked back to the closed door.

"Are you afraid it might not have been wise to leave them alone?"

"They did look as if either one of them could commit murder."

"I hardly think that's likely."

"I hope you're right." She locked her gaze with his. "There's something else I need to discuss with you." She worried her lower lip while she thought how to begin.

His voice caught her attention. "Something terribly important, I gather."

"Yes."

Charfield turned to face her with his arms crossed over his chest. His pose caused the fine cut of his expensive jacket to pull over his broad shoulders. She didn't think she'd ever seen anyone so magnificently formed. Not even her four brothers were so perfect in build. And she'd always considered them the most handsome men in all of England.

Then she made the mistake of focusing on his face.

She swallowed hard. His complexion was a deep bronze. His hair the color of dark coffee. And his eyes a blue as bright as a clear summer sky.

Elly hunted for a word to describe his rugged, yet handsome features and the only word that came to mind was...beautiful.

Her heart shifted. Every horrible experience she'd endured in London haunted her. She remembered the cuts she'd received from the debutantes who didn't want to be sullied by associating with someone so physically inferior. The female gender could be viciously cruel, especially when they were competing for the attentions of the most eligible males in Society.

But what had hurt more was being rejected time and again by the men of the *ton*. She'd naïvely believed the males she'd meet would accept her disability the same as her brothers did.

Instead she'd found the opposite to be true.

Looks were everything. Beauty attracted beauty, and those

less than perfect were considered an embarrassment.

Elly had been an embarrassment.

At first, Harrison and George had tried to include her on outings to which they'd been invited. But it wasn't long before the invitations diminished as people realized there was the possibility their deformed sister might tag along.

And there were always the comments.

Initially she tried to pretend she didn't hear them, tried to pretend she didn't notice everyone was snickering at the unfortunate male who'd drawn the short straw and was forced to be her escort. And nearly always that male was the least handsome man in the room.

Someone as magnificently handsome as the Earl of Charfield would *never* have been forced to be her escort.

Elly lifted her shoulders and rushed to say the words she knew must be said before she lost courage.

"I'd like to apologize. I didn't realize Harrison intended to push me off onto you."

Charfield's gaze narrowed.

Elly raised her chin an inch higher and blurted out the rest of her words before she couldn't. "I know we will probably be forced into each other's company several times over the next two weeks but please understand that I do not expect you to repeatedly partner me."

The expression on his face turned darker, the look in his eyes more frigid. For several long seconds he didn't say anything. Finally, he clamped his hands behind his back and drew a breath that broadened his shoulders even more.

"I won't insult your intelligence or mine by pretending I don't know what you're talking about. You have a slight limp. It obviously doesn't hamper your ability to get from one place to the other and it *definitely* doesn't impede your ability to ride. You handle a horse better than any female I've ever seen. What I don't understand is why you would think such a minor physical imperfection would make a difference to me."

She knew she should be flattered by his compliments. There'd been a time when she would have been. But that was years ago. Now, his insincere comments only frustrated her.

"Because it always has. I spent a whole London Season watching a room empty when I hobbled in."

"You don't hobble."

"I observed everyone avert their gaze so they could pretend not to notice me."

"Well, I'm not looking away. I've noticed you. And I'm fascinated by you."

Elly tightened her fingers around the marble knob of her cane. "Well, don't be. I accepted my future a long time ago."

He paused and cocked his head to the side. "What future is that?"

Elly couldn't answer him. The future she saw for herself wasn't something she wanted to share with him. With anyone.

Luckily, she didn't have to say more because the door flew open and Harrison came down the hall at a pace that gave proof to his irritation. He was escorting Lady Lathamton, but from the expression on his face, having her anywhere near him was the last thing he desired.

Charfield took a step. "This conversation isn't over, Lady Elyssa."

Elly blinked. Did he think her offer to excuse him from partnering her was a test of what kind of man he was? Did he think she evaluated him and he didn't want to seem lacking? Surely not.

"My words weren't a challenge, Lord Charfield. I wasn't testing your gallantry."

"I didn't think you were," he said with more flippancy than his last remark. "I merely think you underestimate me."

"I—"

He held up a finger to stop her words and nodded to where Harrison and Cassandra were coming down the hall. "They don't seem any happier, do you think?"

Elly shook her head.

"I think perhaps keeping a friendly conversation going at dinner may well be a bit of a task tonight," he said as the couple neared them.

Because Harrison wasn't married, the role of hostess automatically fell to her and if the deep furrows on Harrison's forehead were any indication of his mood, they wouldn't get two friendly sentences from him all night.

"If you promise a rematch of our race today, I promise to be at my friendliest during dinner and help you keep the table conversation flowing."

She couldn't help but smile. In fact, what she really wanted to do was lean up and kiss him on the cheek and whisper "thank you" in his ear. She pulled back, appalled that she'd had such a thought.

"Thank you," she said in a whisper that came out far too heavy. "That would be lovely." She paused. "But only because I intend to soundly beat you in our rematch. I've been planning my strategy all day."

His threw back his head and laughed. The sound was so natural and carefree it sent a wave of warmth rushing over her. And drew a threatening glare from Harrison.

"Shouldn't you be inside?" her brother said as he marched

Lady Lathamton past them.

"We thought we'd wait for you, Harrison," she said placing her hand back on Charfield's proffered arm.

"Afraid I might commit murder?" her brother said over his shoulder.

"The thought did cross my mind."

Harrison gave her a look that had the power to destroy a weaker person. Elly just gave Cassandra her most reassuring smile, then she and Charfield followed them into the dining room.

In her dreams, when she was on the arm of a man as handsome as the Earl of Charfield, she was whole again, and her limp was hardly evident. But that was in her dreams. In reality, her gait was decidedly uneven, her limp as noticeable as ever.

Her imperfection remained a blatant reminder not to allow herself to imagine her dreams might be within reach. They weren't and never would be.

She shifted her gaze from Cassie and Harrison to Charfield. This promised to be a very interesting two weeks. Charfield added a complication she hadn't counted on, but everything else was going as planned.

———

Harrison looked down the table at the long line of guests seated to his left then brought his gaze back up the right side. His eyes avoided the person seated beside him. He wasn't ready yet to look at her for any length. Tonight was the first time he'd seen Cassandra since before she'd become the Marchioness of Lathamton more than four years ago.

Tonight was the first time he'd seen her or talked to her since the night she'd left his arms only to be discovered a few hours later in Lathamton's bed.

He stabbed his braised beef tip as if he were practicing for the murder Elly feared he might commit. He was appalled that Cassie not only had the nerve to show up at his home, but that she had every intention of staying.

His gaze wandered down the long table again and lingered briefly on each of his brothers and sisters. One of them was responsible for Cassie being here and whoever it was had outmaneuvered him to a fault.

His blood ran cold and he stabbed at a small potato boiled in crème sauce. He missed his target and the potato slid across his fine china plate, up the small rise, then over the gold rim. It landed on the white linen tablecloth beside his empty wine glass.

Cassandra, who'd seemed to be totally engrossed in a conversation with Jeremy Waverley, her late husband's cousin and only relative, stopped her conversation. With a barely suppressed grin, she motioned to the closest footman and whispered something in his ear. The servant rushed to the sideboard, then returned with a wine decanter and filled Harrison's wine glass.

"If you wanted more wine, Fellingsdown, all you had to do was motion to one of your staff." Lady Lathamton popped an asparagus tip into her dainty mouth and chewed. "There's no need to shoot food at your glass."

Harrison gave her the most glaringly hostile look he could manage then lifted the fresh wine to his lips and drank. He noticed that everyone at the table watched him with renewed interest – everyone except Charfield, who couldn't seem to take his eyes off Elly.

When he noticed the ease with which Elly conversed with London's most notorious rake, he wasn't sure he'd made the wisest decision by inviting Charfield to make her forget the admirer the twins had invented for her.

He took another sip of his wine and vowed to remind Charfield one more time of the conditions they'd agreed to. The object of inviting him had been to keep Elly from being hurt, not put her in greater jeopardy.

He took a larger swallow of wine than usual and set his glass down on the table.

Lively conversations went on all around him. A loud burst of laughter at the other end of the table drew his attention Everyone at the far end of the table was engrossed in a tale the Duke of Parneston was telling.

Toward the center of the table, George and Spence carried on enthusiastic discussions with Lady Brianna, Lady Hannah and a few of their guests.

Only a few seats away, Jules appeared enamored of Miss Amelia Hastings and whatever topic she'd chosen.

Harrison made a mental note to keep a more careful eye on his brothers. Each one of them had made excellent choices in the women they'd asked to have included on the guest list, but Harrison wasn't prepared to handle anything more serious from any of them. He had troubles of his own with Cassandra's attendance. Her presence turned him into the most inept host imaginable, which made him simmer with building fury.

To his relief, whenever there was a lull in the conversation, Elly or one of the twins came to his rescue.

Even the Earl of Charfield was an asset. The fact that he was so at ease at gatherings of this kind seemed to make Elly more comfortable. She joined in the conversations more than Harrison anticipated she might the first night the guests arrived. Hopefully, this party was just what she needed to bring her into the open.

If only the widowed Marchioness of Lathamton hadn't come and spoiled everything.

"Did you attend the race in Grover's meadow last week, Fellingsdown?" Jeremy Waverley asked. Not only was he a neighbor, as the late Earl of Lathamton had been, but he was a close friend of George's.

Harrison pulled his thoughts back. "No, I'd already left to come here. But I heard it was an unbelievable sight."

"That is a monumental understatement. Without a doubt, you missed the race of the year. Roger Wilkes has an Arabian he purchased in Russia he was eager to show off. Then, of course, there was Mattenworth's prize thoroughbred. You couldn't have found two horses more evenly matched."

Waverley turned his gaze to where Charfield sat beside Elly. "You were there, weren't you, Charfield?"

"I was as close to the finish line as I could get without risking being trampled when the horses finished the race. It was amazing."

"Everyone agreed Downing's horse was the most remarkable piece of Arabian horseflesh they'd ever seen... next to yours and Fellingsdown's, of course." Waverley cast a glance from Harrison to Charfield then moved his gaze to Lady Lathamton. All eyes followed him. "Do you still have my cousin's Arabian. Or have you sold it?"

Her arm halted midway to her mouth and she slowly set her wine glass back to the table. "I still have it."

"If I remember correctly, your husband told me his

Arabian's dame was the famous Rouboulet." Waverley leaned closer in his chair and gave her a magnificent smile. "Would you consider parting with him if I made an offer? Since I'm Everett's cousin, the horse would stay in the family."

Everyone watched as Cassandra seemed to consider Waverley's question. "Perhaps. If the offer were right. I don't see much need to keep Everett's horses."

Harrison felt the stabbing of an emotion he couldn't explain. Perhaps anger. Perhaps jealousy. "You would sell Brigado?" he heard himself ask. "He was, after all, your dear husband's prize Arabian. I'd think it would be difficult to part with something that was his."

Harrison watched the color drain from Cassandra's face and knew his words had hit their mark. He wasn't prepared, however, for the announcement she made.

"It would be a lie if I said that my late husband didn't consider Brigado special. But I never shared his affection. Because of a bitter aftertaste left from the rejection of a former acquaintance, anything connected with horses – especially Arabians – is highly distasteful to me."

Harrison's blood turned an icier cold. Cassie hadn't known one horse from another until he'd shown her his stable. *He* was the person who'd given her the first glimpse into the world of Arabians and she'd fallen in love with them the minute she'd laid eyes on them. Just as he'd thought she'd fallen in love with him. Now she hated everything about them.

"It is better to sell the horse, then," he said, unable to keep the bitterness out of his voice.

Cassandra took a sip of her wine then lowered the glass and looked at him. She slowly turned the stem of the wine glass between her thumb and forefinger as her glaring gaze locked with his. "I agree. It is always better to separate oneself from unpleasant memories."

Harrison tried to look away from her but for several interminable seconds no amount of effort could force him to turn his head and back down from the blade-sharp attack she'd issued.

He knew what she was doing. She'd come here as her first step in reentering society after her year-long mourning period. She'd chosen this opportunity to let it be known she was back to take her place as the widowed Marchioness of Lathamton.

She'd walked into his home as if she hadn't shattered his every dream four years ago and left him with nothing. She'd intentionally let this be her first outing to remind him of the fool she'd made of him.

Well, she could bloody well forget it. She'd destroyed his life once. He wouldn't give her a second chance. "Then by all means, sell the horse. You already have an offer."

Harrison concentrated on the food on his plate and ignored the undivided attention Waverley continued to shower on Cassandra, as well as the open smiles she gave him in return.

If she'd come here to find a husband - or a lover - let her pick Waverley. Harrison didn't care who she chose – as long as it wasn't him.

She was a beautiful woman and wouldn't have trouble finding someone to share her bed. The years with Lathamton had been good to her. If there was a hint of shadows around her midnight-blue eyes, he would attribute it to the strain of being out in public for the first time since her husband's death a year ago.

If her smile did not reflect the glow of her inner beauty, he would blame it on the lighting, or perhaps on memories of the husband she'd obviously loved and lost.

But if she thought he would give her a second chance to destroy his heart like she'd done nearly four years ago, she was sadly mistaken. He'd give her over to her late husband's cousin, or anyone else who'd take her, before he'd go through the pain he'd endured when he lost her.

Harrison turned his attention to his role as host and did a better job of keeping the conversation active. He should be happy Elly seemed to get along so well with Charfield. He could almost make himself believe his plan to make her forget her secret admirer might work.

If only he could believe that he'd survive the next two weeks as unscathed as he anticipated Elly would.

But he already knew it was highly unlikely.

CHAPTER 7

When the meal was over, the women rose in a flutter and followed Patience and Lilly from the dining room to a drawing room a few doors down the hall. The men would join them later, but for now they remained to have a glass of Harrison's fine brandy and discuss the rich hunting prospects at The Down.

Elly was never so glad to make her escape in her life. Not only was the atmosphere between Harrison and Cassie heavy enough to drown a hearty swimmer, but Charfield, instead of one of her brothers, had been the one to hover over her all through their meal.

She'd always been able to depend on one of her siblings to come to her aid if she needed help, but during dinner every bit of their attention had been devoted to their guests. Charfield had been the one to engage her in conversation. He'd been the one who motioned for her wine glass to be refilled. He'd been the one who helped her to her feet when the ladies rose to leave. She'd never felt so clumsy in her life.

Sitting and rising had always been the most awkward movements for her, but he acted as if he didn't notice the ungainly way she rose. He even stood motionless when she got to her feet as if he realized she needed a few moments to steady herself. And the smile he gave her when he handed over her cane caused a molten heat to race to every part of her body.

Elly slowed to let the other ladies walk ahead of her.

The focused attention Charfield paid her throughout the meal had caused a rush of excitement as well as a fluttering deep inside her chest.

She hadn't expected him to be such a pleasant companion.

She hadn't expected him to be so adept at overlooking her disability.

She hadn't expected to feel so relaxed around him. So excited just being near him.

And that scared her to death.

Charfield hadn't allowed her to remain a silent observer. He'd forced her to be an integral part of the group as well as a major contributor. In this, he posed a threat she wasn't sure she could combat.

A chill raced up and down her spine. Instead of following the ladies to the drawing room, she stepped into the room Harrison used as a study when he came to The Down, then out onto the terrace that ran the length of the house. She needed to be by herself for a minute to think. She needed to sort out her feelings and decide her best course of action.

She'd never met anyone who could unleash the emotions he brought to the surface. Never met anyone who made her yearn to share the same joys that other females experienced.

Never wondered what it would be like to have a future like every other woman dreamed of having. Because for her those joys weren't possible.

Even men who were desperate for her father's wealth had never shown an interest in her.

Perhaps that was why she'd enjoyed her correspondence with her elusive secret admirer. Perhaps that was why she'd written to her fictitious admirer for so long before requesting they meet.

Because she knew meeting wasn't possible.

Elly walked across the lantern-lit terrace and stared out into the garden. So what did Brentan Montgomery, Earl of Charfield hope to gain by pretending not to notice her limp?

It couldn't be her dowry, for Charfield was reputed to be one of the wealthiest men in England. Nor could it be that marriage to a duke's daughter would raise his worth in London society. Although his rakish character had tarnished his reputation a bit, he was still considered one of the greatest catches of the Season. And she knew why.

She'd been around him for less than one day and already she'd been drawn in by his handsome features and his charming personality. He was intelligent and witty and when he talked to her, it wasn't about the boring things Patience and Lilly told her men talked about when they came to call.

Charfield was interested in horses, of course, as well as the stable Harrison kept, but he'd also asked her how she spent her days. When she explained that most her days were taken up running The Down, he was genuinely impressed. And interested.

He asked her all sorts of questions. If Harrison hadn't ended the dinner so abruptly, she was sure they could have spent several hours discussing any number of topics.

She leaned her injured hip against the cement railing and let the cool evening breeze wash over her. She was enjoying herself ever so much, and for the first time in her life, she yearned for something more than the life she had here. For the first time she had to admit she was a little lonely and thought she might like having someone like Charfield to talk to. She also realized there were things she missed having. Things only a man could give her.

Which was reason enough to be wary. She would be the loser if she let herself dream of things that could never be. Her disastrous London Season had taught her that. She didn't want to go through a similar pain again.

She breathed a deep sigh that hurt as it rushed into the open. The voice of reason shouted that every minute she spent with him put her in greater danger. That voice was right. She knew what she had to do. She'd send a message that she'd decided to retire for the night. Sleep would be difficult enough the way it was since she knew whose face would appear even in her dreams. But dreams were safer than reality.

She turned around to make her way to her rooms and stopped before she took her first step.

Charfield stood in the shadows watching her.

He leaned against the dark stone in a casual pose and drank from one glass. He held a second glass in his hand.

"Would you care for a glass of wine?" He offered her a glass when he reached her.

"How long have you been there?" She took the glass from his hand then lifted it to her lips.

"I was enjoying the view."

"It's dark. There isn't a view."

He smiled. "There is a view."

She swallowed hard. Heavens, he was flirting with her.

Her heart raced and she prayed her shaking hand wouldn't give away her nervousness.

"Your brother has an excellent cellar" He leaned his hip against the balustrade.

He was close. Too close.

Not close enough.

"The cellar is mine," she answered, then nearly laughed at the surprised expression on his face. "And so is Fellings Down."

He smiled. "I'm impressed, Lady Elyssa. I naturally assumed that—"

"...that because of its name, Fellings Down must be entailed," she finished for him. "It's not. It's been in the Fellingsdown family for generations and my father generously deeded the estate to me for my lifetime."

Charfield's gaze never left her face as he took another slow sip of his drink.

"Was deeding you the estate your father's idea? Or yours?"

"Mine."

"You're a very practical woman, aren't you?" He set his glass on the flat stone railing.

"My mother tells me I'm a very independent woman. *Too* independent."

"And what do you think?"

She couldn't help but smile. "I think she's probably right. Being self-sufficient has always been important to me."

"My guess is that it's been an uphill battle. Am I right?"

The corner of the terrace where they stood wasn't brightly lit, but every once in a while the clouds would let the moonlight brighten the sky. She took advantage of one of those times to study his features. "I'm not sure I understand what you mean."

"Your family."

She smiled. "Oh."

He picked up his glass and took a sip. "Only a blind man could fail to notice how closely your brothers watch every move you make. The moment you slid to the edge of the sofa to rise, all four of them instantly came to attention. You had an arsenal of at-the-ready protectors waiting until they were certain you weren't going to object to my assistance."

His smile widened. "I daresay they would have rushed to your side at the slightest indication."

She tried to hold his gaze but couldn't. "I'm very fortunate to have such attentive brothers."

"Have they always been so protective?"

She looked out into the shadows. Even though there was nothing to see, she scanned the horizon as if she could see the vibrant colors of every blooming flower. How could she tell him that they'd left her remarkably alone tonight? That they usually hovered over her as diligently as a mother hen over her chicks.

She tightened her grip around the handle of her cane. No, it would only elicit pity from him if he knew the reason they shielded her so. "Sometimes they forget I am quite capable of taking care of myself."

"So you find it necessary to remind them."

"Perhaps," she said with a smile.

He studied her for a small second then asked a question that seemed to test her confession. "Would you stroll through the garden with me?"

Her gaze snapped to his. "I cannot."

"Because of your leg? Does it pain you when you walk?"

She shook her head. "It's not that. I just—"

"I promise we won't walk far. If you tire, I'm sure we can find a bench where we can sit for a while."

She searched for another excuse. "Being alone in the garden with you isn't proper."

"We'll hardly be alone. In the short time we've been out here, each of your brothers has checked on you from the windows at least once. I'm sure one of them will come to find us before long. Which one do you suppose it will be?"

Elly turned to look over her shoulder just as Spence stepped away from the window to rejoin the men. It was always like this.

Elly felt a clenching in her chest. She was seven and twenty and they still watched over her as if she were eleven and they could undo what had happened.

She looked up and locked onto his gaze. "George."

"Pardon?"

"George will come to find me first. He's my twin and there's a connection that's hard to explain. He'll come."

"Then you have nothing to fear. Shall we?"

She only hesitated a moment. She'd always dreamed of having a handsome man at her side as she walked through a moonlit garden. And there wasn't a man in all of England who was more handsome than Chardfield.

He extended his arm and she stared at it for a quick second before she pulled back.

"There's no need to escort me. I'm not easy to walk beside."

"I've been told I'm an excellent escort."

He had a way of saying the perfect thing for every occasion. She felt so at ease around him the warning bells went off inside her head. She wondered if he had that effect on all women and knew he did. If not, he wouldn't have the reputation he did.

That made him an even bigger threat.

She took an independent step away from him and crossed the smooth stone terrace. When she reached the steps, she used the railing to steady her descent. He followed behind her.

"Would it have been so difficult for you to accept my help?" he said as they walked the cobbled lane.

"I'm quite capable of managing by myself."

"Most women are but they accept a man's assistance because it makes the man feel useful."

"Are you admitting a sense of ineptitude?"

"Not ineptitude, exactly. But helping a female builds a man's self-confidence."

Elly laughed. "I grew up with four brothers, my lord. Not one of them lacks confidence."

"Don't they?"

Elly thought of all the sacrifices her brothers had made to make up for what happened that one disastrous day. But her brothers were different. Charfield couldn't have anything nearly so heavy weighing on him.

She couldn't imagine him lacking self-confidence.

"What if I told you that I do?"

"I wouldn't believe you for a second."

"Oh, Lady Elyssa, let me assure you. There isn't a man alive who doesn't need every opportunity to prove himself to the woman he's trying to impress."

Her footsteps halted. "You're trying to impress me?"

"Of course."

"Why?"

"Because I think you are worth impressing."

Another warning sent a shiver through her. She couldn't

allow him to say such lies. She turned to face him. "What is it you want?"

"You think I *want* something from you?"

"Of course. What is it you want?"

"To be your friend. To enjoy your company for the next two weeks and hope you'll enjoy mine."

She looked up at him and felt a warmth flow through her that washed away every warning she'd issued. She was weakening and the little voice she could usually count on to deliver such stern rebukes was suddenly quiet. Instead, she heard an earthier-toned voice whisper that it would be all right to give herself over just this once. That she didn't have to be totally independent - just this once.

"Have I come close to convincing you that you can trust me?"

Elly stared at his outstretched hand. This was the second time tonight she'd been expected to walk with someone other than one of her brothers. The second time tonight she'd been expected to lean on someone other than herself.

An encouraging seriousness shadowed his features and she slowly lifted her hand and placed her palm atop his muscled arm.

"You won't regret your decision," he said as if he knew the trust she was giving him.

They turned away from the house and took their first step further into the garden.

There was something magical about the harmonious way they moved. His gait seemed to fit with hers even better than Harrison's or George's, or any of her brothers.

With her cane in her right hand and his strong arm beneath her left, Elly could almost forget she walked with a limp. Could pretend she was whole, desirable.

They walked down one path, then another, and Elly could not remember a more perfect night.

After they walked a while, he led her to one of the small stone benches placed along the paths. She didn't need the benches as places to rest. Her leg was remarkably strong. But she sat here in the garden often and read.

He helped her sit, then sat beside her.

"You haven't completely answered my question. Why is it so important to prove your independence to your family? Because you are female?"

No one had ever put it so bluntly. "Yes, and because I am unmarried and refuse to be a burden."

"If I may ask," he said, suddenly seeming closer than he'd been before. "Why are you unmarried?"

Every defense she possessed snapped to attention. Was he serious? Or was he making fun of her? Suddenly he seemed no different than any other man she'd met and her temper soared. "Because I choose to be. Which is no doubt a better reason for remaining single than you have."

She turned to face him squarely and found herself entirely too close to his towering strength. But she couldn't back down. She never backed down. "Isn't your obligation to assure an heir to the Charfield dynasty important to you? I would have thought you'd have found the perfect Countess by now and set up your nursery. Isn't that what every nobleman is expected to do?"

She expected a retort. Instead he laughed.

"Touché," he said, looking at her with a wide grin on his face. "Society says we both have an obligation to wed – you as the eldest daughter of the Duke of Sheridan, and I, as the Earl of Charfield. My reason for not marrying, however, is quite simple. I have a brother who has taken over that responsibility for me. Three sons at last count. Or perhaps it is four by now, since my dear sister-in-law is in a delicate condition once again and expected to deliver any time soon."

"You do not want an heir of your own?"

Elly couldn't believe it. Every titled peerage wanted an heir.

"It isn't that I have anything against providing a Charfield heir. It's the sacrifice one is forced to make to accomplish it."

"And what sacrifice would that be?"

"Marriage."

He spat the word out so solidly it almost seemed like a curse. "You don't want to marry?"

He rose from the bench and took a step away from her. He turned to look out into the moonlit darkness and clasped his hands behind his back. "Were you acquainted with my parents?"

"I never met them."

"But you heard about them."

She felt her cheeks warm and was relieved he couldn't see her discomfiture. Every time her family returned from London they had a new tale to tell concerning the Earl and Countess of Charfield. She'd been shocked at some of the lengths the two would go to disgrace the other. "Society has a habit of embellishing its gossip with each telling so I—"

Charfield's bitter laughter stopped her words. "Oh, believe me. Nothing you heard concerning my parents needed embellishment. The arguments they had in public were legendary, as well as their indiscretions. Their words and actions had but one goal – to humiliate and inflict as much pain as possible on each other."

"Many marriages are not based on love."

"But most other couples do not put their dislike for each other on display for the world to see. And ridicule."

"So you have decided not to marry?"

For several long seconds he didn't answer. When he did, his voice contained a tone she couldn't quite explain.

He returned to the bench and sat beside her. "I'm going to tell you something I've never told another soul. It isn't marriage I object to. In fact, I see many benefits to having a wife. But when I marry, it will be because I have fallen in love."

"And you have never fallen in love?"

She wanted to take her words back the second they left her mouth but it was too late.

"No."

Her breath caught. She didn't want to know that he'd never been in love. She didn't want to know how seriously he took the sanctity of marriage. His words were another indication of how perfect he was.

How perfect the woman he married would have to be.

How lacking she was.

"Why did you tell me this?"

He smiled. "I don't know. Perhaps because I trust you. Perhaps because it was something I finally needed to say out loud. Or, perhaps because it was something I wanted you to know."

She was in uncharted territory and she wasn't sure she was safe there. She quickly erected the wall she always kept firmly in place when threatened. "Your confession is safe with me. But it's not necessary that I know your feelings."

"Isn't it?"

"No."

She wanted to cut him off there but couldn't. She couldn't be so abrupt. Appear to be so unfeeling. So she added, "But I'm glad you shared that with me."

He smiled then looked up at the moon as it appeared from behind a cloud. "So am I."

Her blood turned to liquid heat as it flowed through her veins.

He turned to look at her. The smile was still on his handsome face.

"So am I," he whispered again, then leaned forward and touched his mouth to hers.

His lips were warm and firm and he tasted of fine wine and something else she couldn't explain. She'd never been kissed before so she wasn't quite prepared for such an earth-shattering experience.

Every inch of her body tingled as if a bolt of lightning flashed from the sky and struck her. The blood pounded against her ears like the dull thud of a heavy clanging bell. And the heat...

Her face warmed as though she'd stepped too close to a blazing fire and her heart raced so fast she feared it might leap from her chest.

Emotion boiled inside her nearly to overflowing and she clutched her hands in the folds of her skirt to keep from lifting them. She ached to wrap her arms around his neck and hold him to her. And never let him go.

"*Elly?*"

She gasped when he lifted his mouth from hers and fought the urge to pull him back.

"*Elly?*"

"They're calling you." His voice sounded raspy and hoarse.

"It's... George...," she said, pulling away from him.

She wasn't sure what had just happened. He'd kissed her and she should be shocked, embarrassed. Instead, she wanted him to kiss her again.

"Ah, yes. George."

"I need to go back to the house."

She slid to the edge of the bench and prepared to rise. He was on his feet in a second to stand in front of her just as he'd done before.

"Elly?"

"You'd better answer him or we'll have all your brothers storming the garden in search of you."

She nodded. "I'm here, George." She tried to make her voice sound as normal as possible.

"Are you ready?" Charfield said, holding his arm toward her.

She looked at the arm she needed to hold to rise more gracefully and dreaded the thought of having to touch him. Not because she dreaded touching him, but because she found his touch disturbing. As disturbing as his nearness.

As disturbing as his kiss.

As disturbing as the thoughts his kiss elicited.

She needed time to herself. Time to forget how he made her feel. Time to rationalize what was happening.

Perhaps she was coming down with some malady.

But after she placed her hand atop his arm, she knew what was happening to her was worse than any malady from which she'd ever suffered.

Far worse.

CHAPTER 8

Brent pushed Danza as fast as he dared.

Just as she'd promised, Lady Elyssa had found the most challenging course he'd ever raced.

A copse of trees spanned the meadow ahead of them. According to her detailed instructions at the outset of their race there would be a series of small hedge rows just over the rise, then a narrow stream at the bottom of the hill, followed by a sharp incline before they reached another flat stretch. A stately old maple tree on the opposite side of the open meadow would mark the finish line.

For a fraction of a second, he contemplated letting her win - until he saw the stubborn expression on her face and the fierce determination in her eyes. He knew he couldn't give her that advantage over him.

He looked to his right. Her horse raced neck and neck with his. She was a master horsewoman and exhibited complete control as she crouched low over the huge Arabian. Never before had he met anyone so amazing – male or female – and he knew one fact for certain.

He could not allow her to win.

He urged his horse to run faster and edged ahead. This race wasn't about whose horse was faster. It was a battle of mastery. Of who could master whom.

There'd been fear in her eyes when he'd kissed her as well as confusion. It was obvious that last night was the first time she'd been kissed. The expression on her face when she pulled away told him that she didn't understand the emotions that rushed through her.

Bloody hell. Neither did he!

The fear she experienced would no doubt prompt her to erect more barriers in an attempt to prevent him from breaching her emotions. Allowing her to win the race would strengthen those barriers and put her further out of his reach.

He concentrated on winning with greater determination.

His horse took the first hedge a length ahead of hers, then the second with perfect execution. Her Arabian landed nearly a full second behind his and he vowed he'd give Danza an extra ration of oats when they returned to the stable.

Danza took the stream in a clean leap. But so did Lady Elyssa's horse. And the pounding of hooves seemed closer.

The hill at the top of the rise was as steep as she'd described and he felt his challenger breathing down his neck. He looked to his right and saw her racing beside him. The hardened look of determination on her face reminded him of the look he'd seen on many a rider's face, the look that said she refused to contemplate defeat.

But to him it wasn't defeat. It was equality.

An equality between the two of them.

He pushed Danza up the steep rise, knowing that when they reached the top there was only a meadow to cross and the race would be over.

Bloody hell, but she was magnificent. By this time, most riders would have reached the end of their endurance. But she rode as if she was barely winded.

Danza reached the top of the rise, his lungs pushing out great puffs of air as he charged to a run. When the two horses reached the flat land that stretched before them, both seemed to find a new burst of energy and raced as if they hadn't already been pushed nearly beyond endurance.

Neck and neck, each horse and rider gave everything they had to be the winner in the race.

He leaned over Danza's neck, asking his horse to reach deep down to find the reserve of strength Arabians were known to possess. And Danza did.

His amazing Arabian flew like the wind and reached the stately oak a mere second before Lady Elyssa's horse. But there was no doubt which horse was the victor.

He pulled his horse to a stop beside her and wanted to shout aloud. "You were as magnificent as yesterday," he said, facing her. "Absolutely, magnificent."

He wanted to laugh. He wanted to shout. He wanted to reach out and hug her to him.

"So were you." Her face beamed with pleasure. "Your Arabian is as magnificent as mine! They're perfectly matched!"

There was no anger, or jealousy, or bitterness in her tone – just admiration.

And excitement.

Her cheeks held a deep rosy hue, both from exertion and excitement. She'd tied her hair back with a dark green ribbon but long amber wisps had come loose to float around her face in defiance of her attempt to contain them.

It was her eyes, though, that drew his attention. She should be exhausted, but there was a sparkle in her gaze that indicated that if he challenged her to repeat the race, she would agree.

Never before had he met someone so alive with such a pent-up zest for life.

"I hope you're not disappointed that I didn't let you win," he said.

Not until then did her eyes flash with something other than elation.

"Do you think I am only used to winning, sir? Or that I would admire you more if you'd let me come out the victor?"

"No," he said on a laugh. "Which was why it was so important that I win."

"*Important?* Why was it important?" she asked with an honest frown on her face.

"Because had I lost, I think you would have thought less of me."

A shocked look covered her face. "I would hardly have thought less of you."

"Wouldn't you have? Then what would your opinion of me have been?"

I'm not sure." Her words came out slowly and were filled with contemplation, "But I wouldn't have thought less of you."

He smiled. He couldn't have received a better compliment from her. "Let me tell you what I think. I think that had you won, I would have been easier to ignore." He leaned a fraction toward her. "Be forewarned, Lady Elyssa. I don't intend to make it easy for you to dismiss me."

Her eyes widened and he continued before she had time to

interrupt.

"I also think you're a little bit frightened."

"You think I'm afraid of you?"

"No." His gaze riveted on hers as he finished his sentence. "I think you're frightened of the feelings I force you to face."

She lifted her chin several notches. "I don't know what you're talking about."

The hint of defiance in her expression made him want to laugh. Instead, he swung down from his horse and walked over to her. "The horses are tired. Let's sit beneath the tree for a moment and let them rest."

The first hint of panic crossed her face. "I don't have my cane."

"You don't need your cane."

He lifted his arms to help her from her horse but he didn't touch her. First, he wanted an indication that she would allow him to assist her. He stared into her eyes as a myriad of emotions played inside their gleaming ebony depths; emotions running the gamut from panic to fear to excitement to acceptance.

He almost thought she was going to refuse him. The slight movement of her head indicated she wanted to tell him she had no intention of falling into his arms and letting him hold her, lift her, help her. In the end, though, she leaned forward and rested her hands on his shoulders.

With his hands around her narrow waist, he slowly lifted her from her horse. He was suddenly aware of how small she was, how petite, and how light. Before, only her strengths had been noticeable: her courage, her endurance, her resilience. All the qualities he'd admired from the minute they'd met were inner qualities.

He held her close to him. The pounding in his chest and the thickness in his groin told him everything about her on the outside had the power to affect him too.

He kept her suspended in mid-air, her forearms resting on his shoulders. Her mouth formed a perfectly kissable O, and if he lowered her another few inches, her lips would be close enough to kiss.

He brought her down slowly, reveling in the feel of her body as it skimmed against his. When her toes touched the ground, he lowered his head and touched his lips to hers. He kissed her before she had time to gain her balance, forcing her to wrap her arms around his neck and hold onto him.

It was unfair to take advantage of her like that, but he wanted her at a disadvantage. He wanted her to *have* to hold onto him for support. It was important that she realized she could rely on him, and he would keep her safe.

Their lips met and held, the kiss more intense than the one they'd shared the night before, yet not so desperate as to frighten her.

He pressed his lips to hers more firmly, drinking from her, then he angled his head to deepen the kiss. Her arms tightened around his neck and she held him close.

Brent deepened his kiss even more, tasting the sweetness of her lips, reveling in the soft wisps of air that brushed against his cheek, taking in the small moans of pleasure that came from deep within her. It had never been like this for him before. He'd never kissed a woman who possessed the power this woman had over him.

And he knew, even if he searched the world over, he'd never find a woman to equal her.

He gave her a last brief kiss, then pulled away before his

kisses took him so far he wasn't able to separate himself from her.

Their gasping breaths came in harsh, ragged rushes and he looked into her face, not sure he wanted to evaluate her reaction to his kisses.

But when he did, his heart swelled with joy. The expression on her face evidenced more than he had hoped for. There was a dark glaze of passion in her eyes that told him he'd taken her to a height she wasn't aware she could reach.

Then, at the moment he thought he could rejoice in his accomplishments, a look of confusion clouded her eyes.

"Are you all right?" He held her steady so she could keep her balance.

She nodded, then tightened her grip on his arm before she took a small step away from him. She would have walked away – or run if she had two good legs. He could read her desperation to escape in her eyes but she couldn't walk unassisted. He held her close and let her lean on him, the same as she relied on her cane.

He knew to walk on her right side and led her to a shady spot beneath the giant oak tree that had been the finish line of their race. He helped her sit on the ground, then took a step back and looked down on her.

Her gaze hadn't left his. She studied him as if he'd grown two heads and sprouted horns.

"Let me tie the horses so they don't wander off, then you can tell me what's bothering you."

He tied the horses to a nearby hedge then walked back to where he'd left her and sat down beside her on the grass. "Now, why don't you tell me what's going on inside that pretty head of yours."

She tilted her head and looked at him. She opened her mouth, then closed it again.

"Come on. Out with it." Her hesitation caused the nerves to zing inside him.

She took a breath as if working up the nerve to answer him. Then, in a rush of words she asked, "Why did you kiss me?"

He couldn't hide his surprise. "Why? Because I wanted to. Because it seemed the natural thing to do. Because I couldn't pass up such a perfect opportunity when I had you in my arms." His eyes narrowed as he studied her. "Why do *you* think I kissed you?"

She shook her head as if at a loss to find an answer. "I don't know."

Her cheeks darkened a deep shade of red and she lowered her gaze to her lap. He waited, knowing she had more to say.

"Did one of my brothers ask you to...to...kiss me?"

He couldn't stop the bark of laughter. "Oh, Lady Elyssa. If Harrison or one of your brothers knew I'd just kissed you, I probably wouldn't have any teeth left in my head. Or even a head left on my shoulders, for that matter. No," he said in perfect honesty, "none of your brothers suggested I kiss you."

"Then why did you do it?"

"Do I have to have a reason?"

"Of course you do."

"Didn't you like it?" he asked.

Her cheeks turned even redder. "You know I did."

"Then don't worry about *why* I kissed you but *when* I'll kiss you again."

Her gaze shot to his. "There won't be another time. I won't allow it."

"You won't?"

"No. I don't want to be kissed again."

"By me? Or by anyone?"

"By anyone. But *especially* you."

"May I ask why?"

"I think you know the answer to that."

"Perhaps, but humor me. Explain it to me."

She hesitated, then licked her just-kissed lips. "What happens when you kiss me isn't normal."

"What if I told you it is?"

She shook her head. "You know it isn't."

"Very well." Brent leaned back on his elbows and tipped his head to the sun as if he were completely relaxed. "If you believe it isn't, there's probably nothing I can say or do to convince you otherwise."

She nodded, then looked at him. "How do you feel when we kiss?"

He slowly turned to face her. "As if the sun burst into flames above me and giant fireballs landed at my feet. As if the top I'm riding has refused to stop spinning. As if my legs are made of liquid lava and I'm attempting to climb a mountainside." He turned his gaze and looked at her. "How do you feel when we kiss?"

She lowered her gaze to her lap. "The same."

He smiled.

"Is this the way it always is?" she asked a few seconds later. Her voice came out softer than usual.

His breath caught. He knew the answer he needed to give her would only reinforce her belief that she was right. "No."

"I knew it. That's because what happens when you kiss me isn't normal."

He stretched out on the grass and crossed his hands behind

his head. She was right. If he'd have experienced the raging heat soaring through his body now the first time he'd kissed a girl, he'd have been married years ago. He hadn't reacted to anyone's kiss like this ever before.

He stared up at the clouds as they scurried across the sky and imagined them turning dark and menacing. As ferocious and dangerous as Harrison's temper might turn if he discovered what he'd done.

"*Under no circumstances,*" Fellingsworth had ordered, "*will you risk breaking her heart. If you do...Well, with four brothers who will risk their lives to protect her, the penalty should be vividly clear.*"

And it was. So, what the bloody hell was he doing kissing her?

He turned to his side and looked up at her. She watched him, the look on her face serene, yet filled with the confusion she'd expressed earlier. The blood drained from his head.

Bloody hell. He was falling in love with her.

"What do your brothers have planned for today?"

His change of subjects confused her for a moment.

"The men are going to tour the estate, and Patience and Lilly and I will give the women a tour of the gardens. Then this afternoon, there's a game of croquet scheduled, followed by tea on the east terrace."

"Come for a ride with me. I'll borrow one of your brother's carriages and you can show me your favorite places to escape to on the estate."

Her eyes opened wide. "We can't. My sisters expect me to—"

"Your sisters can manage without you."

She shook her head. "Our absence would be noticed."

She was right, damn it. "Then allow me to be your partner for the lawn games."

Her gaze didn't waver. "I won't be there for the lawn games."

"Why not?"

"Because I have to oversee the preparations for the tea."

"Surely your staff can see to that."

"Perhaps, but I...I don't enjoy outdoor activities."

He wanted to laugh. "I can't imagine anyone who enjoys the out-of-doors more than you."

"I told you," she said, her voice containing a sharpness that was unusual for her. "I don't play."

"Nonsense. Are you afraid we'll lose? We won't, you know. With me as your partner, we're guaranteed to trounce the others."

"No, we won't. Because I don't play. I *can't*!"

She pointed to her right ankle as if that explained everything. And it did.

He struggled to find the air he needed to breathe.

How could he have forgotten?

CHAPTER 9

Elly sat on one of the chairs the servants had moved to the terrace and watched their guests finish their game. Her brothers had always been competitive. Even Lily and Patience had developed an intense aversion to losing whenever they competed. Today was no different. If anything, the rivalry seemed even more intense.

With the guests added to the mix, there seemed to be more impetus to win. Even the females each of her brothers partnered seemed intent on winning. The laughing banter and teasing remarks made Elly smile. Everyone was enjoying themselves – especially Charfield.

She tried not to look at him.

"He's even more handsome than everyone says, isn't he?"

Elly looked up to see Cassie walking toward her. "I suppose so," she answered as if Cassie's question were inconsequential. "Have you and Mr. Waverley finished your round already?"

Cassie laughed. "Cousin Jeremy isn't nearly as determined

as your brothers. The other couples passed us, so he saw no reason to continue."

"My brothers are quite intimidating."

"That's because they are all so expert at the game. Cousin Jeremy doesn't enjoy competing against someone unless he is assured of winning."

Elly's brows darted upward. "That doesn't sound very complimentary."

"I don't mean to sound harsh, but I'm frankly surprised that Jeremy even accepted the invitation to attend. Other than an occasional trip to London, he spends nearly all his time running the estate."

"Is that what he's always done? Even before Everett died?"

Cassie paused. "Everett wasn't cut out to handle such a huge responsibility. Thankfully, his father realized it when Everett was small and taught Cousin Jeremy the skills required to run the estate."

"I don't know who was more fortunate, then. Waverley, because his uncle took him in after his parents died. Or your husband, because he had someone knowledgeable to run the estate."

Elly struggled to put a positive slant on Waverley's position at Lathamton Manor. They'd been neighbors forever, but she'd never developed a fondness for him. The kindest remark she could make was that at least Cassie had someone to help her after her husband died of a fever.

At least there was an heir who would inherit everything.

A lump formed in Elly's throat when she thought of the little boy who was now the Earl of Lathamton. The little boy who had inherited so much at such an early age, yet not nearly as much as he would have if...

But it did no good to wish for something that would never be. At least Waverley would never inherit the title and Cassie and her son would always be taken care.

"Where is Waverley now?" Elly scanned the group of guests but didn't see him.

Cassie nodded to the far side of the terrace where a refreshment table had been set up. Jeremy Waverley was refilling his glass from one of Harrison's brandy decanters.

"Ah, not a gracious loser."

"No."

Elly turned her attention back to Cassie and found her friend studying her.

"Which one of your sisters do you think sent me the invitation?"

Elly swallowed hard. "You think it was one of my sisters?"

"It must have been. I know *you* wouldn't have sent it."

Elly experienced a stabbing of guilt. "Perhaps I would have if for no other reason than to give you an opportunity to come."

Cassie's gaze narrowed. "It's too late to play matchmaker between Harrison and me. Any chance for reconciliation was destroyed four years ago."

"And you cannot forgive him?"

"Nor can he forgive me."

"Perhaps he doesn't know all there is to know."

Cassie's gaze hardened. "He knows all he needs to."

Elly heard the warning in her friend's voice. She was aware that Elly knew her secret, but neither of them ever spoke of it. Perhaps now was the time.

"Maybe if you told Harrison—"

Cassie held up her hand to stop Elly's words. "Don't, Elly.

It's too late. Four years too late."

Elly wanted to defend Harrison but wasn't sure what words would help. He'd jumped to a conclusion when the scandal broke and refused to believe he might have been wrong. For as perfect as Harrison and Cassie had always been for each other, Elly was afraid Cassie was right. It might be too late for any kind of reconciliation.

"Is an invitation all you sent?"

Elly frowned. "I don't know what you mean."

Cassie shook her head. "Never mind."

Elly knew she should cease her questions but couldn't. There was more she needed to know. "Does Waverley have feelings for you?"

The corners of Cassie's mouth lifted. "I'm not sure Jeremy's capable of having feelings for another person. All that matters is the power it gives him to have control over Lathamton Estate. Marriage to me would add to his power. He knows Father left me Hollyvine Keep and he would have control of the property after we married."

Cassie kept her gaze focused on the lawn where the game was nearing an end. From the rise in laughter and jovial teasing, the outcome was close.

Elly followed Cassie's gaze to where Harrison prepared to hit the blue colored wooden ball with his mallet.

"Do you remember anything from that night?" Elly asked.

Cassie shook her head. "I've considered a dozen different explanations but nothing makes sense. All I know for certain is that my brother's life was destroyed that night along with my father's."

Cassie closed her eyes as if she didn't want to discuss that time again. Elly didn't blame her. The events that night had ruined more lives than she wanted to think about.

A loud cheer echoed from the lawn and she turned to watch. Harrison hit his ball with his mallet, then smiled when his ball went through the final wickets.

"Who won?" Elly asked when her siblings and their guests rushed across the terrace.

She'd directed her question to George, who stood closest to her with his partner and chosen guest, Lady Brianna. Jules, however, interrupted, the way he'd often done since he was a youngster.

"Harrison did. But Charfield gave him a run for it. They were tied until the end, then Harrison made a shot from far out. You should have seen it, Elly. Harrison had the devil's own luck. It curved at the very last moment and went through the wickets and hit the stake."

"We were playing partners," Aunt Esther said, fanning her face with her lace handkerchief, "and I'm afraid I wasn't as much help to poor Lord Charfield as I should have been."

"Nonsense, Lady Blume. I was honored to have your assistance. It was because of you that we came so close to winning."

"Thank you, dear boy. I only wish that were true."

Elly tried to keep from turning to where Charfield stood but her gaze seemed to have a will of its own. She turned her head, her gaze drawn to him like a magnet to metal, and her breath caught.

He stood in a relaxed pose with one hip resting on top of the stone railing and his arms crossed over his chest. He'd removed his jacket and wore only a waistcoat and a lawn shirt with his sleeves rolled up to his elbows. The sight of him standing there was magnificent and her heart stuttered.

"Have you seen the new gazebo Elly had built down by the lake?" Aunt Esther asked Cassie when everyone had taken a seat at one of the many round tables set up at various spots on the terrace.

There was room for six at each table and Elly and Cassie had been joined by Aunt Gussie, Aunt Esther, Miss Amelia Hastings, and Lady Hannah Brammwell. The two young ladies were both deep in whispered conversation and Elly knew they were no doubt discussing her two brothers' admirable traits. Elly was glad Jules and Spence weren't near enough to overhear them. They were confident enough of their effect on women as it was.

The men had mostly gathered around the cart where something stronger than lemonade and punch was being poured.

"No." Cassie picked up her glass from the table. "Elly told me about it, but I've not seen it yet."

"Oh, you must," Aunt Esther said. "It's absolutely beautiful. And the view overlooking the lake is magnificent. I can show it to you after tea. Would you like that?"

"That would be wonderful." Cassie smiled at Elly over the rim of her glass as she took a sip.

Elly smiled back. Her aunts were dear, dear people. Both were in their middle fifties and as young at heart as Elly's parents.

Aunt Gussie was Elly's mother's sister and Aunt Esther was her father's. They'd both been childhood friends from their youth and when Elly's parents married, it gave them an excuse to remain close. The Duke and Duchess of Sheridan wouldn't dream of hosting a function without including the two older women. When they were absent, as they were now, Aunt

Gussie and Aunt Esther were the perfect fill-in chaperones.

"Marvelous. We'll go down to the lake then. You'll come with us, won't you, Elly?"

"I wouldn't miss the opportunity to see the expression on Cassie's face when she sees my special project."

Elly reached for her cane, then slid to the edge of her chair. She stopped when Aunt Esther's voice rose above the din.

"Oh, Charfield. Might I impose on you to escort Elyssa while we tour the new summerhouse?"

"Of course, Lady Blume," Charfield answered, drowning out Elly's protest.

"Don't argue," Aunt Esther said, shushing Elly's argument with a wave of her hand. "There's no need for the three of us to go all the way to the lake unescorted when there are ever so many young men capable of keeping us company."

"But I can-"

"You might as well cease arguing," Charfield said, extending his arm. "After partnering your aunt for the past hour or so, I've discovered she is quite firm in her opinions. A trait I admire in a woman."

"Parneston repeatedly tells me I'm opinionated," Aunt Esther said over her shoulder as she hooked her hand through Cassie's arm. "But I'm not sure he means it as a compliment."

"What's this I'm complimenting you on?" the Duke of Parneston asked from across the terrace.

"Nothing, Parney," Aunt Esther answered, leading the way to the edge of the veranda.

The Duke smiled at that last comment, then turned to rejoin the group of young men with whom he was talking.

Elly looked at Charfield's extended arm. If she accepted his help, she'd be forced to battle the emotions she'd struggled all day to forget.

If she placed her hand on his arm, it would only reinforce how wonderful it was to have his strength to rely on. Every time she accepted his help, he made her forget how abnormal she was and glimpse at what it meant to be whole, physically perfect.

"Don't lag," Aunt Esther said as she and Cassie walked past them.

Elly had no choice.

She placed her hand atop Charfield's arm and rose to her feet.

"Good girl," she heard him whisper. When she lifted her gaze, she met the most heart-stopping grin she'd ever seen. "I wondered if you'd be brave enough."

Elly answered his arrogance with a most unladylike snort. "It hardly takes bravery to stroll down to the lake to visit a summerhouse I had built. I've been there a hundred times before."

"I'm sure you have. But this time will be different..." He lifted her hand and kissed her knuckles. "...and you know it."

Elly was ready to argue with Charfield's assumption when Aunt Esther gave a small gasp of discomfort and reached out to steady herself against the railing.

Charfield and Elly turned toward her but Harrison was ahead of them and reached her first.

"Aunt Esther! Are you hurt?" Harrison put his arm around his aunt's waist to support her.

"No, I'm fine, Harrison. My ankle just gave out. Help me to a chair, will you?"

"Of course."

Cassie had hold of Aunt Esther's left arm and Harrison

supported her right as they helped her to a chair.

"Are you all right?" Elly asked when she and Charfield reached them.

"Oh, yes. How silly. It's this annoying ankle of mine. It gives out on me at the most inopportune times. I'll be fine in a little while. I just need to rest the confounded thing."

"Are you sure?" Harrison asked. "I could call for the doctor. We have a very good one in the village."

Aunt Esther waved away everyone's concern. "Nonsense. I'll be right as rain as soon as I rest a moment."

"Can I get you something, Lady Blume?" Cassie asked, kneeling beside her. "A glass of water? Or perhaps something stronger?"

"No, I just need to stay off my ankle for a few moments."

Lady Blume winced when she tried to move her foot. "But I can't bear to think I've prevented you from seeing Elly's magnificent summerhouse. I just won't have it. Harrison, you'll have to take my place."

"No, Lady Blume," Cassie said quickly. "I'll see the summerhouse another time."

"Oh, no. I won't let my clumsiness spoil your afternoon."

"I'm sure Lady Lathamton would rather wait until you are able to accompany her on a tour of the summerhouse," Harrison said, his tone a blatant refusal.

"Nonsense, my boy. She just told me that she'd been looking forward to seeing it. Didn't you, dear?"

"I can see it tomorrow, Lady Blume."

"I won't hear of it, Cassandra. Harrison will accompany you in my place."

Aunt Esther released a sigh that indicated the discussion was at a close.

No one moved.

Elly look at Harrison. His hands were clenched at his sides and the muscles on either side of his clenched jaw knotted in fury. She was afraid he might explode, much like the gunfire at the start of a race.

Next, she lowered her gaze to where Cassie still knelt beside Aunt Esther's chair. There was a mutinous glare in her eyes as her gaze seemed riveted on a blade of grass at the toe of Harrison's boots. Elly thought it was a miracle that Cassie hadn't stormed off and let her retreating back be her answer to spending the next hour or so in Harrison's presence.

Elly finally lifted her gaze to where Charfield stood beside her. His arched eyebrows matched a slight lift to the corners of his mouth. His expression reminded her of someone who was on the verge of laughter. He obviously didn't understand how explosive this situation was.

"Well...uh...then," Elly stammered. "Shall we...go?"

For a very long moment, Cassie and Harrison remained frozen in place, Harrison glaring out onto an area of the perfectly manicured lawn, and Cassie crouched before Aunt Esther.

"Cassie? Harrison?" Elly said a little louder, wondering which one of them would make the first move. Afraid neither of them would give in.

"Come now, Harrison," Aunt Esther said in the same soft voice their mother used when she'd reached the end of her patience and refused to argue further. "You have an obligation to see to your guests."

Elly doubted there was another word that would have convinced Harrison to escort Lady Lathamton anywhere. But duty, obligation, and responsibility had been ingrained in each of the Duke of Sheridan's children from birth. Especially Harrison, the heir.

With a sharp intake of breath, he stepped around Aunt Esther and extended his arm. "Please, allow me," he said, his voice void of any softness.

Elly prayed Cassie wouldn't refuse his offer. Surely she knew the monumental step Harrison had just taken.

Eventually, Cassie raised her arm and placed her fingers in Harrison's proffered hand and rose to her feet.

"Of course," she said with the same lack of emotion as Harrison.

They walked across the terrace and down the path that led to the new summerhouse.

"I think we'd best stay as close as possible," Charfield said with his gaze fixed on the retreating couple.

Elly frowned. "Are you sure it's safe?"

Charfield laughed. "No, but watching the fireworks should be interesting."

He tucked Elly's hand close then started down the path to the summerhouse. As they passed Aunt Esther, Elly glanced at her aunt to make sure she was all right.

The look of triumph on Aunt Esther's face and the wink she and Aunt Gussie shared spoke a thousand words.

They may not have sent the invitation that brought Cassie to their party, but they were somehow involved in the reason she decided to come.

CHAPTER 10

The gloved fingers Lady Lathamton rested on his arm sent one wave of molten heat after another through his body. Harrison wanted to reach inside his chest and throw the painful burden pressing against his heart as far as he could heave it.

Bloody hell, but it hurt to be near her.

He'd been so sure he'd never have to see her again. Or if he did, they'd both be old and gray and far past the age when emotions played any part in their lives. But this was too soon. The pain was too raw.

He cast a quick glance at her from the corner of his eye. She was as beautiful as ever. Even more remarkable today in a green gown that brought out the green in her eyes, and a wide-brimmed straw bonnet that allowed dainty tendrils of her golden hair to frame her face.

He jerked his gaze and his attention to the path ahead of them. He had to stop thinking about her. Had to stop dreaming of things that might have been, but would never be.

Most of all, he couldn't let her know how much her presence disturbed him. "I noticed you and Mr. Waverley dropped out of the game early. Did our company bore you?"

He felt her fingers tighten on his arm as if she hadn't expected him to speak. Or perhaps she wasn't comfortable with his choice of topic.

If Jeremy Waverley was her latest lover, as Harrison suspected, it must be uncomfortable speaking to one of your former lovers about your most recent lover.

"No, it was your skill that intimidated us."

"Surely not you, Lady Lathamton. I remember a time when you were as skilled as any of us."

"I still am."

Harrison wanted to smile. She still possessed an underlying confidence he'd always admired. "Then why did you leave the game so early?"

"Mr. Waverley saw no point in finishing when there was no chance we'd win."

"You quit?"

"No. *He* quit. *I* was left with no choice but to do the same."

He slowed his step and looked down on her with an expression he knew she'd find condescending. "Are the two of you having a lover's spat?"

He knew his question was out of line. Before he had time to react, she jerked her hand from his arm and spun to face him.

"Don't you *ever... ever* speak to me that way again. You have no right."

Before Harrison could utter the apology he knew she deserved, she gave him her back and walked away from him.

The summerhouse was just ahead. He knew that's where

she'd take refuge.

He followed her at a slower pace. She'd been right to become angry. His remark had been beneath him. But it was obvious to everyone who cared to notice that Waverley intended to make her his bride.

Every time he thought of her in someone else's arms – in someone else's bed - he lost control of his composure. If only she hadn't come here. As long as she remained far away, he could try to push the pain of losing her to that dark corner of his heart where he'd locked away all his shattered dreams. It didn't always work, but he had a better chance of succeeding than when she was close enough to touch. Close enough to kiss.

He strode down the path after her, trying to forget how angry she could make him. Instead, he concentrated on the apology he owed her.

He rounded the rhododendron bushes on either side of the stone path and like a vision he'd only half remembered from his last visit, the summerhouse came into view.

He stopped to take in the magnificent site in front of him – to feast his eyes on the beautiful woman staring out onto the shimmering lake.

Elly's design had been remarkable even as a scratched drawing on paper. Today the scene was just as beautiful. Maybe more so with Cassie standing there.

He approached her cautiously, then walked up the two steps and across the floor. He stopped when he reached her but she didn't turn around to acknowledge him.

"I owe you an apology." He hoped she'd look at him.

She didn't.

"I know I no longer have the right to an opinion as to with

whom you choose to associate."

"No, you don't." The chill in her voice was frigid enough to turn his blood to ice.

He didn't wait for her to turn but stepped beside her and braced his hands on the railing to look out onto the shimmering lake. He didn't notice the vibrant colors around him. All he could think about was how close he was to her. If he reached out he could pull her into his arms. If he wrapped his arms around her he could hold her close to him.

If he tipped her chin he could lower his mouth and...

He drew in a harsh breath. "Why did you come here? Is causing me more pain so important to you?"

She turned her head enough for him to see the haughty expression on her face. "You think my intent was to cause you pain?"

"What other reason could there be for you to come to a party when you knew I would be here?"

"I told you that—"

"I know what you told me. That was a lie. Each one of us comes to see Elly often. You've never shown an interest in visiting before. Why now?"

The rosy tint on her cheeks faded slightly and for just one second he thought he saw a flash of emotion between fear and panic in her eyes. In fact, he was sure of it. "Is something wrong, Cassie? Do you need help?"

He couldn't miss the harsh sound of disgust she made before she spoke. "You would be the last person I would come to for help. I learned years ago how much I could rely on you to come to my aid."

"That was different. There was nothing I could do for you then and you know it."

"Are you sure?"

The superior tone in her voice caused a small niggling of doubt to slither through him. How could she think there was something he could have done for her? Bloody hell. She'd been found in Lathamton's bed by her father and half the guests at Lathamton's party.

"Why did you accept the invitation?"

"Believe me. I would rather have ignored it."

Harrison watched the frown deepen on her forehead. He doubted she even realized her expression revealed so much. He tried not to care. But he couldn't manage it. Not with her standing close beside him.

"From your obvious reluctance to be here, something important must have made you come."

She turned away from him and every protective instinct he didn't want to feel rushed through his body. "Is it your son? Is he sick?"

"No! This has nothing to do with my son."

The force of her denial startled him. He turned his gaze to focus on her stiffened posture. Something *was* wrong. Her face was void of color and she stood with her hands hugging her middle as if she needed the support to keep from collapsing.

"Something is wrong. Let me help you."

"You can't." She faced him with the old confidence he was used to seeing from her. "I'm just lonesome for my son. That's all. This is the first time I've left him behind."

"Would you like to visit him tomorrow? I could have someone take you to Lathamton. Then you would be assured he was all right."

"I'm sure he's fine. He's with Nanny Graybrim."

He smiled. He remembered the plump, gray-haired lady

with rosy cheeks and a ready smile. "I didn't know she'd come to live at Lathamton Manor."

Cassie nodded. "When she found out I was going to have Andrew, she wouldn't have it any other way. She's been wonderful."

He tried not to dwell on the child Cassie'd had with Lathamton. But he couldn't help himself. "What's he like?"

"Who?"

"Your son. Lathamton's heir."

"Don't, Harrison." She shook her head and turned away from him.

"I want to know. How old is he now? Three? Four?"

"Nearing four," she answered softly.

"Is he dark-featured? Or light?"

"Don't." Her voice sounded more choked than before.

"Is he bright? Lathamton wasn't a dull fellow and you are one of the most intelligent females I've ever met, so I imagine the boy inherited more than average intelligence. Have you hired a tutor for him?"

"Stop," she cried out.

"I'm only interested. If things had been different, the boy might have been mine."

Harrison heard a small choked sound come from deep inside her. She quickly swiped at her cheek, but not before he saw the one lone tear that streamed down her face.

"Cassie?" Harrison clasped her upper arms and turned her toward him. "What's wrong?"

"Nothing," she whispered as another tear fell from her eyes. "Everything. You're what's wrong, Harrison. You. Me. Everything that happened between us."

She struggled in his arms but he couldn't let her go. How

could she say he was what was wrong? She was the one who'd ruined everything. She was the one who'd shattered their dreams.

Another tear rolled down her cheek, then another, and he pulled her into his arms and held her close.

For a long time, neither of them moved. Having her in his arms again was like a dream come true. He'd imagined holding her like this more times than he cared to remember, thought he'd never have the chance to hold her again. But here she was, clinging to him as if he were a lifeline to save her from the crashing waves.

He wasn't satisfied with simply holding her. Before he had time to evaluate his actions and consider how foolhardy they were, he tilted her chin upward, then lowered his head and kissed her.

The experience was earth-shattering. He'd forgotten how amazing her lips were beneath his. How full and complete she made him feel. How high she enabled him to soar when she returned his kisses.

He opened his mouth atop hers and she followed his lead. She was as hungry as he was, as desperate. As anxious to feast on the earthy passion they'd both gone without for so long.

He kissed her long and deep, taking as much as she'd allow. Offering as much as she was willing to take.

She wrapped her arms around his neck and pulled him closer. He went willingly. Every emotion they'd once shared rushed back to engulf them. Although he thought things might have changed between them, they hadn't. If anything, their feelings for each other had grown more intense.

He reverently touched her, reacquainting himself with her curves and valleys. His mouth worshiped her face, from her high, arched cheekbones, to the strong arch of her jaw. He gently kissed her below her ear, then let his kisses follow the long column of her neck.

He heard her moan as he suckled the tender flesh where her neck met her shoulder. He was beyond allowing reason to control his mind. His brain was the last part of his body he was thinking with right now.

She moaned again, this time louder. Then she flattened her hands against his chest and pushed.

"No, Harrison."

The word 'no' stopped him.

He lifted his mouth and looked down at her.

Her reaction wasn't what he'd expected to see. Instead of the passion they'd shared before her marriage to Lathamton, her eyes were filled with regret. And anger.

"Damn you, Harrison." She pressed the back of her hand to her lips. She sucked in a helpless gasp then took a step away from him. Her arms hugged her middle as if fighting her vulnerability. The color drained from her face. "What have I done?" she whispered as she turned her face away from him.

"Cassie?"

"Leave me alone." Her wide eyes darted toward him. "You had no right. You've ruined everything!"

Her words punched him in the gut.

The full impact of the monumental mistake he'd just made hit him full force. "You're right. I apologize. This is the second time I fell prey to your charm." He couldn't stop the choked laughter. "You'd think I would have learned after the first time."

He jerked on the sleeves to his jacket and adjusted his cravat, then issued her a formal bow. "You need never worry that anything so distasteful will ever happen between us again."

He intended to leave first, but before he could make his excuses, she left him.

She didn't walk away with her head high and her back rigid and straight like he intended to leave her, but she lifted her skirts just enough so she wouldn't trip over them - and ran.

He waited until he was sure he'd given her enough time to return to the house, then walked back up the path.

He met Charfield escorting Elly down to the lake and thought perhaps he should go back with them in case Cassie was still outside on the terrace, finding comfort in Waverley's arms. But he couldn't.

Bloody hell but he'd made a monumental blunder just now.

He stepped off the path to let his sister and the man he'd hired to keep her company walk past. With a short, curt nod, he greeted them, knowing even if Charfield didn't realize something was wrong, Elly would. But he didn't care. He was in no mood to keep anyone company.

He wasn't even sure he could stand to be around *himself* right now.

———

From his hiding place deep in a copse of lush linden trees he had a perfect view of everything that happened inside the open summerhouse. His fondest hope was that Cassie would refuse to let Fellingsdown join her.

She didn't. But neither was she overly friendly.

His gaze remained riveted on the pair as they stared out onto the lake. Neither of them spoke to the other and the smile on his face broadened. *Give him the cut,* he found himself urging her. *Tell him to go away and leave you alone.*

But she didn't. Now the two of them were talking.

He couldn't see their faces, of course, but that wasn't necessary to tell that Cassie and Fellingsdown's topic of conversation was far more intense than a discussion about the weather.

His blood boiled when Fellingsdown reached out for her and Cassie let him hold her. And touch her.

And kiss her.

Then she kissed him back.

White lights exploded behind his tightly-squeezed eyes. Damn her.

Damn her!

He couldn't watch more. He spun on his heels and made his way back to the house, making sure no one saw him. He had plans to make.

She was his.

His!

And no one would take her away from him.

CHAPTER 11

The sun shone brightly the following afternoon and Elly sat alone on one of the comfortable wooden benches placed throughout the park. Everyone had gone on the planned trip to town to watch Mr. Devon make his crystal pieces. It was a fascinating process so she knew they'd be gone a long while. Much longer than she wanted to be on her feet. She'd stayed home and had come outdoors to enjoy the sunshine.

She leaned her back against the bench's white-painted railings and stretched out her crippled leg. She'd overcome many of the nightmarish events from her accident. She'd even learned to walk again, though every doctor her parents took her to told them she wouldn't. But the panic that engulfed her after she fell through the rotten boards covering the abandoned well was something she'd never been able to conquer.

The long, terrifying hours she spent in the dark, her unanswered screams, the cold, the unbearable pain, and most of all, her disability, everything resulting from the fall still remained.

Elly slowly pulled up the hem of her green muslin skirt and looked at her deformed ankle and foot. She seldom allowed herself to look at it. The odd angle of her foot and the unnatural tilt of her ankle wasn't a pleasant sight.

It no longer pained her as it did when she was younger and still growing, but there were times when she tired more easily. Times when her limp was more pronounced. She hated those times. Especially during the cold winter months if she stayed in the damp too long.

She tried to turn her foot, tried to force her ankle to move enough so her toes were straight ahead of her, the way her toes on her left foot were. But her foot refused to move.

It was just as well she'd stayed home today while her siblings and the rest of their guests went to the village.

Besides, it would be good for Charfield to partner someone else for a change. She didn't know why, but he seemed content – no, almost *eager* to escort her in to dinner each evening. And for the three days since he'd arrived, he'd met her early each morning so they could race. And yesterday afternoon—

Elly's thoughts spun back to the hours they'd spent together admiring the view of the lake from inside the open summerhouse. They'd talked of any number of things and she'd shared thoughts with him she'd never shared with anyone else. Not even George. Or her sisters.

All the while she'd been with him she felt...beautiful.

She looked back to her foot. Oh, if things were different she might let herself believe...

But things were not different. She possessed nothing to draw his affection. In fact, it was quite the opposite.

She examined her foot one more time, then quickly

dropped her skirts over her ankle when she heard a noise behind her.

"Fitzhugh said I'd find you here," the Earl of Charfield said as he walked toward her.

Elly turned on the bench to watch him approach. A warmth wrapped around her heart and she was even more aware of how perfect he was.

How imperfect she was.

"I thought you went with the others." She made sure her ankle was completely covered. "You're going to miss seeing Mr. Devon's crystal creations. They're quite remarkable, you know."

"I'm sure they are. But as long as I am near, your brother and Lady Lathamton ignore each other as if the other doesn't exist. Without my presence, your brother has no choice but to step up as escort. He and Lady Lathamton now have no choice but to be cordial to each other. At least in public."

She giggled. "Oh, that's marvelous." She smiled broadly, realizing he'd played right into Aunt Gussie and Aunt Esther's plan without even knowing it. She looked at his hands and saw the wooden croquet mallets he'd used the other day. "What are you doing with those?" She nodded toward his hand.

"These? They're the mallets one uses when one plays croquet."

"I know *what* they are. I asked what you were doing with them."

"I'm going to play croquet."

"Did some of the others remain behind?" She looked around for any of the other guests.

He smiled a heart-stopping smile that shifted her heart in her breast.

"No. You and I are going to play."

She felt her cheeks warm. "I don't play croquet."

He took a step toward her and held out his hand. "Then it's time you learned."

She lifted her chin and gathered all the fortitude she needed to hold her position. She was never surprised when people who didn't know her well expected things from her she couldn't do. But she thought he would have realized by now what she was capable of and what she was not.

Croquet was something she was *not* capable of doing. She needed her cane to balance herself and she couldn't hold a cane and swing the mallet at the same time. Besides, she wasn't about to risk falling to the ground just to prove to him how physically impossible playing was for her.

She didn't move. Neither did he. He simply stood before her with his hand extended and that perfect smile on his face.

"I *can't* play," she said more forcefully than before. "It is something I cannot do."

"That's because you didn't have me to help you."

He said the words with such nonchalance Elly had to blink to make sure he was serious. "Do you think that just because you're here to give me instructions I'll suddenly be able to do something I've never been able to do before?"

He broadened his smile. "Are you brave enough to find out?"

He issued a challenge as if he knew there was little she wouldn't try if challenged.

She took the arm he held out to her and rose to her feet. "What I am," she said, shifting her cane to her other hand until she regained her balance, "is brainless enough to make a fool of myself to prove you wrong."

"What you are," he said, swinging the mallets in one hand while they walked down the terrace steps and toward the open lawn, "is one of the bravest people I've ever met."

Elly was at a loss for words. There was nothing brave about her. And he'd find that out when she swung the mallet the first time and landed on the ground.

She walked at his side, trying not to let him see how apprehensive she was. The stakes and metal wickets were still up from their match two days ago. Or perhaps he'd asked one of the footmen to put them back. She wasn't sure.

He led her to the starting spot and placed two wooden balls on the ground. One was red, the other green.

"Which color would you like?" he asked.

"The color isn't important."

"Good. Then you take the red. Green is my lucky color."

"Any color would be your lucky color with me as your challenger."

"Where is your confidence?" he said as if she were a child who needed scolding.

"I lost it, along with my common sense." She snatched one of the mallets out of his hand, then leaned on her cane to position herself behind the red ball. She debated whether to keep her cane in her hand to steady herself as she hit the ball, knowing a one-handed swing would be well off the mark. Or whether she should hook the cane over her arm and swing the mallet with both hands. Swinging the mallet with only one hand would limit her power but at least she had a chance to stay on her feet.

She opted to swing one-handed to save her dignity.

"What are you doing?" he said, stopping her from swinging her mallet.

She lowered her mallet and glared at him. "I am showing you *why* I do not join in lawn games."

"Have you forgotten that I said I would help you?"

She rolled her eyes and turned back to the ball. Help her what? Help pick her up from the ground? She leaned on her cane again and prepared to swing.

"Give me your cane," he said from behind her.

She ignored him and concentrated on how hard she could swing without toppling over. The feel of his hand on her arm stopped her.

"Give me your cane."

She stared at him. His expression told her he was serious. He held out his hand as if he expected her to give her cane over.

"I need my cane for support," she whispered, hating how weak the words made her sound. "My foot is not strong enough to hold me."

"I will be your strength."

She lowered her gaze to the hand he held out. He expected her to trust him to hold her steady. He expected her to trust that he would not let her fall.

Her heart raced in her chest. Even her brothers hadn't asked her to trust them so completely. She was suddenly terrified. And at the same time, excited beyond words.

She took a deep breath and slowly handed her cane over to him.

Before he took it, he stepped behind her and placed his free arm around her waist. She didn't have time to react before he took her cane from her and hooked it over his forearm. Then, he stood directly behind her and placed his hands on either side of her waist.

"What do you think?" His face was so close to her cheek she could feel his warm breath against her skin.

"I'm frightened." She stood without the fingers of her right hand clamped around her cane for the first time since she was eleven years old.

"Don't be. I won't let you fall."

"But—"

"Trust me."

Trust me.

She'd never stood this close to a man who made her blood race through her veins like someone had opened the floodgates and there was nothing to stop the rush of emotion from flowing to every part of her body. She'd never felt so alive in her life.

Every nerve in her body sang in celebration.

"What do you think?" he said.

She held out her empty right hand and smiled. "I don't know what to do with it." She was aware of how useless it felt without her cane in it.

He chuckled and she turned her head to look over her shoulder. He was smiling at her.

"Are you ready?"

She matched his smile with one of her own and nodded.

"Place both your hands around the mallet."

Elly curved her fingers around the mallet the way she'd seen her brothers and sisters do hundreds of times.

"Slide your right hand down a little," he instructed her.

He had his hands clamped tightly around her waist and she felt steady and secure. And free. The feeling was amazing.

She slid her right hand down, then placed the head of the mallet on the grass directly behind the red ball and leaned forward.

"Widen your stance. That will give you better leverage."

She moved her legs, then leaned over the ball again.

"Now take a slow swing at the ball and don't stop when your mallet comes into contact. Follow through with your swing."

She bent down and shifted to position herself, then rose again. "Are you sure?" she asked.

"That you should follow through with your swing?"

"No. That I am not too heavy for you. That you won't... won't—"

"I won't let you fall, Elly," he whispered in her ear. "I promise."

She sucked in a fortifying breath and took aim at the ball. Before she lost her confidence, she pulled the mallet back, then swung in a swift forward motion.

His hands tightened around her waist the second she moved, then he stepped close behind her the instant she hit the ball. He moved with her – or perhaps she moved with him – and she followed through with her hit.

But most important of all, she didn't fall.

"I did it!" She watched her red ball sail across the thick, green lawn. "I did it!"

His hands remained firm around her waist and she stood as free and solid as if she had two good legs on which to balance herself.

She was as excited as a small child at Christmas time. She wanted to jump for joy. Or race through the meadow. Or do any of the things she knew were impossible for her to do. But most especially she wanted to thank him for what he'd done for her.

She wasn't sure whether she was the one who turned in his arms or if he was the one who turned her, but she found herself standing close to him, his hands still anchored on either side of her waist. They were pressed to each other, her thighs touching his, her stomach pressed to his hips and her arms held out from her body because if she moved them where they wanted to go they would be clamped around his waist. Or draped across his shoulders. Or wrapped around his neck.

"You were wonderful," he said, then lowered his head and kissed her.

His lips were warm and firm atop hers, the feeling the same as the first time he'd kissed her. Yet different. He seemed to be demanding something more from her, something very intimate, yet he was asking in a most tender way. Her blood heated as it rushed through her body.

He didn't hold his kiss long. Not so long that it left her breathless as it had done before. Nor so long that her knees turned weak as they had done before. Just long enough to cause her heart to lurch in her breast. Then he lifted his mouth from hers and smiled down at her.

"You were wonderful." And he kissed her again, this time lightly on the cheek.

There was nothing sensual in the second kiss. It was rather the same as a greeting or farewell kiss she exchanged with each of her siblings or her parents when they arrived or departed. This second kiss was as ordinary as any she'd ever received, and he gave it as if he had every right to exchange such intimacy.

She smiled as she fought the euphoric bubbles that sputtered in her breast.

"I didn't know it would be like this."

"Hitting a ball with such freedom? Or the kiss?"

There was a glimmer in his eyes. He was teasing her. Wasn't he?

She opened her mouth to answer but he placed his finger across her lips to stop her.

"Don't say anything. I prefer to think it was my kiss."

She smiled and looked down at the narrow space between them.

"Would you like to practice hitting the ball again?"

"Oh, yes. I'd like to see if I can hit the next one over by that tree. Do you think that's too far?"

"For you, my dear, nothing is *too* far, or *too* high, or *too* anything."

She smiled up at him as something warm and soothing wrapped around her heart.

He stepped behind her and anchored his hands around her waist. "Take your stance," he instructed. "Point your left shoulder to the spot where you want your ball to go."

She did just that.

"Let me know when you're ready."

"I'm ready," she said when she was in position, then hit the ball.

This second time was ever so much easier. She wasn't nearly as timid or as apprehensive.

Trust me, he'd told her. And she did. More than she had ever trusted anyone in a long, long time. At least since the accident, she thought with a growing sense of hopefulness. And it was a good feeling.

She hit the next ball with a hearty swing and nearly squealed with delight when it went even farther than she thought it would. The next one went even farther and the one after that was nearly perfect.

"All right, Miss Show-off. It's time you had some competition."

"Are you challenging me?"

"Be assured I am."

She looked him in the eyes and laughed. "Very well, sir, but be warned. I don't intend to let you win."

"Nor do I intend to let you best me, either."

"And to show you what a sporting person I am," she said taking her cane from his arm and leaning against it, "I'll let you go first."

He looked shocked. "I wouldn't dream of going first. I will give you no reason to accuse me of taking advantage. You, my dear, will hit your ball first. And that," he said, tapping her gently on the tip of her nose, "will be the only time you are in the lead."

She gave him a toss of her head and got into position. When she was ready, she gave him the signal to hold her. After his hands were firmly anchored at her waist, she pulled her mallet back and swung.

It wasn't important that she win. It was enough for her to hold her own against him. Or maybe it was enough simply being with him.

He'd shown her how it felt to be courted by someone who considered her the same as any other woman. He made her feel young, and desirable, and...whole.

She would always be grateful to him for that.

CHAPTER 12

Brent escorted Elly to the terrace and seated her before he collapsed into the chair next to her. He couldn't remember enjoying himself so much. And it was all because of her.

"You cheated, you know," she said, taking a tall glass of lemonade a servant rushed out to serve them.

Brent took several swallows of the cool liquid then set his glass onto the table. "I did not cheat. I've already explained, a very large, fierce-looking insect landed on my arm just as you were making your last hit. I jerked my hand to prevent it from taking a huge bite out of my tender skin."

"You ruined my shot on purpose. Admit it."

"I'll admit nothing of the sort." He took another drink from his glass. "Do you think I would resort to such an underhanded and deceitful trick as tickling you just to prevent you from winning?"

"I do," she said looking at him through narrowed eyes. "I think that's exactly what you did."

"I'm wounded." He clutched his hand to his heart. He tried to look severely insulted but from the expression on her face she made it plain she was having none of it. He couldn't help it. The look on her face made him laugh.

She paused with her glass midway to her lips.

"What?" There was a look of wonderment in her expression that confused him.

"Your laugh. It was different."

"Different? How?"

She cocked her head to the side and studied him. "You laugh often, but the way you laughed just now was different somehow. More sincere, perhaps. As if this laugh was real."

"Was it?"

"Yes."

He sat back. How could he explain that everything he did and felt when he was with her was real? How could he make her understand that for the first time in his life he was alive with happiness?

He studied her. He'd spent all afternoon with her, but he realized it hadn't been long enough.

"Do you know what I think?" She looked at him as if he were a puzzle to be decoded.

"I'm afraid to ask."

"I think you should be on stage."

"You think I'm acting?"

She held his gaze another few seconds and the longer she looked at him the more he was convinced she could see through him. No, not *through*, but *into*, him. And for the first time in his life he truly wanted someone to see the *real* Brentan Montgomery.

"I think you are adept at putting on an excellent front, one you've perfected over the years. What I'm trying to decide is who is the *real* you, the man you are when you're in London or the man you are when you're away from the prying eyes of the *ton* and the snatching claws of the matchmaking mamas."

Brent couldn't help but laugh again. "Which one do you think?"

"I'm hoping it's the one you are here. I'd hate to think I'd become fond of a fraud."

He couldn't think of one thing to say to that. A part of him wanted to assure her that she hadn't, that the man she'd met here was the real Brentan Montgomery. That the rogue and rake he was reported to be wasn't who he was at all, but who he'd become to keep from being caught by one of those matchmaking mamas she'd mentioned.

"I can't believe you've never married."

Her statement caught him off guard. Even though he'd been repeatedly asked, he'd never believed the questioner was interested in why he'd avoided marriage. Until now.

He crossed his right ankle over his left knee and took another long swallow of his lemonade, wishing the liquid were something stronger.

"If you could describe marriage in just one word," he said, keeping his gaze focused on her face, "what would it be?"

"Oh, I'm not sure I could find just one." She wore a truly puzzled look.

"Then two. Or even three."

"Well, there would be love. And, of course, trust. And above all, friendship."

"Do you know what word I would use?"

"You could describe marriage in just one word?" she said with a smile on her face.

"Very well, two. At the top of my list would of course be hatred. Then, very close behind that would be bitterness. And the third would be—"

He stopped. The smile left her face and there was a look of pity in her eyes. Bloody hell, but he couldn't stand for her to pity him.

"Were your parents never kind to each other?"

He answered her in his most flippant manner. "They must have been at least twice. I have a brother, you know. Unless my father was also guilty of committing rape."

Her gaze lowered to her hands in her lap and her cheeks turned a brilliant scarlet.

"I apologize, my lady." He bolted from his chair and stepped to the cement railing. "I had no right to speak to you in that manner."

"Does your brother feel the same?"

"He remembers our parents the same as I, if that's what you're asking."

"Yet, he fell in love and married. Or did he not fall in love, but just married?"

"Yes, Michael fell in love. Head over ears in love, if the truth be told. To a wonderful girl, who has given him a houseful of children."

He turned back to her and smiled. "Which gives me an excellent reason to remain single. Michael has already done his duty to provide the future Earl of Charfield."

"You do not want children of your own?"

"I haven't given it much thought. Children aren't important to me."

He turned before she recognized his words for the lies they were. Every time he went to visit Michael, he couldn't help but wonder what his own children might look like. Or how many sons and how many daughters he would be blessed with. But never had there been a woman in his dreams. Never once had there been a mother to his children.

Perhaps that was because he and Michael had never had a mother. Not really. Not in the way Elly and Fellingsdown and George and Jules and the rest of the Prescott siblings had parents who loved them. And loved each other.

"Have you ever been in love?"

"Have you?" he asked turning her words on her.

"No."

"Why not?"

"Because I am still searching for the man of my dreams."

She looked up at him. "Do you ever dream of finding your perfect woman?"

He laughed. "That particular dream was shattered long ago."

How could he tell her that was one dream he wouldn't allow himself to have. Or, as impossible as it seemed, that he hadn't met even one female in his lifetime with whom he would consider risking his future.

Until now.

That thought pulled him up short. Could he actually be considering a future with her? Was it possible for him to dare to dream that he'd found someone with whom he could share his life?

There were so many questions he wanted to ask her, so much he wanted to find out, but now wasn't the time. It was too soon. Besides, the guests were returning from their trip to town and the special afternoon he and Elly had spent alone together was at an end. Brent stood as Elly's siblings and their female guests gathered around them.

"Oh, Elly," Amelia Hastings, cried out as she came across the terrace. "You should have gone with us. Mr. Devon's shop is a marvel."

"Yes, Amelia can say that," Jules teased, placing his hand beneath her elbow in what Brent noticed was a very possessive, intimate manner. "Devon's going to have to spend all of the next six months restocking his inventory."

"I only purchased two pieces. Nearly everyone else came back with more than that. And Brianna purchased the most exquisite crystal bowl. If Mr. Devon would have had another like it, I would not have been able to resist."

"I'm sure Archibald can have another done before—"

Brent nearly laughed out loud when a panicked expression covered Jules Prescott's face and he frantically motioned for Elly not to say more.

"Before when?" Amelia asked with a glimmer in her eyes.

"I'm sure he can have another bowl done by this time next year," Elly finished.

"That long?" she said, the disappointment obvious in her voice.

"Perhaps we will have another summer gathering next year," Jules said, "and you can visit Mr. Devon's Crystal Shop again. I'm sure he'll have another by then. Plus even more of his creations."

"Wonderful." She gave Jules an endearing expression. "I'll save all my pin money until I come again."

Brent scanned the terrace. Each of Elly's brothers seemed exceedingly fond of the female they'd asked to have invited. All except the marquess.

Fellingsdown stood a short distance from them, talking

with Viscount Parkridge and the Earl of Berkingham, his two brothers-in-law. Brent had no idea what the three men were talking about but it apparently wasn't interesting enough to hold Fellingsdown's attention because his gaze kept gravitating to the other side of the terrace, where Lady Lathamton stood talking to Elly's two aunts. From the twinkles in both aunts' eyes, Brent couldn't help but wonder if Fellingsdown or Lady Lathamton realized the matchmaking scheme the two women were hatching.

He doubted it.

As if suddenly aware that he'd been the focus of Brent's thoughts, Fellingsdown took that moment to glance in his direction. Fellingsdown excused himself from his discussion with his brothers-in-law and came toward him.

"We missed you on the tour of our town," Fellingsdown said, stopping far enough away from Elly that Brent was forced to step several feet to converse with him. Their spot on the terrace left them quite isolated, which he was sure was what Fellingsdown intended.

Brent smiled. "When I realized your sister had elected to remain behind, I decided to return to keep her company."

"I see," Fellingsdown answered, then walked to the far edge of the terrace and down the three stone steps that led to a small side garden. Brent had no choice but to follow him.

Fellingsdown stopped when they were far enough from the rest of the group to keep from being overheard. "You've done an admirable job of fulfilling your obligation, Charfield. I applaud your ability to become such good...friends in such a short time."

"You didn't think it was possible for your sister to consider me a friend?"

"I wasn't worried that she wouldn't consider you a friend. Nor you, her. Anyone who's ever taken the time to know her is aware it's hard not to like her and consider her a friend shortly upon meeting."

"Then what exactly is your concern?"

"Our purpose in inviting you—"

"Our?" Brent asked, feeling that he'd been the target of a scheme much larger than he'd anticipated.

"George knows of our agreement. And Jules and Spence, of course."

Brent felt a niggling of something he didn't quite understand. "Of course," he answered, and from the lift of Fellingsdown's right brow, he knew his sarcasm hadn't been lost on Elly's brother. "And what about your sisters, the twins? Do they know why I'm here, too?"

"They're the reason this gathering was necessary in the first place."

Brent clasped his hands behind his back and turned to look out onto the colorful garden. Elly's summerhouse was out there, to the right of this path. He remembered the time they'd spent there two afternoons ago. Then their visit again after dusk last night.

Brent hadn't thought any of Elly's brothers were aware of their escape from the planned evening of board games and musical entertainment. Now he wasn't so sure.

"What is your concern?" Brent asked, turning to face Fellingsdown.

"Our agreement was that you would partner Elly enough for her to forget an admirer we all considered inadequate for her."

"And you don't think I've lived up to my end of the

agreement?"

"I think you've *more* than lived up to your part. In fact, I'm not sure she's given her secret admirer a second thought since meeting you."

"Then I'm not sure why you object. Isn't that what you intended me to do?"

Fellingsdown cleared his voice. "What I didn't intend... what *none* of us intended, was for you to take Elly's admirer's place."

Brent arched his brows. "And if I have? You would object?"

"You forget. I know your reputation. According to the bargain that brought you here, when these two weeks are over you will leave The Down with far more than when you arrived. What I don't intend is for you to leave my sister behind with a broken heart."

Brent felt his temper rising. "I have no intention of that happening."

"See that it doesn't." Fellingsdown gave a curt nod then took a step toward the terrace where the guests were still discussing their trip to the village and the purchases they'd made.

Brent watched Elly's brother walk away. He was more confused than he'd ever been in his life. And more frustrated. He hadn't handled the exchange with Fellingsdown at all well. This had been the perfect opportunity to explain his feelings for Elly. Except...

...he had no idea what those were.

He tried to make sense of his emotions as he followed Fellingsdown to the terrace but couldn't. The emotions raging inside him were all so new. So foreign.

When he reached the bottom step he looked up. Elly's brother, George, stood at the edge of the terrace holding one of the mallets he and Elly had used to practice.

"Look, Harrison." George lifted the mallet high. "I think the reason Charfield stayed behind today was to practice his game."

"Perhaps he intends to challenge you to a rematch," Spence said. The gathering on the terrace cheered in avid expectation.

Jules stepped forward and held up his hand. "Place your wagers here. This promises to be the rematch of the summer."

The shouts and cheers increased.

Brent couldn't stop a grin from covering his face. Everyone was truly enjoying themselves and he was glad for such frivolity after the serious conversation he'd had with Fellingsdown.

Fellingsdown slowly turned, then crossed his arms over his chest. "Have you been practicing behind my back?"

Brent couldn't help but look at Elly to see her reaction.

She shook her head several times as if pleading for him to keep her secret, but she was also laughing behind her hands clasped over her mouth.

Brent couldn't help but laugh, too.

"I've been found out," he said. He struggled to look as humble and guilt-ridden as possible. "I'd intended to wait until an opportune time to challenge you to a rematch, but I see I've been discovered."

"Rematch! Rematch!" the group lining the edge of the terrace cried out.

Fellingsdown let the cheering go on for a few seconds, then raised his hand to quiet them. "I've been challenged to a rematch by the esteemed Lord Charfield...and I accept!"

Another loud cry went up.

"Choose the time, Charfield."

Brent nodded gravely. "In two days."

Another cheer went up, this one even louder than the one before.

"Two days it is," Fellingsdown decreed when the guests had quieted. "On the side lawn."

Brent nodded again. "Agreed."

"Very well. We will have a replay of our croquet match in two days, immediately after our noon luncheon."

Another loud cheer erupted and Fellingsdown gave Brent a dismissive bow then turned.

"One moment, please!" Brent raised his hand to gain the crowd's attention as well as Fellingsdown's.

Fellingsdown stepped level with Brent and waited until the crowd quieted.

"Since our last match was not a singles match, I would like to propose that our rematch not be one either."

Fellingsdown arched one brow. "You are suggesting we each have a partner?"

"I am."

Fellingsdown arched both brows. "Do you have a certain partner in mind?"

"I do."

Brent didn't look at Elly. He knew her reaction wouldn't be positive.

"Very well. Name your partner."

"Choose me!" a female voice cried from the crowd.

"No, me!" another voice echoed.

"If you truly want to win, Charfield," Elly's brother, Spencer, said in a loud, commanding voice, "you'll pick me to be your partner."

"Hardly," Elly's brother, Jules boasted. "I best Spence every three of four matches. You'd be better off with me as your partner."

"Make your choice, Charfield." Fellingsdown smiled, obviously finding genuine humor in this odd turn of events.

"Very well. I choose—"

Brent turned and looked at the chair where Elly sat. Two bright circles dotted her cheeks and she frantically shook her head to stop him, but Brent refused to let the pleading in her eyes deter him.

"I choose Lady Elyssa."

There was a sudden hush from the group. Fellingsdown took a menacing step toward him as if he'd uttered a profane word in polite company. "How dare you," he said through clenched teeth. "You know Elly hasn't mastered swinging a mallet."

"I know nothing of the sort."

Brent ignored Fellingsdown's anger and locked his gaze with Elly's, willing her to accept his invitation. "Will you agree to be my partner, my lady?"

For a long time she didn't answer. The longer the seconds stretched, the more fearful Brent was that she intended to refuse. From the looks of fury in George, Jules, and Spencer's eyes, Brent considered that if she didn't make her choice soon, he might not be around to hear her decision.

As if George thought Brent had humiliated his sister enough, he took a step toward him. His clenched fists were the evidence Brent needed to realize George's mission was to either plant a fist into his jaw, or bodily remove him from the premises. He hoped Elly would not hesitate any longer.

At just the right moment, she rose to her feet.

With her hands anchored on the edge of the table, she pulled herself up. Everyone turned their attention to where she stood. Even George halted a few feet from Brent.

"Will you agree, my lady?" Brent repeated.

She did not rush to give her final answer, but responded nonetheless with a firm response. "I will."

Lady Lathamton was the first to react to Elly's astounding news. With a broad smile on her face, she rushed the few steps that separated her from Elly and wrapped her arms around her friend's shoulders. That was the beginning of the well-wishes and words of congratulations.

"Are you sure, Elly?" Fellingsdown asked when the noise quieted.

"Of course," Elly answered. "I'm honored to be asked. Now I'd like to know who you intend to pick for *your* partner."

Fellingdown looked shocked.

"I'll be your partner," Jules and Spencer said at the same time.

"No, I'll be his partner," George said, asserting the authority he assumed his age gave him.

Several of the female guests protested that it would hardly be a fair match if one of his brothers partnered him, that his partner should be a female.

Fellingsdown then turned to where his two aunts sat together at a table. "Aunt Esther, would you or Aunt Gussie please do me the favor of being my partner?" he said, his expression indicating he found more humor in the situation with each passing minute.

"Oh, we couldn't," they both countered at the same time.

"Our talent is not nearly adequate," Aunt Gussie said.

"And you really should choose someone younger than either of us doddering old women," Aunt Esther added.

"Neither of you are—"

"Might I suggest someone I consider equal in talent to Lady Elyssa?" Brent suggested, eager to see the issue resolved.

Fellingsdown nodded. "Of course."

Brent shifted his gaze to the woman standing beside Elly. "Lady Lathamton, would you do us the honor?"

Fellingsdown made a choked sound from beside Brent and Elly's friend opened her mouth as if to object, but both Aunt Gussie and Aunt Esther chimed in before their nephew or Lady Lathamton could say anything.

"Excellent choice, Charfield." Aunt Gussie clapped her hands in excitement.

"Absolutely," Aunt Esther echoed with a gleeful expression on her face.

"I presume you have no objection," Brent said to Fellingsdown, knowing the Marquess of Fellingsdown would never embarrass a guest by refusing her assistance.

"Of course not," Fellingsdown responded with unusual stiffness. "But the lady has not agreed. Perhaps she does not wish to be the other half of my party."

"Of course, she'll be your partner. Won't you, Cassie?" Elly asked. Her enthusiasm made it impossible for Cassie to say no.

Lady Lathamton's answer was not nearly as fervent as Elly's had been, but she nonetheless agreed – if not reluctantly.

A round of applause and genuine cheers went up and Jules and Spence were left with no choice but to record the wagers the others placed on their winning preference. Then everyone gathered into excited groups to discuss the remarkable happening and wait for the day of the match to arrive.

CHAPTER 13

Excitement over the croquet match consumed dinner that evening and the next. It continued each evening even after everyone went into the drawing room for the evening's entertainment.

By the time the eve before the match arrived, Cassie couldn't pretend excitement any longer so she made her escape through a side door and onto the terrace to be alone. She spun around when she heard a noise from behind her. Harrison stood in the shadows.

"May I join you?"

She nodded and he walked toward her.

"I saw you come out here and thought I'd take this opportunity to talk to you privately."

He stopped when he reached her and looked out into the garden instead of looking at her. She was thankful. Because of the soft, gentle breeze she could smell the intoxicating cologne he always wore. The unique fragrance always had an affect on her.

For months after her marriage to Everett she'd sworn she could smell Harrison's special cologne. Each time her sense of smell betrayed her she looked about, hoping to find him. Praying he'd finally come to rescue her.

But he hadn't. Having him burst through the door to save her had been a figment of her imagination.

It was still the same. She wondered why it couldn't be different now. Nearly four years had passed and nothing had changed. The emotions she'd felt when she was young and carefree and...happy were still there.

Seeing him again after four years had opened the door behind which she'd locked all her memories. They'd only been in each other's company for five days and every dream and longing she'd ever yearned for rushed back in the form of desperation and need.

Even though she'd attempted to avoid him, it had only taken that one kiss in the summerhouse to know she would never be over him.

She would never stop wanting him.

She would never stop loving him.

But that love held no hope. Her dream of a life as Harrison's wife was shattered four years ago.

"Was there something you needed?" she asked, keeping as much emotion from her voice as she could.

"Yes. I'd like to apologize."

She turned to look at him. "Apologize for what?"

"For not thinking of a way for you to avoid being my partner tomorrow."

Cassie shrugged. "Charfield hardly gave you an opportunity."

"No, and neither did my aunts. But I should have been able to think of a solution. I'm sure you'd rather be as far from me as possible."

Each painful word stabbed into her like a dull needle pricking through tender flesh. "I doubt I resent your company any more than you resent mine."

"Perhaps. Which is all the more reason I should have thought of a solution so we wouldn't have to spend the afternoon together."

The moon was a small crescent shape that gave a bare minimum of light. Cassie fought the tears that blurred the little sliver of light. She refused to weep in front of him. Tears had never done any good.

She should know. She'd shed enough of them when she realized Harrison wasn't coming to save her. She'd shed even more when she realized he had believed every horrible word of the scandal and abandoned her to face her fate on her own.

"Do you ever think about the plans we made when we were younger?" she asked.

"Of course. To me, they weren't just useless words. They were dreams for a future I thought we'd have together. Obviously, I was the only one of us who took them seriously."

His words hit their mark and she felt a weight drop to the pit of her stomach.

She wanted to respond with an equally hurtful remark, but before she could get out her scathing retort, he surprised her by issuing another apology.

"I'm sorry. I came out here to apologize, not to throw stones. Besides, what I mistakenly thought was between us is far in the past. I've put it behind me."

Cassie swallowed. "I'm glad."

She knew it was too late to resurrect the feelings that had once been between them, but she had one more question she needed him to answer. "Why didn't you at least come to talk to me? Why didn't you come to ask if the rumors were true?"

"Why didn't I come to—"

He stopped his words in mid sentence, but not before she heard the anger and hurt in his voice. When he resumed talking he spoke each word with tempered caution.

"I did. More times than I could count. But each time your father had me removed like so much garbage."

He raked his fingers through his hair. "Would it have been so hard for you to explain what had happened? Couldn't you have at least sent a note?"

A part of her died. *Couldn't you have at least sent a note?* Hadn't he gotten any of her frantic pleas for help? Somehow not one of the messages had been delivered.

Had her father done that?

Or Everett's father?

Or both of them?

Heaven only knew. They were both desperate enough. For a reason she only *thought* she understood, the two of them were responsible for the lies and the scandal that destroyed her future. As well as her brother's. Not only had her father disowned his only son, but he'd allowed his only daughter to be married off as if she were nothing more than a piece of horseflesh to be sold to the highest bidder.

How could she tell Harrison that? How could she expect him to believe they'd both been pawns in a terrible tragedy?

She couldn't. It was too late, because nothing would undo what had been done – even telling the truth. But she had one more question she needed to ask.

"If I had sent a note to...to ask for your help, or to...explain, what would you have done?"

"I'd have come, of course. I'd have walked through hell and back if you'd wanted me. But you didn't. When I wasn't allowed to see you, I waited for word from you; any sign that the scandal involving you and Lathamton was a mistake. But no word came." He paused. "Then you married him and it was too late for me to do anything."

He stopped and she searched for the right words to say, but there were none.

"Why, Cassie? Why did you let me believe you loved me when you loved someone else?"

"I did love you, Harrison," she heard herself say even though she swore she'd never say those words to him again.

"Obviously not enough," he threw back at her. "Or perhaps just not as much as you loved Lathamton."

"Harrison, I—"

"There's no need, Cassie. The time for explanations is well past. Besides, that's not the reason I came in search of you. I came to assure you that I won't let our lack of feelings for each other affect the fun everyone seems to be having because of the challenge."

"Everyone *does* seem to be having quite a grand time with this."

"Yes. Even Elly."

"She never told me she'd mastered swinging a mallet," Cassie said.

"None of us knew." Harrison was quiet for a moment before he shared his thoughts with her. "Do you think it's possible she won't be able to play?"

Cassie thought for a moment. "I don't know. I haven't

given it a thought. Surely she wouldn't have consented to be Charfield's partner if she couldn't."

"Perhaps, but I can't imagine how she'll manage keeping her balance without her cane. Or holding on to her cane and swinging a mallet at the same time."

Cassie felt Harrison's worry. He and George had always been the most protective of Elly's brothers. Perhaps that was because they were the oldest. But more than that, she thought it was because they considered themselves the most responsible for what had happened to her. She knew Harrison did. He'd admitted that to her a long time ago.

But he'd told her many things when he thought her heart belonged to him.

How she missed the closeness they'd once shared. How she missed having someone in whom she could confide her thoughts and dreams.

"How serious do you think Charfield's intentions are toward Elly?" she asked. Even if she would never realize any of her dreams, it wasn't too late for Elly to find her happily-ever-after.

"What do you mean? Charfield has no designs on Elly."

She couldn't help but laugh. "Surely you've noticed how he looks at her, and how eager he is to keep her company. Even if how he reacts to her isn't plain enough for you, you can't tell me you haven't seen how she looks at him."

"Charfield's being polite. And Elly's enjoying his attention. That's all."

"Oh, Harrison. There's far more to it than that. I can't speak for Charfield for I don't know him on a personal level, but I do know Elly. It's plain to everyone, including your two aunts, that Elly's falling in love."

He shook his head. "No. Elly's never shown any interest in a man before."

"Just because Elly's never shown interest in a man before doesn't mean she doesn't have the same feelings as every other woman."

"Even you, Cassie?"

She hesitated, but couldn't resist answering him. "Yes. Even me."

She knew how he'd interpret her answer; knew there was only one way he would take what she said. His reaction was exactly what she prayed it would be.

He stood next to her, close enough to gather her in his arms. When he reached for her she didn't fight him, but moved toward him, even though she knew stepping into his embrace was like jumping off a cliff into the rocky crags below.

He held her close for several long minutes, her cheek pressed to his strong, warm chest and her ear taking in every thundering beat of his heart. His muscular arms bracketed her in a secure embrace that made her feel safer than she'd felt in a very long time.

But being in each other's arms wasn't enough. They both needed something more from the other.

Harrison placed his finger beneath her chin and tilted her head upward. With a lazy, half-lowered gaze he looked into her eyes to read her expression.

Then kissed her.

His lips were firm and sensual against hers, his kiss demanding. He tilted his head and deepened his kiss as if he'd gone without her for too long and couldn't take in enough of her. There was nothing gentle in his kisses, yet he was the gentlest man she'd ever kissed.

He was the *only* man she'd ever kissed.

He pulled her closer, then opened his mouth atop hers. She followed his lead and allowed him to enter.

This is what she'd relived time and again during the long, lonely nights when all she had were her memories. She'd gone without the strength of his arms around her, the pressure of his lips atop hers, and the power of his thundering heart beating against and through her too long. For so many days and weeks and months after the scandal, this is what she'd thought she'd never learn to live without.

Now she didn't know how she'd survive giving it up again.

He lifted his mouth from hers but didn't release her. "After kissing you the other day in the summerhouse, I told myself I wouldn't make the same mistake again."

"So did I." She tried to control her breathing so he wouldn't know how much his kiss weakened her.

"I'm not sure it's possible to keep that vow."

"Neither am I."

"That's what I was afraid you'd say."

Being near him was too dangerous. She had a son to consider.

"Then perhaps it would be best if we use as much self-control as we possess when we're together."

His statement gave her pause. "Yes. That would be in both our interests."

Cassie looked into Harrison's eyes and knew she could never allow their renewed friendship to become anything more. For her son's sake she couldn't let Harrison become part of her life. "Yes, I think there's a chance that will work," she whispered with the same shyness she'd felt as an inexperienced debutante during her first ball.

"So do I," he answered. He dropped his arms from around her. "We'd best go inside." He took a step away from her. "Tomorrow will be a big day."

"You go ahead. I think I'll stay outside a little longer."

"Very well."

Harrison nodded, then walked into the house.

Yes, she thought. If they both practiced self-control, there wasn't a reason they couldn't remain on friendly terms until the end of the party.

Cassie stayed outside for several minutes after Harrison left her. She'd been sure that after all this time his kisses would no longer affect her. But they did. Even more now than they had four years earlier.

She closed her eyes and mentally reminded herself it was too late for a future with Harrison. Their shared past made it impossible. Her son made it more impossible.

She took a deep breath then straightened when she heard someone approach from behind her. She turned, then stopped.

"It's a pleasant evening, isn't it?" Jeremy Waverley said walking toward her.

She watched him approach and decided to make a hasty departure. "Yes, very pleasant. But I was just ready to go inside."

"Oh, don't go in yet. I've hardly spent any time with you this whole week."

She raised her eyebrows. "I'm sure there's nothing we need to discuss concerning the estate now. Surely whatever it is can wait until Fellingsdown's summer party is over."

"Do you think the estate is the only topic I'd like to discuss with you?"

"Perhaps not, Mr. Waverley. But as I've indicated before, I'm not interested in furthering a personal relationship with you."

Fire flashed from Waverley's eyes. She wasn't sure if the reason for his anger was because she'd called him Mr. Waverley, which he hated, or because she'd rebuffed him yet again.

"Then perhaps you should consider how essential I am to the running of Lathamton Estate. Or that I am next in line for the Lathamton title – after your son, of course."

How dare he!

"Are you issuing a warning?"

"What would I have to warn you about? I'm just stating a fact. Developing a friendship with Lord Fellingsdown may not be beneficial to you. Or to your son." He paused. "Or to Fellingsdown."

Cassie couldn't find her voice. Was he serious? "What are you saying?" she finally asked when she could speak.

"Nothing, Cassandra. Except that from the day Lord Lathamton took me into his home, I've controlled the estate. I was trained to take care of it because it was obvious Everett would never be capable. I'm not about to hand everything over to an interloper who already has more than he needs or deserves."

Cassie clenched her hands at her sides and faced Waverley with all the bravado she could muster. "I'm going to forget you said something so foolish. And so threatening. Lathamton Estate belongs to my son, the Earl of Lathamton. If you ever make such traitorous remarks again, you will find yourself banned from setting foot on Lathamton property ever again."

The look in Waverley's eyes held more hatred than she'd ever seen before. She was suddenly terrified.

"If you'll excuse me," she said and walked away from him. Her legs trembled and her stomach lurched, and she thought she'd be ill.

What if he were serious? What if he posed a threat to her son? To Harrison?

She had to think. She had to figure out what she could do to protect them.

CHAPTER 14

The next day was as perfect for the big competition as anyone could have ordered. The temperature wasn't too warm, nor was it too cool. The breeze wasn't too brisk, but gentle enough to make an exquisite day.

Even the moods of the guests sitting around the luncheon table contributed to the almost carnival-like atmosphere. There was an abundance of laughing and joking, and the never-ceasing buzz of conversation that centered around only one topic – the croquet match.

Elly wished it were over. She wasn't sure how she would survive until it was.

She looked up and down the table. Even Harrison seemed resolved to enjoy the challenge. He took the light ribbing from the other guests with a humorous attitude and accepted the teasing comments from his siblings with a smile.

Cassie, of course, remained quiet, and even a little remote, but Elly could understand that. Cassie was probably as nervous as she was. But they seemed to be the only ones. Everyone else talked of nothing except the match.

George, Jules, and Lillian placed their wagers on Harrison and Cassie. Spence, Patience, and both Elly's brothers-in-law opted to back Elly and Charfield.

Even their two aunts were divided, Aunt Gussie convinced that Elly and Charfield would come out the winner and Aunt Esther equally convinced the victor would be Harrison and Lady Lathamton.

And so the banter went. It had begun, of course, the minute Jules called for a wager. Talk throughout dinner last night had been of little else, and even though Elly hoped everyone's excitement would die down, it hadn't. Now, just minutes before the match was to begin, everyone seemed, if anything, even more excited.

Everyone except her. She was so nervous she hadn't been able to eat much of her breakfast and even less of her lunch.

The twins had planned a superb menu of cold meats and cheeses served with a variety of warm breads, and for desert, a special iced lemon custard. She tried to do justice to their exquisite planning but it was impossible. Having everyone gathered together in the same room only added to the guests' excitement as they discussed the upcoming croquet match.

The close outcome of the previous match between Fellingsdown and Charfield only fueled the debate over which team would come out on top. Of course, special care was given to avoid commenting on Elly's inexperience – or inability. Or on the fact that Lady Lathamton hadn't played much of the previous match so no one knew how she would react under pressure. Thankfully, at least for now, the comparison was between Brent and Harrison.

That should have made her feel better, but it didn't. All she could do was push the food around on her plate and pretend to eat. Anything more would probably cause her churning stomach to revolt.

"Perhaps you'd like to try a bit of *my* cold chicken," Charfield said, inching his plate toward her. "It's really quite delicious."

She looked into his smiling face. "I have my own, thank you."

"I thought perhaps there might be something wrong with your food."

"No, it's excellent."

"Then there must be something else that's keeping you from eating. Perhaps you ate too much this morning for breakfast?"

She narrowed her gaze and gave him a narrowed glare.

"Oh, that's right. You hardly ate anything for breakfast either. Do I have cause for worry? I'd hate for my partner to faint during our match from lack of food."

He was teasing her – again. "You know perfectly well I'm fine." She smoothed the linen napkin on her lap. "I'm a little nervous, if you must know."

"Nervous over what?"

She gave him a look she hoped was more deadly than the last, but from the way he continued to devour the food on his plate, she doubted he even noticed her annoyance. Even though her heart raced every time he came near her, she was glad he'd escorted her in to eat and sat beside her. His relaxed presence and confident manner were all that kept her from announcing to the entire gathering that she couldn't participate in their croquet competition.

It would be easy enough to do. Everyone knew she wasn't

accomplished enough. Her family would understand that she didn't want to do something that would cause people to stare at her.

"Surely you don't doubt your ability."

"Of course I doubt my ability. I only just learned to play. I'm not good enough by half."

"Your shots are more accurate than any player I've ever played against - with the possible exception of your brother of course."

"Which is exactly why you should have chosen someone with whom you stood a better chance of winning."

"Is winning so very important to you?"

She slid a piece of fruit from one side of her plate to the other. Finally she breathed a deep sigh and lowered the fork to her plate. "No. It's not the winning or the losing I care about."

"Then I fail to see why you are so concerned?"

"It's me. It's the assistance I need to swing the mallet. It's the way I allow you to hold me to keep me from falling. It's—"

His burst of laughter stopped her words and drew the attention of everyone sitting near them. With a unison turn of heads, the couples on either side and directly across from them turned to see what was so amusing. Elly picked up her fork again and stabbed at a piece of chicken, then put it in her mouth and chewed as if nothing were the matter.

She concentrated on her food until conversation around them resumed then said, "Do you know what people will think when you hold me?"

Charfield was in the process of lifting his glass to his mouth and he stopped, then slowly turned his head to look at her over the rim of his glass - and smiled. His eyes contained more than a bit of humor, as well as the most suggestive look she'd ever seen.

"Yes. Every man here who is not your brother will think I'm the luckiest man in the world."

"Hardly!" Her loud guffaw caused half the table to look at them again. Elly pretended she didn't notice and lifted her water and took a drink. The liquid was cool and clean and tasted like sawdust when it went down.

"You have nothing to worry about," he whispered. "You play like an expert."

"Beginners luck," she mumbled.

"Perhaps it was the first time you played, but you were better yesterday. Even better when we practiced this morning at dawn."

"But what if—"

Charfield turned in his chair, causing her to stop.

"You might as well give up, Elly. I'm not going to let you talk me into finding another partner."

She clenched her hands in her lap and he placed his long, strong fingers over hers and gave her a gentle squeeze.

When had he started calling her Elly?

When had his touch calmed her like no other touch could?

"You'll be fine. Better than fine. You'll be marvelous."

Elly doubted she'd be fine, but it no longer mattered. Besides, she couldn't risk talking any more. They'd drawn enough attention as it was.

The staff served the iced lemon custard, which the guests devoured in no time, and when they finished, Harrison rose to his feet.

"Are you and your partner ready, Charfield?"

Charfield gave Elly's fingers another squeeze beneath the table followed by a quick wink before he turned his attention to Harrison.

"My partner and I have finalized our winning strategy."

This boast of confidence brought a round of cheers and jeers, depending upon which couple a bet had been wagered.

"Then I suggest we get this competition under way."

There was an even louder rumble of excitement, then the men pushed back from the table to help the ladies rise. Before Elly could take a calming breath, the room was empty except for her and Brent and Harrison and Cassie. But they were at the other end of the table.

Charfield stood at her side wearing one of the most endearing smiles she'd ever seen. "Are you ready?" he asked, extending his arm.

"As ready as I'll ever be. Just don't say you weren't warned when you take hold of me so I can take my first swing and one – or all – of my brothers challenge you to a duel."

"Haven't you heard? Duels are illegal."

"So was French wine not that many years ago and we all enjoyed it in abundance."

Charfield laughed. The deep, rich...genuine sound was the most intoxicatingly wonderful thing she'd ever heard. She couldn't help but revel in the sense of composure that washed over her. Without the dread she'd felt earlier, she placed her hand on his forearm and rose to her feet.

Harrison stood at the other end of the table. "Are you ready to face your defeat?" It was as if he were intentionally adding a bit of fuel to the already charged challenge and Elly suddenly realized that he was actually enjoying this.

"You're very confident for a brother who's never seen his sister hit a ball before," Charfield said.

"What I *am* confident of," Harrison answered, crossing his

arms over his chest, "is *my* talent combined with my partner's. I'm afraid you will find us quite undefeatable."

Elly caught the wink Harrison gave Cassie and the shy smile she answered in return. The air suddenly seemed charged with something quite magical.

No matter what had happened to tear them apart four years ago, there wasn't a doubt in Elly's mind they still loved each other and fate had played a very nasty trick on both of them.

She didn't know what had made Cassie accept the invitation she'd sent, but she vowed she would do whatever she could to play matchmaker.

"Come, Lady Elyssa," Charfield said, holding out her cane. "It's time to show this braggart what *real* talent is."

Elly walked at Charfield's side across the terrace then down the steps and around the house to the east lawn where the croquet course was set up. The other guests were already there, chatting and laughing about the marvelous fun they would have this afternoon.

"Since I supposedly issued the challenge," Elly heard Charfield say to her brother, "I insist that you and your partner go first."

Harrison gave them both a perfectly executed bow and came up with a smile on his face. "On behalf of my partner, I accept the courtesy."

A cheer erupted from the guests. The gathering was positioned far enough from the players not to interfere with the play, yet close enough that Elly was certain she could feel them breathing down her neck.

But at least she didn't have to hit her ball first.

She exhaled a huge sigh of relief. She wasn't sure she'd have the courage to go first.

Cassie'd chosen yellow as her color and she started the game. She tapped her ball through the starting wickets, then took aim and hit her ball toward the first station. Her shot was perfect, stopping a short distance from her goal.

A loud cheer went up and she turned to give the crowd a nod of appreciation.

Harrison was next. He'd chosen the blue ball and his shot landed even closer to the goal, as expected. Another rousing cheer went up from the onlookers and Harrison turned to give them a regal bow, befitting his station as the future Duke of Sheridan.

Elly was next.

She'd chosen the red ball and Charfield placed it at the starting position.

"Are you ready, my lady?"

There was a soft look in his eyes; a calm, encouraging expression on his face. His intent was to put her at ease but she was far too tense for her fears to evaporate.

She nodded, and took her position behind the ball. The group applauded encouragingly, whether to show support for an achievement no one thought she'd be brave enough to attempt, or to encourage her to do her best, regardless of how ungainly her swing might be.

She knew not one of her family or their guests expected perfection. They probably didn't imagine she'd get her red ball close to its target.

A few even shouted words of encouragement, and she smiled when George's voice came through with distinction over the rest of the group. She had the best family in the world. They wanted her to succeed at whatever she tried.

Elly swallowed hard, then looked over her shoulder to

where Brent stood. "We might as well start." She prayed she wasn't making a huge mistake.

The crowd was still cheering her on, urging her to make her first hit. Brent stepped closer to her and placed his left hand on her waist.

The riotous noise coming from the onlookers turned noticeably softer.

Brent held out his right arm and Elly hooked her cane over his forearm. Then, he stepped up even closer and placed his right hand on the other side of her waist.

The silence from the crowd was deafening.

Elly froze.

"Hit the ball, sweetheart," he whispered in her ear, "or you may not get a chance to."

Elly shifted her position, then with Charfield holding her steady, she hit the ball.

Brent didn't release her, but kept his hands around her waist. It took a while for everyone to move their gazes from the improper way Charfield held her, to how expertly she'd hit the ball.

Her ball was almost even with Harrison's.

Charfield gave her a little squeeze around the waist and leaned forward to whisper in her ear. "Wonderful, sweetheart. Simply wonderful."

He handed back her cane, and when she'd regained her balance, stepped away from her.

At first, Elly wasn't sure she had the courage to turn to look at the gaping crowd. She wasn't sure she could hold her temper if any of them made a comment on the indecent way Charfield held her. But she didn't have a choice. She'd have to face their censure sooner or later.

She turned, then staggered when she looked at her family and friends. Charfield placed his palm beneath her elbow to steady her.

Aunt Esther stood with her hand over her open mouth while one lone tear streamed down her cheek.

Patience and Lilly both clung to their husband's arms while tears rolled unabashedly down their faces.

But the sight that affected her most was the look of pride on Harrison's face.

And George's.

And Jules's.

And Spence's.

Since the day of the accident there'd been an underlying tinge of guilt in their eyes, as if they were each responsible for each difficulty she faced.

Today, there was a different look in their eyes. A look of... admiration.

She felt her cheeks turn warm and knew she'd turned embarrassingly red. She'd always hated when people stared at her and there wasn't one pair of eyes looking anywhere but at her.

She tilted her head upward and looked into Charfield's beaming gaze. The crowd of gathered watchers remained silent, but suddenly that wasn't important. All that mattered was the pride she saw in Charfield's eyes.

Then, as if on cue, her family and their guests broke out in thunderous applause. One by one, her sisters and brothers rushed forward to give her a warm hug. Harrison was first and George next. None of them were shy about showing their excitement at her accomplishment.

"I see you've kept my sister's talent hidden from us,"

Harrison said to Charfield after the last of her siblings released her.

"I warned you she was exceedingly talented."

"So you did," Harrison said on a laugh. Then he turned to Cassie, who'd come to give Elly a hug and was still holding her hand. "From the expertise my sister exhibited, I think we have our work cut out for us if we intend to win this match."

"I think you're right. I'll redouble my efforts." She looked over her shoulder as she walked to the spot her ball had stopped. "And I expect you to do the same."

The gathering laughed wholeheartedly, which eased the tension created by the preceding emotional scene.

Harrison took a few steps then stopped to issue a statement that made Elly smile.

"Our match just rose to a different level, Charfield. Neither my partner nor I intend to give you any quarter, so I suggest you make each shot your best."

"We'll be sure to do that."

Harrison walked away and Elly noticed there seemed to be a lighter spring to his step. She wasn't sure if it was because of her surprising accomplishment, or if he was happy to be spending the afternoon with Cassie.

Charfield tapped his ball through the double wickets, then lined up like he'd taught her to do and hit his lucky green ball. It stopped inches from Harrison's and the crowd erupted with cheers and applause.

Charfield stepped close to her and offered her his arm. They walked together across the lawn and she realized this was the most perfect day she'd ever had.

She turned her head and looked at him. "Do you care if we don't win?"

He gently squeezed her hand. "We've already won."
And she knew he meant it.

CHAPTER 15

Brent lined up to take his next swing. If he truly believed his green ball was lucky, he'd have to credit it for the advantage he and Elly had over Fellingsdown and Lady Lathamton. But he'd never been a superstitious person and the credit for their lead belonged to Elly. She was amazing.

She put her body into every swing, trusting him to keep her from falling; knowing that if he lost his grip she'd land on the ground in an embarrassing heap. He'd never met anyone who trusted him so completely.

"Do you think I should aim for Harrison's blue ball to knock him out of line, or should I try to knock Cassie's yellow ball further from the goal?" she whispered as she lined up to hit her ball.

Brent loved the feel of her next to him. He loved the way her backside fit snugly against him. He loved the opportunity supporting her gave him to wrap his arms around her waist and hold her.

Yesterday, when they'd practiced, he'd mistakenly thought the shock waves zinging through him were a natural reaction to having a beautiful woman in his arms. This morning he'd tried to convince himself that was still the case. Now he knew it wasn't.

If having a woman in his arms caused such a startling effect, he would have experienced this same heaviness every time he asked a beautiful woman to dance. Or each time he escorted one of London's numerous beautiful young women for an afternoon drive through Hyde Park.

No, this was different. Much different.

Brent tipped his head until his mouth was close to Elly's cheek then he whispered in her ear. "I think it would be best to try to knock your brother out of the way. Then, if I can manage a good shot, I may be able to add to our lead."

She nodded, then shifted her position behind her red ball.

"Lady Lathamton," Harrison said loud enough to draw everyone's attention. "I think my sister's strategy is to spoil my superb position."

"Do it, Elly!" one of her brothers yelled from the sidelines.

"Knock Harrison as far as you can," one of the twins added.

Elly giggled as she looked into his face, and it was almost more than he could do not to lean down and kiss her.

Although kissing her would have been enjoyable, it was a far cry from what else his body wanted to do. Holding her in such an intimate manner was a torture surpassing what he thought he could endure. Even kissing her in front of her family was stretching the limits of what they would allow.

"How quickly my siblings forget where their family loyalties lie," Harrison said with a stoic expression on his face. "I won't forget this, George."

This brought a loud chorus of ribbing, aimed not only at Harrison, but at George and Elly's other brothers and sisters who'd encouraged her to knock Harrison out of contention.

"We should have placed a wager on the outcome of this match," Elly said while the friendly banter was still going on.

Brent laughed. "What would you have wagered?"

A slight frown etched her forehead before she smiled. "Nothing. I have everything I want." She broadened her smile. "What would you have wagered?"

Brent knew. Without a second thought he said, "I'd have asked for a colt from El Solidar."

"Oh, yes. That would have been a wonderful wager. Perhaps it's not too late?"

He looked at her and felt his heart hitch a notch in his chest. "Perhaps it's not."

With his hands still at Elly's waist, he turned to face his competition. "Fellingsdown," he shouted loud enough to be heard over the exuberant crowd. "My partner and I would like to propose a wager."

There was a moment of silence, then the group of guests cheered loud enough he was sure they could be heard all the way to London.

"A wager! Yes!" they all shouted at the same time.

Fellingsdown tipped his head back and laughed. "What wager would you and your partner like to make, Charfield?"

Brent looked Elly's brother square in the eyes. "If we win, I claim an offspring from El Solidar."

The guests erupted into a louder burst of cheering and yelling and clapping. Only Fellingsdown remained motionless. And one other. Elly's brother, George.

George must have known what the payment was for Brent

to be Elly's partner for the party. He must also know what Brent meant when he wagered what had already been offered – that Brent considered the conditions of their former wager null and void. This included his agreement to make Elly forget her anonymous suitor, that he wouldn't let her fall in love with him, and that he wouldn't risk breaking her heart.

Brent was sure he'd already accomplished his first objective. Elly hadn't mentioned an anonymous suitor since they'd met, and Brent knew she would have spoken of it at some time during the hours they'd spent together.

As to the other conditions...

No one had to worry about him leaving her with a broken heart because he had no plan to leave her - *ever*.

And the stipulation that he wouldn't allow Elly to fall in love with him...

Brent couldn't stop a smile from forming on his lips. He had no intention of trying to keep that condition. He intended to do everything in his power to make her fall in love with him. As in love with him as he was with her.

He loved her. He knew without a doubt that he did. Now her brothers did, too. His wager made that clear.

Brent kept his gaze focused on Fellingsdown. The real meaning behind what he'd just proposed wasn't lost on Elly's brother, or on George. From the looks on their faces, they both realized Brent was asking permission to court their sister.

"And if you lose?" Fellingsdown asked, his tone decidedly serious.

"I lose my horse." Brent paused, then added. "But I still win."

Fellingsdown's reaction was slow, but when it came it was unmistakable. Elly's brother smiled, then his broad smile turned to laughter. "Lady Lathamton," he said, turning his attention to where his partner stood. "We've been challenged. Do you object to my accepting Lord Charfield's wager?"

The onlookers stood in silence, waiting for the wager to be confirmed. When Lady Lathamton answered with a decided "No," they erupted into applause.

Brent felt as if he'd grown wings and could fly over the highest mountaintops. Fellingsdown had accepted his wager. Which meant...

Brent lowered his gaze to the woman in his arms. He'd been granted permission to court Elly. His heart rejoiced inside his chest.

As he looked at Elly, her smile turned to a puzzled expression. "Did you see the look Harrison gave you?"

"Yes."

"Did I miss something?"

"It's a private wager between the two of us."

She looked at him with a questioning lift to her eyebrows. "Do you intend to share it with me?"

"Of course. You're my partner." He gave her a playful tap on the tip of her nose. "But first we have a match to win."

He took his place behind her and clasped his hands to her waist. Perhaps he held her closer than he ought. If she noticed she didn't say.

But he wasn't sure he would have stepped back if she had. Having her in his arms was where he wanted her to be for the rest of his life.

———

Elly's heart pounded as she watched Cassie prepare to

make her last shot. If Cassie missed, the match was over and she and Brent won. If Cassie made her shot, the game would continue and Elly would be next.

Elly looked to the crowd watching every play. She thought some of them might tire of standing in the sun and go back to the terrace and drink lemonade in comfort, but no one did. When the twins realized no one wanted to miss any of the excitement of the match, they'd ordered blankets to be brought out. Even Aunt Gussie and Aunt Esther sat on the grass with the young people, drinking the lemonade the staff brought out to them.

"Hit Elly's ball hard enough to knock her out of Harrison's path, Lady Lathamton," Jules shouted from his spot on a blanket next to Amelia Hastings.

Elly gave her brother a glaring look that made Miss Hastings giggle behind her hand. Obviously Jules's wager was on Harrison and Cassie.

Elly couldn't help but laugh when the half of the group who'd placed their money on Brent and her jeered Jules.

Cassie stepped up to her yellow ball and took aim. Harrison stepped back from where he'd been next to her, giving her some last-minute instructions. He tried to look calm and collected but Elly knew he was as nervous as the rest of them.

"What if she knocks my ball far off the path?" Elly said, leaning back against Brent. She knew she was taking advantage of having him so close but she didn't care. She was enjoying every minute of today, every second of being near him.

"You'll play like you have all day and come back to challenge her."

"But your wager?"

His hands clasped around her upper arms and he

gently turned her so she could look at him. "The wager means nothing. It is not yours to win or lose. The wager is insignificant compared to how we are enjoying ourselves. Do you understand, Elly?"

She nodded. "But I know how much you want a colt from El Solidar."

"There are other ways for me to get a colt. Ways that have nothing to do with the outcome of this game. So don't concern yourself with what happens."

Elly didn't have an opportunity to respond before Cassie took aim and swung.

Elly watched the yellow ball sail across the lawn and race toward her red ball. With a loud whop that echoed in the silence, yellow blended with red, then Elly's red wooden ball whizzed away from its perfect position and didn't stop until it was far out of line of the goal.

A loud mixture of cheers and moans rose from the gallery of onlookers. Harrison rushed to Cassie's side, lifted her in the air and twirled her around in a circle.

"It's all right," Brent whispered. "We haven't lost yet."

Elly nodded, but she knew winning would be much more difficult now.

Harrison gave Cassie another congratulatory hug, then placed his arm around her shoulders as they walked toward her ball.

Elly smiled. A part of her was happy. Today's match seemed to bring her brother and Cassie closer to each other. The rest of her, however, couldn't forget that she and Brent were a step further away from winning their wager.

"Your turn, Fellingsdown," Brent said, his voice calm and optimistic.

"Are you worried?" Harrison said on a laugh as he walked to his blue ball.

"Of course not. Your sister is my partner."

Elly smiled to thank Brent for the compliment, then turned to the onlookers to curtsy in appreciation for the applause they added.

Harrison lined up behind his ball.

This was it. This hit would almost determine the outcome of the game.

Harrison pulled his mallet back in a wide arc and began his downward swing.

Before his mallet connected with its target, a muffled pop sounded from somewhere to their right and Harrison crumpled to a heap on the ground.

————

The second Fellingsdown went down, Brent pulled Elly in front of him and dropped to the ground. He covered her body to protect her.

They lay there for a few moments, listening for another shot, but there wasn't one. The only noises were the screams of surprise and terror that came from the guests.

Brent lifted his head and scanned the area. He watched for some movement from the line of trees from which the bullet had come, but the only movement he saw was Jules and Spencer racing in the direction of the trees. George had already ushered the guests toward the house.

Brent lifted himself from her. "Did I hurt you?"

"Harrison's hurt."

"I know. Stay here and I'll go to him."

"But—"

"Don't move, Elly." He pressed his hand against her shoulder when she tried to rise. "We don't know who else the idiot will shoot at."

He rose to his feet and raced to where Harrison lay.

Lady Lathamton was already there, her eyes wide with fear. She pulled on Fellingsdown's jacket with trembling fingers and removed the material from his arm. A dark spot dampened the sleeve of his shirt just below his shoulder.

"Get Cassie and Elly away from here," Fellingsdown said in a ragged voice.

He was obviously in pain but at least he was conscious. Brent didn't know a lot about bullet wounds, but he knew that was a good sign.

Brent looked up as George reached them. Elly was on his arm.

"I thought I told you to stay where you were." He pulled her to the ground and tucked her next to him.

"I couldn't."

"Why doesn't that surprise me?"

Elly moved toward Harrison. "How badly are you hurt?"

"I'm fine." He tried to sit but Brent held him down.

"Don't move. If that bullet was intended for you, then let the man who pulled the trigger think he accomplished what he intended. Besides, Elly and Lady Lathamton are too close. If he tries to shoot at you again he might hit one of them."

Fellingsdown sagged back to the ground. He stayed quiet until Jules and Spence reached them.

"Did you find anything?" George asked.

Both brothers shook their heads.

"Maybe it was an accident," Cassie offered.

"This wasn't an accident," Jules interrupted, looking again toward the thicket of trees for any sign of movement. "Someone intended to shoot Harry."

She shook her head. "I didn't think he was serious," she whispered.

Brent studied Lady Lathamton. Her face was pale, her eyes filled with terror. A wave of unease washed over him.

"What do you mean?" he asked, leaning closer to her. "Who didn't you think was serious?"

She jolted as if she'd suddenly realized she'd spoken aloud. She swiped a tear from her damp cheeks and backed away. "No one. I...misspoke."

Fellingsdown reached for the lady's hand and held it. "I'm sure it was an accident, Cassie. No one would be so thoughtless."

Several footmen came with a makeshift sling. Lady Lathamton clutched Fellingsdown's hand as they made their way to the house. Her face still lacked color, and several times she swiped at the tear that ran down her cheeks.

The lady was hiding something.

———

Cassie paced the carpet that ran the length of the hall outside Harrison's bedroom. The doctor was still with him along with Harrison's three brothers and the Marquess of Charfield.

Harrison could have been killed.

She had to warn them. She had to make sure they stood guard outside Harrison's room. And inside.

She clasped her cold hands to her hot cheeks. She didn't

think Waverley was serious when he issued his threat. She didn't think he'd try to kill Harrison.

But he had.

She paced the floor at a faster speed.

"Why don't you sit for a while," Elly said, looping her free hand around Cassie's waist. "It won't be much longer now."

She stepped out of Elly's grip. She couldn't let her hold her, comfort her. Everyone would hate her when they found out it was her fault Harrison had been shot.

"What's taking them so long?" She waited for the door to open so she could rush in to see for herself that Harrison was all right.

"The doctor's being thorough."

"But it shouldn't take so long. Maybe Harrison was hurt worse than we thought."

"No. He was walking when they brought him in. That has to mean his wound wasn't too severe."

"George said he'd lost a lot of blood. Maybe..."

Cassie knew she was being irrational but she couldn't help it. This was her fault.

She swiped her fingers over her damp eyes. When she looked up, Elly's hooded gaze locked with hers. "Why did you send me an invitation, Elly?"

Elly took an uneven step toward her. "To give you an opportunity to mend whatever tore you and Harrison apart. I'd hoped you would accept, but I doubted you would."

"You were surprised to see me?"

"Very." Elly smiled. "I was nearly as surprised to see you as Harrison was."

Cassie searched for the right words to ask her next question. She knew how much she would reveal if she said the wrong words. "Was the invitation all you sent?"

"All?"

"Yes. Did you follow your invitation with a letter?"

"I'm not sure I understand."

Cassie studied the confused expression and knew Ellie wasn't responsible for the letter. Dear God, she said as a prayer, as a plea. That meant someone else knew her secret.

"What letter did you get, Cassie?" Ellie stepped closer and placed her hand over Cassie's in a comforting manner.

"I shouldn't have come," she said. "I should have been satisfied with things the way they were."

"No, you shouldn't. You and Harrison have made remarkable strides to heal the hurt between you. If you are in any kind of trouble, this is exactly the place you need to be."

Cassie wished Ellie were right. She wished she and Harrison could go back in time and forget everything that had torn them apart. And she thought maybe that was happening.

She remembered how he'd swung her around in the air after she'd made her last shot. She should have known Waverley was watching. Their show of affection had undoubtedly been the impetus he'd needed to carry out his threat. If only she hadn't let Harrison touch her or hold her. Perhaps if she hadn't agreed to be his partner...

She squeezed shut her eyes and considered her alternatives. She had to tell Charfield and Harrison's brothers that Waverley was responsible even though he'd deny it when confronted. Without proof there was nothing anyone could do. And Waverley would be free to try to kill Harrison again.

Her heart raced even faster.

"I have to leave. Harrison won't be safe until I'm gone."

"You're not thinking clearly, Cassie." Ellie grasped her by

the shoulders and held her.

She spun away. "Yes, I am. I only came because of the letter. But that no longer matters. Nothing is worth Harrison's death."

"What letter?"

Cassie shook her head. The sooner she left, the better.

An abnormal calm settled over her. The most terrifying part of any tragedy was not knowing what action to take to fix it. But she was past that. She knew now what she had to do.

She took a relaxing breath when the door opened. She heard George thank the doctor for coming, followed by his order for Fitzhugh to be sure to feed the doctor before he left. When Fitzhugh and the doctor left the room, Cassie entered.

She rushed across the room and didn't stop until she reached the bed where Harrison lay.

He wore no shirt or nightshirt and his upper arm was heavily bandaged in clean, white cloth. She looked from the bandage to Harrison's face and her breath caught in her throat.

He was beyond pale, no doubt from the doctor's painful ministrations as well as the loss of blood, but he appeared to be all right.

"How are you?"

"Better now that the doctor's finished torturing me."

Cassie knew he'd intended his last remark to be a joke, but she couldn't form a smile.

He frowned. "Are you all right, Cassie?"

She nodded. "I'm going home, Harrison. My maid is packing now and I intend to leave as soon as my luggage is loaded."

Harrison's eyes closed on a regretful sigh, then he opened them and faced her. "Of course. No one can blame you for wanting to leave after what just happened. I'll have my staff assist you with whatever you need."

Charfield stepped forward. "I'm afraid we can't allow you to leave, Lady Lathamton."

He leveled a stern look in her direction. "At least, not until you tells us who shot Lord Fellingsdown."

CHAPTER 16

All eyes focused on Cassie and she felt the blood rush from her face.

"Cassie?"

Harrison whispered her name but she couldn't bring herself to look at him. If she did, he'd know it was her fault he'd been shot.

"I think you need to tell us what you know," Charfield said.

The impact of his words caused her to stagger. "I can't."

"You don't have a choice."

It was suddenly impossible for her to keep her balance. If George hadn't been near enough to steady her, she would have slumped to the floor.

"Jules, would you please close the door?" Charfield ordered. "And make sure the hall is empty of any guests."

Jules rushed to close the door.

"Spencer, perhaps you can find your sister and Lady Lathamton a chair. I'm sure they'd be more comfortable sitting."

Elly's youngest brother went for chairs.

"George, help me up," Harrison said, already trying to raise himself.

George hesitated. "Are you sure, Harry? You've just been—"

"Help me up," he demanded.

Charfield moved to one side of the bed and George to the other. Together they moved Harrison to a sitting position and Elly rushed to prop a pillow behind his back.

"What's this...about, Charfield?" Harrison's voice was ragged but exhibited a strength Cassie was glad to hear.

Charfield turned his attention toward her. His expression remained serious. He knew.

"Why don't you explain what's going on, my lady?" he said when Spence brought in two chairs and Elly and she sat.

All eyes shifted to her. Sheer willpower was all that kept her upright in her chair.

"Cassie, what do you know about the shooting?" Elly asked. The frown on her face matched the question in her voice.

Cassie took a deep breath and focused her pleading gaze on Charfield. "I have to leave The Down. It's the only way Harrison will be safe."

"Safe from whom?" Charfield asked.

She shook her head. She couldn't tell them. She couldn't.

"Tell us," George demanded in an uncommon display of forcefulness.

"I can't," she cried out. "If I leave, everything will be all right. He just wants me away from here." She paused. "Away from Harrison."

Tears fell from her eyes and she swiped them from her cheeks. "I didn't think he was serious. I'm so sorry."

Harrison's gaze narrowed. "Who, Cassie?"

"I can't tell you. You'll do something foolish." She swiped her hand to include all of them. "And it will only make things worse."

"If someone intentionally shot Harrison, we don't intend to ignore it," Spence said.

He was the most outspoken of Harrison's brothers and had the quickest temper. He was also the one to forget a wrong the fastest. But Cassie knew he wouldn't forget this. None of them would.

"Telling you won't do any good." She wiped her tears with the handkerchief Charfield handed her. "And you can't go to the authorities. He'll only deny he shot Harrison."

"We have no intention of going to the authorities," Jules said. "We'll handle this ourselves."

"No! You can't! I'm the only one who can keep Harrison safe!"

Harrison reacted with the strength of a man whose arm wasn't in a bandage and who hadn't just had a doctor sew his flesh together. "Bloody hell, woman!" he said, slamming the fist of his uninjured hand down beside him on the bed. "Do you think I'm the kind of man who'd hide behind a woman's skirts?"

She slid from the chair and knelt on the floor beside the bed. She reached for his hand and wrapped her fingers around his fist. "What happened is my fault. I should have known he meant it, but I didn't think he was serious."

"Who, Cassie?"

"Waverley."

"Waverley?" George said in disbelief. "What does Waverley want so badly that he'd try to kill Harrison to get?"

For a moment no one spoke, then Charfield answered George's question. "You're looking at her," he answered, then nodded to where she knelt.

"Waverley's in love with Cassie?" Harrison shifted on the bed as if he wanted to rise. George placed his hand on Harrison's shoulder and he settled back against the pillow.

"I don't think love has much to do with Waverley's motives. Am I right, Lady Lathamton?"

She nodded.

"When did you realize what Waverley's intentions were?" Charfield asked.

Another stabbing of fear spiked through her and she gazed at him with a pleading look that begged him not to say more.

"Answer Charfield's question, Cassie," Harrison said, the hardness in his voice leaving no room for mistaking his determination. "How long has Waverley bothered you?"

"A little more than six months," she said softly. "His comments were innocent at first. He began by reassuring me that he'd always be there to help me." She breathed a sigh that shuddered. "Then his suggestions became more personal. He told me that since it was unthinkable for me to remain alone, I should give some consideration to remarrying. Especially with a young son to raise and two estates to manage."

"Two?" Spence said.

Cassie rose from the floor and sat on the edge of her chair. "I'm sure you heard the rumor that my father disowned my brother, Benjamin. It happened the night before...my marriage."

"Do you know why?" Charfield asked.

She shook her head. She tried not to remember anything about that night. It was the second worst night of her life.

"Benjamin came to see me before he left England. He'd been disowned by Father and was on his way to the docks. He had passage to Boston, in America.

"I didn't know until Father died two years later that he'd left everything to me. I'd always hoped Father would forgive Ben for whatever he did and leave him Hollyvine Keep. But he didn't."

She looked into Harrison's eyes and prayed he'd tell her she'd told enough.

"Go on, Cassie."

"Hollyvine Keep isn't entailed and neither is our London property. I have control of everything until my son reaches his majority. Then it goes to Andrew."

"Does Waverley know this?" Harrison asked.

"I'm sure he does. He's managed the Lathamton holdings for years. Even though Hollyvine has its own steward, I'm sure he's kept abreast of how it's being managed."

"How did you know Waverley intended to harm Harrison?" George asked.

"He told me."

"He told you!" Spence slammed his fist against the small table closest to him. "When?"

"Last night." She turned her gaze to where Harrison lay on the bed. "He saw us...on the terrace."

"What did he say?" Harrison asked.

She shook her head. "I don't remember exactly, but he mentioned that developing a friendship with you wouldn't be beneficial to me. Or to you. I didn't dream he meant to harm you."

"There's no way you could have known," Harrison said. "None of this is your fault."

"Perhaps not. But I can prevent anything more from happening." She rose to her feet and faced them. "I need to leave here."

Charfield answered her announcement with a rebuttal. "I'm afraid we can't allow that, Lady Lathamton. You need to stay."

"But Harrison won't be safe if I stay."

"We'll make sure nothing happens to him. Or to you."

She shook her head. They didn't understand Waverley's desperation for power. Or his desire for wealth. "How are you going to do that? By guarding Harrison night and day?"

"No," Charfield said. "By eliminating the threat."

George took a step forward. "It would be my pleasure to ask Waverley to leave The Downs."

"We'll help," Spencer said, giving Jules a nod.

"Asking him to leave won't make him any less dangerous," Charfield said. "He has to admit his guilt to someone whose reputation is beyond reproach and whose word carries enough weight to force him to reside far away from here. Preferably out of England."

"Do you have someone in mind?" Harrison asked from the bed.

Charfield smiled. "You have among your guests some of the most influential members of the House. Your two brothers-in-law, for example."

"They're related," George reminded him. "I'm afraid their word won't carry as much weight as someone who's not."

"The Duke of Parneston isn't," Charfield added.

"No, he isn't." George said with a serious grin on his face. "But Waverley's hardly likely to admit to any of us that he tried to kill Harrison."

"No," Charfield agreed. "There's only one person who can get him to admit what he did."

Everyone in the room was quiet as they considered who that might be.

Cassie's heart beat faster, her pulse pounded in her head. Charfield was right. There was one person to whom Waverley would boast.

Harrison was the first to realize who that person was. "No. I won't allow it."

"Allow what?" Jules asked.

"It's the only way," Charfield said in a soft, calm voice.

"Then we'll find another way," Harrison said.

"Would someone explain what's going on here?" Spence demanded.

"There's nothing to explain," Harrison said, trying to sit up in bed. "I won't allow it."

Cassie stood. "Yes, you will, Harrison." She tried to keep her voice as steady as possible. "Because I'm not required to ask your permission."

"We'll think of something else, Cassie."

She ignored Harrison's protest and looked at Charfield. "I take it this plan of yours involves me."

Charfield nodded. "Yes. It also involves a certain degree of danger."

She wanted to laugh. "As compared to what? Harrison dying the next time Waverley shoots him?"

"Cassie, no," Harrison said. "We'll think of something else."

She sat on the bed and reached for Harrison's hand. "I'm not about to let Waverley threaten you if there's something I can do to stop him." She gave Harrison a decisive nod, then turned to Charfield. "Please explain what you'd like me to do?"

"In order to eliminate Waverley as a threat, we must get him to admit he shot Fellingsdown, and will do so again."

"When would you like me to meet him?"

"As soon as possible. Tonight. He'd be a fool not to realize you suspect him. Especially since he threatened Fellingsdown last night."

George stepped closer. "There will be musical entertainment after dinner. A chamber quartet. Perhaps Lady Lathamton can ask to speak privately with Waverley during the performance. We'll leave the yellow drawing room door open and the room brightly lit." George turned to look at her. "Do you know which room I'm talking about?"

"Yes."

"That room will be perfect," Jules added. "There are connecting doors on either side that lead to Elly's study on one side and the library on the other."

"There's even a small office space in the back where Father's secretary works when he comes from London," Spencer said. "It will be the perfect place for the Duke of Parneston to hide so he can overhear Waverley's confession."

"Do any of you realize the danger Cassie will be in?" Harrison glared at everyone surrounding his bed.

George crossed his arms over his chest. "She won't be in any danger, Harrison. We'll keep her safe."

Cassie was touched by Harrison's concern. She lifted his hand and held it close to her breast. "I won't allow Waverley to think he got away with nearly killing you. He needs to be stopped."

"If anything happens—" Harrison started to say, but Charfield held up his hand to stop him.

"It won't. We'll make sure we're nearby so nothing goes

wrong."

It was settled, then. She would do whatever it took to stop Waverley. One question still bothered Cassie, though. She looked at Harrison, then Charfield, hoping they could give her an answer. "What can Waverley possibly hope to gain that is worth committing murder?"

Charfield was the only one to offer a solution. "I don't think Waverley intended to kill Fellingsdown. If murder was his intent, he could have done it easily enough. Fellingsdown was an open target more than once."

"Then what was his goal?" Spencer asked.

"I'm only guessing here," Charfield said, locking his hands behind his back. "I think his goal was to frighten Lady Lathamton into leaving The Down. He can only achieve his goal to control Lathamton Estates and Hollyvine Keep if he marries Lady Lathamton. When he saw a friendship growing between the two, he was desperate to stop it. His intention in shooting Fellingsdown was more than likely to injure him severely enough for the party to be called off."

Cassie felt her disgust for Waverley intensify. "Even if we married, it would only give him Hollyvine. Lathamton Estate is entailed. When Everett died, the estate as well as the title passed down to Andrew. The only way for him to gain possession would be if something were to happen to—"

Her heart stuttered for several beats. "No!" The terror that raged through her stopped her breath. "He intends to kill Andrew!"

Harrison squeezed her hands. "He won't get the chance. When the Duke of Parneston hears Waverley's confession, the authorities will have all the proof they need to lock him away for the rest of his life."

With a great deal of effort, Harrison pushed himself to sit straighter on the bed. "George, you and Spence and Jules take turns watching Waverley. Don't let him out of your sight."

"We won't," George said. "Jules, go down now and keep an eye on him."

Jules started for the door. "What should I tell everyone when they ask about you?"

"Tell them I just received a scratch. That I'll be down for dinner tonight and am looking forward to the evening's entertainment."

"Are you sure?" Cassie asked. Harrison's injury wasn't severe compared to how grave it could have been, but he'd lost a great deal of blood and that wasn't something to take lightly.

"I'm sure. Go, Jules. I want Waverley to know his plan to call off the party failed."

When Jules left the room, Charfield focused again on Harrison. "Having you fit enough to join us for dinner should work to our advantage. Hopefully Waverley will be so furious he'll let down his guard when Lady Lathamton speaks to him."

"I'm fit enough. I'm going to come down for dinner and allow Cassie to make a great fuss over me."

She was sure no one missed the look of affection on Harrison's face.

"And when the time comes," Harrison continued, "I want to be the one to give him the option of leaving England and never coming back. Or spending the rest of his life in prison."

Everyone agreed that this was the perfect way to handle the evening.

"Then perhaps we should leave," Elly said, "so Harrison can rest for a few hours before dinner."

They filed from the room, but Cassie stayed. She didn't

move until she heard the door close, then rose from the bed and walked to the window. "I'm sorry," she whispered.

"Don't, Cassie. This isn't your fault."

"Perhaps I didn't cause Waverley to do what he did, but I should have told someone what he said. I didn't dream he was serious."

"I don't want you to risk being alone with him."

She saw the concern on his face and walked to his side. "You have nothing to worry about. Your brothers won't let anything happen to me."

"I know," Harrison answered. "I can't help but worry, though."

She smiled. How like him. He was always thoughtful like this. It was one of the traits she loved about him.

"I need to go now so I can practice what to say tonight." She leaned over and gently kissed him. "And you need to rest."

"I would rest better with you here."

She smiled. "No you wouldn't."

She walked to the door. "Rest now," she said, then closed the door behind her.

How had she let this happen again? How had she allowed herself to fall in love with him again?

She remembered the warmth of his hand holding hers, of his lips pressed to hers and she knew she hadn't fallen in love with him again.

She'd never fallen *out* of love with him.

CHAPTER 17

Elly cleared the papers from the desk in the middle of the small office where her father's secretary worked and put away anything that might make noise if someone moved it. It wasn't that the Duke of Parneston was clumsy, exactly, but he wasn't the most graceful man in the world. The last thing Elly wanted was for His Grace to knock something over and give away their hiding place. That would ruin everything.

She tried to convince herself that tonight's plan would go off without a hitch, but she couldn't make the uneasy niggling inside her go away. Cassie was taking a huge chance talking to Waverley alone, but what else could she do? He'd already shot Harrison. Whether his intent had been to kill him or simply warn him away from Cassie didn't matter. His desperation to possess Lathamton Estate as well as Hollyvine was obvious. And the only way he could possess both was to marry Cassie.

And eliminate the Lathamton heir.

Elly finished making the room ready, then closed the

door behind her. The string ensemble was already set up in the music room at the end of the hall. Discordant tones sifted through the closed door as the musicians tuned their instruments. After a slight pause, they struck up a lilting tune that made Elly want to sway in rhythm.

Dancing was the one activity she'd never been brave enough to try. When she'd first been injured every doctor her parents took her to told them she'd never stand. She not only managed to stand, but learned to walk.

Then she learned to ride, even though the doctor told her staying atop a horse was impossible.

Her latest challenge had been to climb the hillside to the east of The Down. She always challenged herself to do something no one thought she could do.

But she'd never been brave enough to attempt to dance. Not only would the turns be impossible, but limping in a man's arms would embarrass her as well as the poor man who'd been foolish enough to ask her.

She couldn't help but wish, though, that just one time she could experience dancing in someone's arms as she moved across a ballroom floor.

The enthralling strains of the music became more enticing. Elly propped her cane in front of her and placed both hands on the ivory handle. She looked over her shoulder to make sure she was alone, then swayed in time to the rhythm.

She didn't move from her spot in the center of the room but swayed back and forth. As the music became more intense, she closed her eyes and dreamed she had two healthy legs and was in Brent's arms. She dreamed that the two of them were gliding across the floor.

She wasn't sure when she became aware that Brent was

behind her. Perhaps it was when her flesh warmed as it always did the moment he was near.

Perhaps it was when the skin at the back of her neck prickled with excitement.

Perhaps it was simply when the rapid beating of her heart increased in tempo.

Whatever the reason, she stopped with a start and jerked her head to look at him. The action threw her off balance.

Elly tried to compensate but knew the result was going to be disastrous. She stumbled, then prepared for the floor to rise to meet her.

Instead, she found herself in Brent's arms.

"I shouldn't have surprised you." He held her close. "But I'm glad I did."

His arms wrapped securely around her waist and his thick, muscled legs bracketed her. She'd dropped her cane and had no choice but to reach out and hold him.

He pulled her closer and smiled down at her. "If I hadn't surprised you, you wouldn't have lost your balance and I would have had to search for an excuse to hold you in my arms. I should thank you for being accommodating."

"Oh," was all she was capable of saying. She was embarrassed that he'd seen how ungraceful she could be, and yet, she was just as glad to be in his arms as he claimed he was to have her there.

"You were dancing to the music."

She shook her head in denial. "I don't dance."

"Have you ever tried?"

"Dancing isn't something I am capable of doing."

"Just like you couldn't play croquet?"

Elly opened her mouth to argue, then closed it. When she

spoke it was to admit something she very seldom said out loud. "The reason I don't dance is because even if I mastered keeping my balance while doing the steps, which I very much doubt I could, the clumsy way I move would embarrass me as much as it would my partner."

Brent raised his left eyebrow and looked down on her with a disbelieving gaze. "I sincerely doubt that."

"Oh, don't. The poor man wouldn't know whether to reach for my hand when doing the steps or my cane."

"Perhaps you've never considered doing the right dance. Or having the right partner."

Elly ignored his comment about having the right partner. "And what dance would that be?"

"A waltz."

She tried to think of a rebuke that would tell him how foolish an idea he'd come up with, but she couldn't. She'd always wanted to dance and she'd always dreamed of dancing in the arms of a tall, strong man.

Suddenly, her dreams seemed about to come true. She was in the arms of the strongest, most handsome man she knew. A man with whom she was afraid she'd fallen more than a little in love, and the orchestra had just started playing a waltz.

"May I have this dance?" he asked, bowing ever so slightly.

She shook her head. She couldn't. He'd been able to accept many of her most ungainly actions, but dancing was something he wouldn't be able to ignore. He'd feel every jerky step she took.

"Trust me, Elly," he whispered. "The music is playing and we're all alone. No one will see you."

"You will," she whispered as softly as he had.

"I don't count."

Oh, he counted. He more than anyone.

"Please," he whispered.

Her gaze locked with his. Suddenly dancing in his arms was more important than any degree of embarrassment she might experience.

She slipped one hand to his shoulder and placed the palm of her other hand in his.

"If it makes you feel more secure, you can place your arm around my neck."

She nodded and wrapped her arm around his neck.

Then he moved.

The first few steps were clumsy and far from the graceful vision she'd imagined in her dreams, but she was dancing.

"Place your other arm around my neck," he whispered as they moved in time to the music, "and relax."

Elly placed both arms around his neck and he wrapped his arms around her waist. She seemed to float across the small, open area in the morning room. She couldn't imagine what it would be like to dance in the wide expanse of a ballroom. But here it was magical.

In London, a man as handsome as the Earl of Charfield would never give her a second look. In polite society, a man so sought after would have his sanity questioned if he asked her to dance. Every instinct told her to wonder why he was so intent on escorting her in to every meal, why it was so important to teach her to swing a mallet, and why he'd put himself through the torture of teaching her to dance. But that same instinct warned her not to question his reasons, but take advantage of the experiences he offered her.

She leaned her head against his shoulder and forgot all the misgivings that gnawed at her. Instead, she absorbed every wonderful sensation of being in Brent's arms and enjoyed the euphoric feeling that she was a whole person.

"The music has stopped," he finally whispered.

"Oh."

They stood, locked in each other's embrace until he spoke. "Elly?"

"Hmm?"

She looked up and the minute her eyes met his he brought his mouth down over hers.

His kiss was hungry, an all-consuming desperation that begged for something she was eager to give.

She wasn't sure why she was less in control with every kiss, but she was. His touch, his kisses – everything about him affected her with an overwhelming intensity. She knew allowing him to become so important to her was dangerous. She was living in a dream world and falling in love with a man who could never love her in return.

He was an earl, for Heaven's sake. He was expected to spend part of every year in London, expected to take his seat in the House, oversee his affairs, attend a required number of social events. He could hardly be expected to be seen in public with a cripple hanging on his arm.

She thought of her jerky motions as she walked across a room. Of the clumsy way she had to climb stairs. How she had to lean against the railing and pull herself up each step. How her foot would drag when she was overly tired.

She was an invalid and all the wishing in the world wouldn't change what she was. All her dreams combined wouldn't make her Charfield's perfect match.

She slid her arms from around his neck and turned her head to break his kiss.

"What's wrong?" he asked, his breathing ragged. He wrapped his fingers around her upper arms to keep her steady and looked at her with a concerned frown on his face. "Are you worried about tonight?"

She didn't answer him. She couldn't. Not once had she felt sorry for herself. Her brothers didn't need her self pity added to their already-overwhelming sense of guilt. But tonight for some reason she couldn't explain, she felt a deep sense of regret.

"Do you think Cassie will be able to get Waverley to admit he shot at Harrison?" she whispered.

"I don't know."

Brent pulled her close to him and she leaned her cheek against his chest and listened to the thundering of his heart.

"I want you to promise me something, Elly."

His deep, rich voice rumbled beneath her ear and she thought how special it would be to be held like this forever; how perfect it would be to listen to the soothing sound of his voice for the rest of her life.

"What?"

"I want you to stay out of sight tonight."

She lifted her gaze. "I will. I'll be with the Duke of Parneston in the small office."

"Yes, and I want you to *stay* in the office. No matter what happens out here, or what you hear, you are not to step foot from that room until I call for you. Do you understand?"

"Yes, but—"

"No. Do you understand?"

Elly took a deep breath then nodded.

"Good."

He gave her another tight squeeze then held her away from

him and looked into her eyes. "Perhaps it would be best if we went in for dinner. I'm sure the first of the guests have already gathered and we don't want to draw attention to this room. Or to ourselves."

While Brent bent to retrieve her cane from the floor, Elly looked around the room. A lot would happen here yet tonight.

Even more had already happened that she would never forget.

She took her cane in one hand and slipped her other arm through the bend at his elbow. Together they walked toward the door.

"Elly," he said before they left the room.

"Yes?"

"You dance superbly. Thank you."

"Thank you," she said. "That was something I never thought I'd do."

"I have a feeling that with the right inspiration there's very little you can't do."

"I'll try to remember that."

"Oh, I intend to make sure you do," he said, giving her hand a gentle squeeze.

A rush of molten heat raced through her veins. With him holding her, she could almost believe she was whole, was perfect. But she couldn't forget that she wasn't.

When he told her he intended to make sure she didn't forget that with him she could do anything, he didn't mean it. Not the way her heart wanted him to mean it.

But even if he did, allowing him to play a part in her life wasn't something she could contemplate. She was with friends and family here. Everything would be different if they were ever amidst strangers.

He would be embarrassed to have her near him. And she would understand why.

———

Cassie lifted her glass of wine and took a small sip, then set it back on the table, but not before placing her hand over Harrison's arm and leaning over to whisper in his ear.

"Is Waverley still watching us?" she asked, smiling in a most flirtatious manner.

"His eyes haven't left you for more than a second or two all evening. All I can say is I'm very lucky he took a shot at me before this evening. From the angry scowl on his face, he's so jealous his goal wouldn't have been a warning, but murder."

"Don't tease like that, Harrison."

"I'm sorry." He placed his hand over hers and tucked her fingers beneath his. "Are you nervous?"

She shook her head and kept a bright smile on her face. "I know I should be but I'm too furious to be nervous. I can't believe Waverley is so malicious. Did he really think he could force me to marry him?"

"That's exactly what he thought. He knows how protective you are towards your son. With a few pointed threats to Andrew's welfare, he could force you to do anything he wanted. A mother will make many sacrifices when her child's safety is in jeopardy."

"At this moment I despise him more than I thought it was possible to hate anyone. Do you know how hard it's been not to stand up·and expose what he did to you?"

Harrison lifted his chin and laughed.

Cassie couldn't resist the urge to cast a glance at the other end of the table to see Waverley's reaction to Harrison's laugh.

His face was tinged scarlet and the hand that rested on the white linen tablecloth was clenched into a tight fist.

"What happened to us, Cassie?"

Harrison's question startled her and she slowly turned her gaze back to his. The look in his eyes was filled with such intensity the blood flowing through her veins warmed. "Nothing either one of us had the power to stop."

"Do you think it's possible for us to once again find what we shared?"

Her heart raced in her breast. "I don't know. Perhaps."

He gave her hand a gentle squeeze, followed by a reassuring look filled with hopefulness. "Then I think we need to find out."

Tears filled her eyes and his handsome features blurred in front of her. "Yes, I think we do."

Harrison looked back down the long line of guests seated around the table. "But first we have a task to take care of. Are you ready?" He placed the napkin from his lap onto the table.

"Yes. I can't wait to expose him."

"Be sure to give Elly and Parneston time to get situated before you approach him."

Cassie nodded as she studied Harrison's face. "Are you all right? You seem a little paler than before."

"I'm fine. It was only a scratch and Doctor Brunswich took good care of me."

Cassie smiled, then leaned back in her chair.

The play was about to begin. She'd rehearsed what she intended to say for hours after she'd left Harrison and now it was time for her performance.

Harrison's life depended on her success.

And so did his son's.

CHAPTER 18

Cassie paused outside the formal dining room in a prearranged meeting with Jules and Amelia Hastings. Everything that happened was part of their well-devised plan. After dinner she was to talk to Jules and Amelia long enough to allow the other guests to enter the music room ahead of her. This would give Elly and the Duke of Parneston time to make their way to the small room where they'd be sure to overhear everything Jeremy Waverley said.

She wasn't worried that Waverley would go in to the musicale without her. He hadn't let her out of his sight all night and now he stood a few feet away feigning interest in one of the Fellingsdown ancestral paintings. He was biding his time until he could ask to escort her inside.

Now that she knew his true intentions, he was as easy to read as if he announced his next move. His underhanded maneuvers sickened her.

Suddenly, there wasn't one thing she liked about him.

She finished her conversation with Jules and Miss Hastings, then let them walk away from her. She turned as if she were in a hurry to enter the music room, then paused when his voice stopped her.

"Cassandra." He rushed to her side. "May I have the pleasure of sitting beside you during tonight's entertainment?"

She turned and glared at him with all the hatred she'd stored inside her. "No, you may not." She faced him squarely so he would realize the full impact of her hostility. "In fact, I've been searching for an opportunity to talk privately with you. I think right now would be the perfect time." She spun away from him and headed toward the yellow drawing room.

She wasn't worried he wouldn't follow. Every move he made had one objective: to get her to rely on him while eliminating everyone who came between him and his ambitious goal of acquiring the Lathamton title and the land that would go with it.

Now she knew that not only included Harrison, but her son.

She fought to keep her knees from buckling beneath her. There wasn't anything she wouldn't do to keep Andrew safe. That thought gave her the courage she needed to confront Jeremy.

She stormed down the hallway and passed the first door. It was dark inside as Harrison had guaranteed her it would be. So was the second room. But the third room was brightly lit. This was the drawing room where Harrison and the rest waited to overhear Jeremy's confession.

She stepped inside.

Waverley followed, then closed the door behind him. The minute they were alone Cassie spun to face him. "What have you done?" she said in an accusing tone.

"Done? I don't know what you're talking about."

He took one step toward her then another.

"Stay where you are!" She held up her hand to stop him. "I don't want you anywhere near me."

"You don't mean that," he said in a sickeningly smooth tone.

"Oh, I mean it. And more!" She took a step closer to the door behind which the Duke of Parneston hid. "I know what you did, Mr. Waverley. What I don't understand, is what you thought to accomplish by something so devious?"

She called him Mr. Waverley on purpose, knowing how much he hated the degrading title. He never let her call him anything but his Christian name. Now she knew why. He would settle for nothing less than being called by his Christian name or the Lathamton title – a title he intended to acquire by murdering her son.

"I have no idea what you think I did."

The gleam in his eyes told her getting a confession from him wouldn't be easy. He was playing with her, hoping to make her doubt herself. But she wouldn't. She had to stop him now or forever live in fear.

"I am not a fool, Mr. Waverley."

"Stop calling me that! My name is Jeremy and that is what I choose to have you call me."

"*I* choose to call you Mr. Waverley. And what *I* choose to do will be what happens. *I* am the Marchioness of Lathamton and my son is the Marquess."

Cassie stiffened her spine and prepared to say what she knew would open the door to his admission. "Lathamton Estates belongs to my son and I want you to remove yourself from his property."

She saw that her words took him totally by surprise. He reacted with more anger and fury than she'd imagined possible.

"No!" he bellowed. "Lathamton Estate is *mine*! *Mine*!

"It will *never* be yours."

"It will. And so will *you*!"

Cassie laughed. She realized how furious he was and reached for every ounce of courage she possessed. Laughing in his face, however, achieved the objective she wanted. His glare hardened and his face turned a mottled red.

"Lathamton Estate has been mine since my uncle took me in. *I'm* the one who always took care of it."

"Do you think that gave you the right of ownership?"

"I have more right to it than your weak husband did. Even my uncle realized that. If he hadn't died so soon after Everett, he would have made sure I got it."

"No," Cassie said, raising her chin. "The title and the estates belong to my son."

"Your son! He'll *never* inherit Lathamton! I won't allow it!"

He stopped. His face lost several shades of color. He knew he'd said too much.

Cassie focused all her fury on him. "From this moment on you will not step foot on Lathamton property except to collect your belongings. And you will be watched every moment you are there."

He shook his head and smiled. "You don't have the authority to enforce that, Cassandra."

"Then I'll find someone who will help me."

"Who? Fellingsworth?"

Cassie didn't respond. Threatening to evict Waverley had

caused him to become dangerously agitated. She suspected it might not be safe to provoke him further.

"Do you think I don't see what's happening between the two of you?" He clamped his jaw so tightly the knots on either side of his face bulged. "Do you think I don't realize you've fallen in love with him again?"

He took a step toward her. She wanted to run but she didn't dare. She needed him as close to the room where Elly and Parneston hid as possible.

"Today was your warning, Cassie. Next time Fellingsdown won't be so lucky. Next time instead of wounding him, I'll kill him."

"Do you intend to kill everyone I show an interest in?"

"I won't allow you to ruin what I've spent my whole life working to achieve. Lathamton Estate will belong to me. I've managed every inch of it from the time my uncle took me in. I knew it was only a matter of time until it would be mine. Then the scandal broke out and I—"

Waverley stopped.

Cassie knew she should allow his partial sentence to go unfinished but she couldn't. She was desperate to know what had happened that night. She needed to know why her father disinherited his only son and why he allowed his only daughter to be caught up in a scandal that was sure to ruin her life.

"What do you know about the scandal?" she asked, anxious - yet dreading to hear what happened.

Waverley smiled. It wasn't a friendly smile or an open smile, but a sinister grin.

"I know it all," he said, taking another step toward her. "I know every single sordid detail. Which part would you like to hear first?"

She didn't answer him. He enjoyed this and she knew he wouldn't need prompting to continue.

"Should I tell you first why your father disinherited your brother and forced his only son to leave England? Or would you rather know the details of what happened to cause you and Everett to be discovered naked in each other's arms?"

She reached out to steady herself against the wall. She wanted him to stop – Harrison would hear every revolting word of this, and yet, *she* needed to know. *She* needed answers to the questions that had plagued her for four years.

She looked up into Waverley's eyes. He relished being the one to tell her every disgusting detail.

"Ah, I see you'd rather know what happened the night you and Everett were found together. I know you don't remember because—"

His malicious grin broadened.

"You were drugged, my dear Cassandra. Both you and Everett. That was the only way the world would ever find Everett in bed with a woman...considering his abnormal preferences."

Cassie thought she might become ill. She clutched her hand to her stomach and held tight. She wanted him to stop. She didn't want to hear another word, yet knew she had to let him continue.

"You knew that, though. Didn't you, my dear?"

She forced herself to glare at him as if his words didn't destroy her.

"Everett's unusual practices were at the root of this whole tragedy. Everett's penchants...and your brother's."

"My brother was not—"

Waverley shrugged. "Perhaps not, but I had to make your

father believe he was for my plan to work."

The bottom fell out of her world. "You intentionally destroyed my brother's reputation so my father would disown him?"

"It was part of my plan, Cassandra. Once I discovered Hollyvine wasn't entailed, I realized I had to have it. Combining the land from Hollyvine with Lathamton would make me one of the most influential landowners around. Even more influential than Fellingsdown."

Cassie burned with rage. She hated him more than she'd ever hated anyone in her life. "You evil liar. You won't get away with this."

"Oh, but I will. My plan is perfect. Once I make you my bride..."

Waverley reached for her. The feel of his hands on her caused a reaction she'd never experienced before. Before he knew what happened, she pulled back her arm and slapped him.

———

The loud crack of flesh hitting flesh echoed in the small room where Brent hid along with Harrison, George and Spencer. Harrison reached for the door to go to Cassie's aid, but George and Spencer placed a reassuring hand on his shoulders. Brent held up his hand to motion to everyone to stay still.

"Don't you ever touch me," they heard Cassie say and Brent looked through the small opening he'd made to watch what was going on in the room. What he saw almost made him smile.

Waverley staggered back several steps and rubbed his left cheek. "You shouldn't have done that Cassandra. It's going to give me great pleasure some day to tame that temper of yours."

"You'll never get the chance."

"Won't I? I've worked too hard to let anything stop me. Your late husband nearly destroyed the Lathamton title when his abnormal preference was discovered. The severity of the situation required drastic action. It was all I could do to clean up the mess Everett created."

Waverley shoved his hands in his pockets. "Lucky for all of us that I was an expert at covering for him. I'd done it my whole life."

He paced in front of the door where they hid and Brent moved everyone back. He didn't want Waverley to realize they were there. But he didn't have to worry. Waverley was so focused on his rantings he passed them by without a glance.

"Poor Uncle Henry's first instinct was to send his son away on a permanent excursion, but I couldn't have that. If Everett went away, I'd never inherit his title. Everett needed to be eliminated. That was the only way I could become the Marquess of Lathamton."

"You killed Everett?"

Waverley didn't answer for a few moments and everyone held their breath while they waited for him to answer Lady Lathamton's question.

"Oh, Cassandra. What do you take me for?"

"A murderer!"

Waverley laughed. "No, I'm not nearly so calculating. Your husband's health was always questionable. He died of the influenza, just as the doctor said. Of course, the special medicine I concocted probably didn't help him as much as the medicine the doctor intended him to take would have."

"How could you!"

"Oh, Cassandra. Don't tell me you weren't at least a little relieved when dear Everett died. You never loved him. How could you? He was so pathetically weak."

"He was a human being who didn't deserve to die!" Lady Lathamton cried out.

"You have such a soft heart. I've always known that about you. From the very beginning I regretted having to involve you in my scheme, but you were so perfect for the part. And so was your brother."

Lady Lathamton shook her head and opened her mouth. But Brent could see she was past speaking.

"It didn't take much effort to force your father to disinherit your brother and send him away. His pride in the Hollyvine name worked to my advantage. Besides, the generous amount I offered to support your brother in his new life convinced your father that his son would never lack for anything."

"Losing my brother killed my father."

"I regretted that, Cassandra. Honestly, I did. But I had no choice if I wanted to gain control of Hollyvine."

Waverley paced the floor from one side of the room to the other. "After your brother was gone, I put the next step of my plan into motion."

"You sent the note saying my father wasn't well and needed me to come."

"There's no need to sound so angry, Cassandra. You have to admit my plan was brilliant. When you arrived at Lathamton's townhouse, I showed you to a small parlor and gave you a glass of wine."

"Which you'd drugged," Lady Lathamton said.

Brent had to hold Fellingsdown from charging through the door.

"Oh, it was nothing harmful. Only something to make you sleep."

"You bastard!"

"Now, Cassandra. That's no way for my future wife speak."

"I'll never be your wife."

"But you will. If you want to make sure Fellingsdown stays healthy, you'll agree to marry me."

"Or you'll what? Kill him?"

"Of course. This afternoon was just a warning. Next time I won't just put a bullet in his arm. I'll aim for his heart."

"No!" Lady Lathamton cried out, and Brent realized the lady had gone through as much as she could handle.

With a nod, Brent threw the door open and Harrison, George and Spence stepped out behind him. The door from the opposite side of the room opened at the same time and Jules and Harrison's two brothers-in-law stepped out.

"What the—"

Waverley's wide-eyed gaze darted from one side of the room to the other. The hatred in his glare was unmistakable.

"I'm afraid you've done as much damage as you'll ever do." Brent moved until he stood between Waverley and the door. He wasn't about to let the blackguard escape. But first he had to get Lady Lathamton out of Waverley's reach. "Lady Lathamton," he said, "please, step aside."

Fellingsdown lifted his arm and Lady Lathamton ran to him.

"How touching," Waverley said, "but I've had enough of your theatrics. I think I'll join the rest of the guests. The music sounds first-rate."

"You'll go nowhere." Harrison stepped in front of Lady Lathamton to remove her from Waverley's threatening glare. "Except to prison."

Waverley barked a harsh laugh. "On what charge?"

"Two charges of attempted murder."

Waverley shook his head. "On whose word?"

"Any of us. We all heard you," Jules said.

"I don't think so. If any of you accuse me of any wrongdoing, I'll deny it."

"You can hardly deny harming Everett and shooting Harrison when so many of us heard you admit it," Spencer said.

"Who do you think would believe you when I told them your family conspired against me because Lord Fellingsdown was desperate to eliminate me as a suitor to his lost love?"

The Duke of Parneston stepped out of the small office behind Waverley. "Then my testimony will be of invaluable service. I can assure you I will be believed. My word is held in the highest regard."

Waverley staggered back. "Damn you! Damn all of you!"

Waverley's eyes contained a frantic fear. His gaze darted from one side of the room to another as if looking for a way to escape.

Parneston stepped forward. "As the person prepared to bring charges against you, I feel it necessary to offer an alternative. On behalf of Lord Fellingsdown, I give you the choice of leaving England and never returning. Or staying here to face a charge of attempted murder."

"No!" Waverley's gaze darted to each exit. "You can't do this to me."

"We can," Parneston continued, "and we will. Your actions

are detestable and I will not allow you to go unpunished."

"Lathamton is *mine! Mine!* I worked too hard to get it. You can't take it away from me."

Waverley made a frantic movement toward one exit, then the other, but there was no escape. Every means of escape was blocked - except the door leading from the small office where Elly hid.

Waverley focused on the open doorway – the doorway behind which Elly hid – and realized it was his only means of escape.

Brent lunged forward, but before he could reach Elly, Waverley grabbed her by the arm and pulled her from the shadows. He held her in front of him and pressed a pistol to her temple. "I suggest that all of you step aside to let me leave. Lady Elyssa will, of course, accompany me."

Brent lifted his hands in a conciliatory gesture. "You can leave and no one will follow you. But we will not allow you to take Lady Elyssa with you."

"You won't?"

Waverley jerked Elly toward him and she lost her balance. She reached out but there was nothing but air, and when she started to fall, Waverley jerked her arm to hold her upright. She cried out in pain.

"Let her go!" Brent demanded. "I'll go with you."

Waverley laughed. "No, Lady Elyssa will be much less trouble. For a reason I cannot understand, you have all formed a fondness for this poor creature. I'm sure I'll be much safer as long as I have her with me."

Brent locked his gaze with Elly's and tried to give her as reassuring a look as he could, but the terror in her eyes stole his breath. He knew she saw through his false bravado to the fear he couldn't hide.

Brent tried bartering again. "You're free to go, Waverley. No one will follow you. Just leave Lady Elyssa here."

Waverley answered his plea with a laugh. "I'm not a fool, Charfield. Do you think I don't know the minute you have this poor creature back you'll come after me? No, she stays with me. And if you want to see her alive again, you won't come after us."

There was a demented look in Waverley's eyes, madness in his reasoning.

Brent knew he'd lost his grip on sanity, and from the looks on Elly's brothers' faces, so did they. Dealing with an insane man frightened him more than he wanted to consider. There was a chance they could reason with him if he still retained a shred of stability, but Waverley was past that point. In his mind, he thought reaching Lathamton would provide safety.

And ridding the world of the current Marquess of Lathamton would make him the titled heir.

Brent considered every possibility and couldn't think of one that wouldn't put Elly in more danger than she was now.

"Don't move. Any of you! If you try to follow me, you'll regret it."

Waverley pulled her toward the door and Brent knew he was running out of time. When Waverley turned to reach for the latch, Brent made an attempt to rush him. He couldn't let Elly out of his sight.

Before he took even one step toward Elly, Waverley slammed the pistol against the side of her head. Elly cried out in pain.

"No!" Brent cried out and pulled up short. He lifted his hands in surrender and struggled to control an eruption of anger that was nearly beyond his control.

Waverley pressed the pistol hard enough against Elly's temple that she winced. "I'll kill her if you try to stop me!"

He looked at each of them as if to emphasize his point. When Waverley's gaze met his, Brent couldn't stop his threat from spilling into the open. "You're a dead man, Waverley. I don't care what I have to do, or how long it takes me, you're a walking corpse."

"Come after me, Charfield, and she's dead."

Brent stood helplessly by while Waverley pushed Elly into the hallway and slammed the door behind them. Lady Lathamton's soft sobs were all Brent heard over the thunderous pounding of his frantic heartbeats.

If Waverley killed her...

He couldn't finish the thought. He wasn't sure how he'd be able to go on if he lost her now.

He heard Waverley drag Elly down the hallway and strong hands clamped around his upper arms and held him back.

"The man's demented," Spence said, through clamped teeth. "What does he hope to gain now? We're on to him."

"He doesn't care," Jules answered. "He wants to own Lathamton Estates."

"But he can't!" George bellowed. "Lathamton had a son. The land and the title are secure as long as—"

George stopped without finishing his thought.

"Bloody hell!" Brent heard several of the group who'd gathered behind him say. It didn't take but a second longer for Lady Lathamton to realize the danger her son was in.

"Harrison!" she cried out. "He's going to kill Andrew!"

"Shh, Cassie. We won't let him harm the boy."

Brent raced to the door. The minute he could no longer

hear Elly's unsteady gait, he rushed from the room. Elly's family was close behind him.

George placed a firm hand on Brent's arm. "Waverley said he'd kill her if we followed."

"Do you think there's a chance in hell he intends to let her live once he reaches Lathamton?"

The second the words were out of his mouth a feeling of dread weighed down on him.

A deafening silence fell over the men. They knew he was right. Once Waverley reached Lathamton Manor, Elly would be of no further use to him.

"We'll need weapons," Brent said. He was desperate to reach Elly as quickly as he could. He was frantic to reach her before Waverley killed her.

"I'll get them," Spence said and rushed off.

"And the horses saddled."

"I'll take care of that," Jules said and was gone.

"One for me, too," the Duke of Parneston said in a tone with which no one would dare to argue.

Brent nodded, then ran down the wide hallway that led to the entryway.

He looked to the open foyer door and felt a loss greater than he thought he could withstand.

Elly wasn't in sight.

CHAPTER 19

Elly's foot and leg throbbed with unrelenting pain and her head ached where he hit her.

Waverley hadn't given her limitations a thought as he dragged her across the cobblestones to the stable. Nor had he taken her disability into account when he pushed her to mount the horse.

She prayed they'd ride separately. She could have outridden him with no problem, but before she was securely in the saddle, he mounted behind her and took off at a wild gallop.

She knew their destination. He was taking her to Lathamton Manor. In his warped thinking, he assumed there was a chance he could live the life he dreamed of having if he reached the safety of Lathamton Manor. But his dreams were impossible. He would fail with this one last desperate attempt to achieve the title and the estates that went with it.

What she feared most was that he'd kill little Andrew before

Brent and Harrison arrived to stop him. She wasn't sure how they intended to rescue her, but they would. She didn't doubt it for a second.

It was up to her, though, to slow Waverley down in order to give Brent and her brother time to catch up with them.

When they arrived at Lathamton Manor, Waverley pulled his horse to a sudden halt and jumped to the ground. He didn't give her time to prepare to dismount but jerked her down. She landed at an odd angle on her injured leg and collapsed to the ground. A stabbing of pain to her knees shot through her.

"Get up, dammit!"

She thought of feigning an injury so severe she couldn't get to her feet but she couldn't risk Waverley going in to the house without her. Little Andrew was alone with just his nursemaid to protect him.

She pushed herself to her knees without his aid, but couldn't stop the cry of pain when he grabbed her by the arm and jerked her to her feet.

"Move!" He pulled her along behind him. "You didn't seem to have nearly so much trouble moving when you walked with Charfield."

"I need my cane," Elly gasped as she limped to keep up with him. Her leg ached and she'd scraped her knees when she'd fallen on the cobblestones. Ahead of her were three stone steps to the house. She'd never make them without falling.

Waverley didn't seem to care. He pulled her after him as he stormed toward the house.

She tripped on the first step and fell.

He looked down at her as if she were an insect that needed to be eliminated. He hesitated a moment as if deciding whether to let her live or smash her under his boot. He must have thought it was more beneficial to allow her to live because he dragged her up the remaining two steps.

The Lathamton butler opened the door and gaped in shock. "Lady Elyssa? Sir?"

"Get out!" Waverley bellowed. "And take everyone with you! Now!"

"No," Elly cried out, trying to struggle out of Waverley's grasp. "Don't leave!"

"Out!"

When the butler hesitated, Waverley pulled the pistol from his pocket and fired over the frightened man's head.

Elly heard screams from the hallways and back rooms of Lathamton Manor then the scurry of feet that grew fainter with each second.

"Don't leave!" she cried out, but she knew from the silence there was no one left to hear her.

Waverley pulled her across the marble foyer floor toward the twin winding staircases. His destination was the third floor nursery where three-year-old Andrew was with Nanny Graybrim. Elly couldn't let Waverley reach them. She and the elderly nurse wouldn't be a match for an armed man with a gun.

"Move!" Waverley shouted when they reached the base of the staircase on the right.

Elly intentionally dropped to her knees and pretended she was unable to get up.

"Get up, dammit!" he bellowed, then yanked on her arm to force her to her feet.

She screamed in pain then covered her head with both arms as his hand came down to strike her. Her arms took the brunt of the blow, but the jar to her head caused her vision to blur.

"Get up!"

He slapped her hard across the face then jerked on her arm again. This time Elly rose to her feet. Another blow like the last one and she was afraid she'd lose consciousness. She had to remain alert for Andrew's sake.

She took the first step but lost her balance on the second when he yanked on her arm. She fell hard. The pain was severe. Beneath her skirt, warm blood ran down her legs.

"I need time to climb stairs," she gasped.

"We don't have time!"

She didn't know how she managed, but eventually they reached the top of the first flight of stairs. She sank to the floor and grabbed her aching leg.

"Get up!"

"I can't!"

She held on to the banister that ran the length of the balcony and overlooked the foyer. The nursery was another flight up. Her leg throbbed so hard she knew she wouldn't make it. She looked up the long flight of stairs and thought how impossible it would be to climb any more stairs.

"Get up, I say, or I'll—"

The sound of horses approaching stopped his tirade.

"No!"

The flight of stairs that led to the nursery was a short distance from her. Waverley's focus turned to reaching young Andrew before anyone arrived to stop him and he dropped his grasp from around her. Killing the boy was more important to him than she was.

Elly couldn't let him get away from her. She struggled to her knees and wrapped her arms around his legs when he took his first step.

He kicked out, lifting her in the air and slamming her body against the newel post.

She screamed in pain but didn't let go. She knew if he reached the nursery he'd kill little Andrew before anyone arrived to protect him.

"Let go, dammit!"

When Elly didn't release her hold he slammed his fist against her head. She nearly lost her grip but she clamped her arms around his legs and held on. The pain from his blow was unbearable. He slapped her again then reached down, clasped his fingers around her arms, and lifted her in the air.

She heard the muffled sound of footsteps pounding on the floor below her. She heard the bellowing sounds of voices demanding that Waverley release her. She heard Brent's panic-filled roar and knew he'd do everything he could to help her. But he'd be too late.

She glanced down the long flight of stairs and knew the next time he kicked her she'd tumble to the bottom with no chance of stopping herself.

But he didn't kick her. Instead, he pulled her up by the arms and held her in front of him.

"All of you! Get out! This is *my* house. *Mine!*"

With his arm clamped around her waist, he dragged her with him to the stairs that led to the third floor nursery. One by one he pulled her up each step.

"Stop, Waverley," the Duke of Parneston ordered but Waverley continued climbing. Even though there were eight armed men making their way up the first flight of stairs, he was determined to reach the nursery. In his demented mind, he actually believed that if he killed the three-year-old Marquess of Lathamton he could inherit the title and achieve everything he thought he was entitled to have.

Elly looked to the foot of the stairs to where Cassie stood. Tears streamed down her pale cheeks as she waited for this terrible ordeal to be over so she could run to the nursery and gather her son in her arms.

"Put the gun down, Waverley," Harrison said, climbing the stairs behind Brent. "Release Elly and we'll let you leave England a free man."

"No! The title is *mine*!" Waverley moved his gaze to Cassie. "Did you really think I'd let your bastard son inherit the Lathamton title, Cassandra? Do you think I don't know your dirty little secret?"

"Leave Andrew be, Jeremy. He's just a babe." Cassie took the first few steps toward him.

"No! He's a fraud. An imposter! I'm the last remaining Waverley. *I* deserve the title. Not him!"

Waverley pulled Elly up a few more stairs.

Brent took another step. Then another. "You won't succeed, Waverley. We won't let you. Even if you shoot one of us, there are seven others who won't hesitate to kill you."

"Put down your gun," the Duke of Parneston said. "We're giving you a chance to go free."

"You don't understand. None of you realize what she's done."

Elly knew what Waverley meant with his accusations. She knew the secret Waverley threatened to expose.

She fought the dizzying circles spinning inside her head and kept her gaze focused on her friend. Cassie's face turned ashen as her wide-eyed gaze darted from Waverley to the step in front of her where Harrison stood.

"Did you think I didn't know, Cassandra? I knew Everett

better than anyone. I knew it was impossible for the child to be his."

Waverley looked to the closed nursery door then dragged Elly up one more step.

"Your accusations have nothing to do with Lady Elyssa," Brent said. "Let her go."

Waverley tightened his hold.

"You'd like that, wouldn't you? The minute I let her go I'm left with nothing. Just like Uncle left me with nothing."

Waverley pulled her up another step.

"Uncle was so desperate to play along with her deceit he claimed a bastard as his legitimate heir." He spewed an ugly sound of disgust. "He thought the child would prove to the world that Everett wasn't as depraved as everyone knew he was."

Waverley laughed. The sound of his laughter sent chills down Elly's spine.

"But I knew."

Waverley turned his gaze to Cassie again. "Did you think I'd allow you to pass your bastard son off as Everett's? I'd rather see the Lathamton title die."

"Stop it, Jeremy," Cassie cried out.

"No!" His gaze darted toward the nursery door then back to Cassie. "Did you think I'd allow a child without a drop of Waverley blood in him to inherit the Lathamton title?"

Elly shifted her gaze to where Harrison stood. She knew the exact second he realized what Waverley insinuated. The gasping breath he took was similar to that of a drowning man struggling for air.

"Cassie?" Harrison said, turning toward her.

Waverley bellowed another demented laugh. "Oh, I am

truly enjoying this. Do you see now why I can't allow the boy to inherit my title, Fellingsdown?"

Harrison leaped two steps toward him. "If you hurt him—"

"Stop!" Waverley pushed Elly closer to the edge of the stairs. "Or I'll let her fall."

Harrison stopped.

Elly locked her gaze with Brent's. She was losing consciousness. She was weakening and needed his strength. She wanted the sight of him to be the last sight she saw before Waverley threw her down the stairs.

"Release her," Brent said, the look in his eyes nothing short of murderous. "Release her now and you can walk out of here and leave England."

"If I don't?"

"You're a dead man."

Waverley laughed. "Do you think I don't know I'm a dead man no matter what I do?"

Waverley took the last step before reaching the third floor then stopped. The nursery was the second door down the hall - a short run to where the boy stayed with his nursemaid.

He pressed the gun beneath her chin and forced her to look at him. There was a smile on his face.

"You know what's going to happen, don't you?" His smile broadened. "This is why I brought you with me."

Elly understood Waverley's intent with vivid clarity. Her fall would be the distraction that allowed him time to kill Andrew.

She reached out, hoping to grasp the railing but it was too far away. She struggled with greater desperation.

Waverley slapped her hard then jerked her back.

A malicious grin lifted the corners of his mouth. His eyes

contained an icy coldness that stole her breath. "You won't succeed," she gasped. "They'll stop you."

"No, they'll be too concerned with saving you."

"Not...all of...them."

He pulled her closer to the edge of the stairs. "Shall we see?"

Everything after that happened in rapid succession.

Waverley shoved her away from him and ran toward the nursery. At the same time a loud explosion of gunfire rent the air.

Cassie's scream echoed over the gunfire while the roar of her brothers' voices rose above it. But Brent's voice was the one she listened to hear. It came through her hazy consciousness like a soothing breeze on a warm summer day.

"Elly!"

She wouldn't die alone. Brent would be with her.

That was her last thought before she tumbled forward down the long flight of stairs.

CHAPTER 20

"No!"

Brent was living his worst nightmare. His heart dropped from his chest when Elly tumbled forward. He moved as fast as he could but it seemed as if his boots were filled with sand. As if he moved in slow motion. She lost her balance and plummeted down one step. Then another. And he was helpless to do anything to save her.

Gunfire blasted around him but he didn't take time to notice, or care what happened to Waverley. He raced up the stairs. All he wanted to do was keep the worst from happening.

He reached out and prevented her from falling down the entire flight of stairs, but wasn't able to catch her before she twisted at a harsh angle and slammed her head against the wall.

"Elly!"

He picked her up and held her in his arms then cupped his hand against the back of her head to assess the damage.

"How badly is she hurt?" Harrison asked rushing toward them.

"I don't know." Brent pushed the hair from her forehead. A stream of blood trickled down the side of her face.

"Here!" another brother said, handing him a clean, white handkerchief.

Brent pressed it to her temple and watched it turn dark with her blood.

Lady Lathamton rushed past them. "Bring her up here. We need to lay her down."

Brent rose with Elly in his arms and followed Lady Lathamton down the hallway, far away from where Waverley's body lay. The room was bright and cheery and seemed a perfect place for Elly to wake up.

If Elly woke up.

Brent shook his head to clear it.

Of course she'd wake up. Elly was strong. She'd been through much worse and survived. Then Brent looked down at the bruises on her face. The ache inside his chest hurt even more. She shouldn't have been the one hurt. She hadn't done anything to deserve this.

"Has someone gone for a doctor?" he asked when he placed Elly on the bed.

"Yes. And Parkridge and Berkingham went for the twins," George said. "They'll want to be here."

"Is there water in that basin?" He nodded to a small washstand on the opposite side of the room.

Fellingsdown rushed away and brought back the basin and several clean cloths.

Brent rinsed one out and placed it on Elly's face. It removed the blood, which made the cut on her forehead appear less severe. But as he washed away the blood, the bruises on her face became more evident.

"Bloody hell," he said, gently placing the cool cloth on the discoloration below her eye. "If the bastard weren't already dead, I'd kill him over again."

"He's dead. Each one of us can attest to that. Although Parneston insisted we allow him to take the credit."

Brent nodded, then wiped away another streak of dried blood. "We need to remove Elly's shoes. I'm afraid her foot might be injured."

George moved to the side of the bed. "Let me. I used to rub her foot when we were younger and it ached."

He sat on the mattress next to Elly and lifted her injured foot. "She might not want you to know what her foot looks like." He looked at Brent. "I was the only one she ever allowed to see it."

"Then we won't tell her."

George nodded and worked silently until the laces were undone. When he finished, he lifted Elly's foot to remove her boot. The minute he touched her foot she moaned.

"Ah, hell," George said through clenched teeth.

"What is it?" Harrison looked at the foot, then uttered a curse even more foul.

"It's all right, Elly, my sweet," Brent said, holding her still. She tossed her head from side to side as she fought for a release from the pain.

When she calmed, Brent released his hold on her shoulders and turned his attention to the foot of the bed. The sight stole his breath.

Her foot was gnarled and misshapen but he'd expected to see something similar because of how she limped when she walked. He hadn't, however, expected to see her bruised and swollen foot, or the blood that soaked through her stockings.

"Lift her skirt," Brent ordered.

"We can't. Elly would never—"

"Lift it! At least to her knees. Uncover both her legs."

George didn't argue further but slowly lifted Elly's skirts away from her legs.

"Damn him," he said again, then ordered Harrison to get more water and cloths.

"I wonder how many times the bastard threw her to the ground?" Harrison said when he returned.

"Several, from the looks of this," George said.

They turned when the door opened. It was Lady Lathamton.

"The doctor's on his way," she said, closing the door behind her. "How's Elly?"

"The doctor needs to hurry."

Lady Lathamton rushed to the side of the bed. Brent saw her expression change the minute she looked down.

Tears welled in her eyes then trickled down her cheeks. Her expression changed to pity.

This was what Elly meant. People who didn't know her considered her a freak. Strangers avoided her. But the people who loved her were the worst. They pitied her, and pity was the emotion she could least accept.

This was why she kept her disability from the world. This was why she was content with her life at The Down. Not because she didn't like people – she loved people. She just couldn't live with their pity.

"She'll be fine," Brent heard himself say.

"Of course she will," Lady Lathamton answered, wiping

the tears from her cheeks, then rinsing out a clean cloth and handing it to him. She rinsed out another cloth and handed it to George.

"I don't think anything's broken," Brent said, pressing a cloth on Elly's torn knees. "But I wish the doctor would come. Her ankle is swelling rapidly."

The door opened and Spence and Jules ushered in the doctor.

"Doctor Brunswich, we're glad you're here," Harrison said, greeting the doctor. "Elly's had an accident."

"Parneston explained about her *accident*. I'll see to Waverley's body when I'm finished here."

Without pausing to greet any of the people in the room, the doctor looked down at Elly and asked, "Is Nanny Graybrim still here?"

"Yes," Lady Lathamton answered.

"Good. Send her in to help me. The rest of you, out."

Brent hesitated, but the doctor looked at him and in a softer tone said, "Go. I'll send for you as soon as I'm done."

Brent nodded, then followed Lady Lathamton and Elly's brothers from the room.

"Nellie," Lady Lathamton said to one of the servants waiting in the hall. "Find Nanny Graybrim and send her in to help the doctor. Then go to the kitchen to have the footmen bring up plenty of warm water and anything else the doctor might need."

"Right away, my lady." Nellie bobbed a polite curtsy then rushed off to do her mistress's bidding.

"We'll wait for the doctor downstairs. We'll be more comfortable there."

Lady Lathamton turned to lead the way down the stairs

but stopped when Fellingsdown's voice interrupted. "Is your son all right?"

Lady Lathamton nodded. "Nanny Graybrim hid him in a toy chest. He thought they were playing a game."

"Perhaps before we leave you could introduce me to him."

Lady Lathamton's face blanched a shade of white.

Brent thought she might refuse, but she didn't. As if she realized having her son meet Fellingsdown was inevitable, she unclenched her hands and dropped them to her sides.

"Of course. I would be happy to have you meet him."

The group had only taken a few steps toward the stairs before the nursery door opened and a small lad rushed out pulling Nellie's hand. The minute he saw Lady Lathamton he dropped the young girl's hand and ran toward them.

"Mother! Mother! Guess what?"

Everyone looked at the little boy running toward them.

"What?" Lady Lathamton asked lowering herself to the youngster's level.

"Nellie's going to take me to the pond to watch the fish."

"She is?"

"Yes. Nanny said Nellie should take me for a walk because she has to help the doctor. Is someone sick?"

"No. A friend of mine had an accident and the doctor came to take care of her."

"Oh," the boy answered then slowly lifted his gaze as if he just realized there was a crowd of adults staring at him.

"Andrew. I'd like to introduce you to some friends of mine."

The little boy with hair the exact dark shade as Harrison's, and eyes the same color as Harrison's took his mother's hand and came forward. The resemblance between the Marquess of Fellingsdown and the boy was unmistakable.

She stopped in front of Fellingsdown. "Andrew, I'd like you to meet the Marquess of Fellingsdown. Fellingsdown, my son, Andrew, the Marquess of Lathamton."

"Hello, Andrew."

"Lord Fellingsdown."

The boy executed a superb bow of respect, then waited for his mother to continue the introductions.

Other than a slight nod of each head when they were introduced, there wasn't much conversation from any of them. They were all too stunned as they looked from Fellingsdown to the small lad standing in front of him.

"Are you friends of my mother's?" the child asked when the introductions were finished.

"Yes," Fellingsdown answered.

The boy seemed to ponder that answer, then decide it met with his approval.

"Did you know my father, too?"

Fellingsdown nodded. "Yes, I did."

The young Marquess's shoulders seemed to sag. "I wish I had." There was a hint of disappointment in his voice. "I was too little when he died to remember him."

The boy stopped and a smile lit his face. "Would you like to come with me to the pond to see the fish? Bertie said one of them's as big as a sea monster, but I've never seen it."

"Bertie?" Fellingsdown asked.

"He works in the gardens, and he takes me fishing sometimes."

"Do you like to go fishing?"

"Oh yes. I caught a real big fish the last time. But Bertie had to help me. I wasn't big enough to do it by myself. Some day I will be though."

"Maybe we can go fishing sometime."

"Oh, yes! I'll even show you where the best place to fish is."

"I'd like that," Fellingsdown said.

"Did you hear that, Mother? Lord Fellingsdown wants to go fishing with me."

"Yes, I heard. That's wonderful." She gave her son a quick hug then turned him around. "Go with Nellie now, and be good. We'll have gingersnaps when you return."

"Oh, boy," he said as he skipped down the hall and out of sight.

No one said anything. Brent knew it was most likely because they were unable. Finally Lady Lathamton broke the uncomfortable silence.

"If you'll follow me," she said, "we'll wait in the drawing room until the doctor calls for us."

Upon that statement, she walked away from them to go downstairs.

"I'm going to stay here," Brent said before Lady Lathamton had gone far. "The doctor may need something."

That was the truth but he also wanted to stay close to Elly.

"I think I'll go outside and wait for the twins," George said, perhaps needing fresh air. Perhaps wanting to give Harrison and Lady Lathamton time alone.

"I'll go with you," Spence said.

"Me too," Jules added.

Fellingsdown's three brothers walked down the stairs and out the front door. Fellingsdown followed Lady Lathamton down the flight of stairs and to a drawing room below.

Brent stood on the balcony and began the worst torture known to mankind.

Waiting.

————

Harrison closed the drawing room door behind him but couldn't find the courage to walk across the floor. Somehow, he knew when he discovered the truth of what happened that night nearly four years ago, it would be something he wasn't sure he could live with.

"Cassie?" He swallowed past the lump in his throat.

The woman he'd loved his whole life stood on the opposite side of the room with her back to him as she watched out the window. Over her shoulder he could see a little boy skipping across the grass on his way to the pond.

"He's mine," Harrison said, not as a question because he knew the answer, but as a statement. It was important that he acknowledge his son even though he could never publicly claim him.

Cassie nodded without turning around. "Did you hear Waverley admit he'd drugged me that night?"

"Yes."

"I can't tell you what happened because I don't know. The whole ordeal was a nightmare. I woke up in a strange room, in a strange bed, with a strange man. My head throbbed while a crowd of strangers pointed at me and accused me of scandalous behavior. I didn't understand what they meant. I hadn't done anything."

She turned around to face him and tears streamed down her face.

He made a move to go to her but she stopped him with a lift of her hand.

"I sent you a message right away," she said.

"I didn't get it."

"I know. Waverley admitted he intercepted it."

She dabbed at the tears falling from her eyes and took a shuddering breath. "I knew I was carrying your child and I...I told my father and Lord Lathamton. I was certain they wouldn't force me to marry, knowing I would be passing off another man's child as Everett's. Instead, the news pleased Lathamton."

"That's because it was unlikely Everett could father a child. But what would make your father go along with Lathamton's scheme? Did he owe him money?"

Cassie shook her head. "It was my brother."

"Your brother?"

"Waverley accused Ben of being Everett's lover. It wasn't true, of course, but I realize now that Waverley must have threatened to spread the rumor if Father didn't disown Ben. To save Ben's reputation, Father agreed to Waverley's plan."

Cassie took a step into the room and sat on the edge of the sofa. Harrison sat beside her but remained far enough away not to intimidate her.

"Before he left, Ben came to tell me goodbye. He made me promise not to believe anything the old marquess said about him. I had no idea what he meant at the time but now I know. Waverley was behind it all. He wanted to get his hands on Hollyvine and Lathamton Estate."

"Do you know where your brother went when he left England?"

Cassie lifted her gaze. "He went to America. I think a place called Boston. But I hear America is immense, and most of it barren and desolate."

"It doesn't matter how large America is or where your

brother is living. We'll find him, and we'll bring him home. He's the rightful Earl of Hollyvine and deserves to be acknowledged as such."

"You would do that?"

"Absolutely. What happened isn't his fault any more that it was yours or mine."

She almost placed her hand on his, but stopped before they touched. "Thank you, Harrison."

Neither of them spoke for several long minutes. Finally he turned to her. "Was Everett good to the boy?"

He had to ask, had to know that his son hadn't been mistreated.

"He wasn't cruel, if that's what you want to know. He wasn't anything. The only demand Everett ever made after we married was that I keep the boy out of his sight. I honored his request. He never saw Andrew."

They both sat quietly on the sofa, Cassie on one end and Harrison on the other. If they'd wanted, they could have reached out and touched each other, and yet... It was expecting too much to ask that either of them make the first move to span the distance.

Finally Cassie looked at him with eyes filled with emotion. "I waited for you to come for me. Even after I was forced to marry, I thought you'd come."

"I came to see you after the scandal broke," he said.

"When?"

"The next morning." It was the first time he'd admitted how desperate he'd been to get her back. "I went to your London townhouse but was refused admittance. I barged in anyway and ran through the house like a madman."

"Father had already removed me to the country. We left

before sunrise."

"That's what your butler told me when I threatened to break his neck."

More tears fell from her eyes.

"He told me you'd gone to Lathamton Manor to marry."

"I didn't want to marry Everett. I kept hoping you'd ride into the church and carry me off and we would live happily ever after."

"I was too proud. I'd made a fool of myself when I went to your townhouse. I refused to follow you to Lathamton Manor and beg you to choose me."

"Didn't you know I loved you?"

"I should have, but I was too hurt." He turned on the sofa and reached for her clenched fingers.

She turned her head and their gazes locked.

"Andrew is the Marquess of Lathamton," Cassie said in a soft, quiet voice. "You can never claim him."

"I know."

Harrison thought he knew pain. The pain he'd experienced when he thought Cassie had betrayed him had been an ache so cavernous and debilitating he wasn't sure he'd survive. But this was a different pain. A deeper, rawer pain.

"I never stopped loving you," he said, exposing his heart to her.

She released a loud sob, then flew into his arms. "I love you. I was furious with you and I tried to convince myself I could hate you. But I couldn't.

Harrison kissed her on the cheek then down the side of her face and finally on the lips. "You shattered every dream I had for a life with you, but no matter how hard I tried, I could never stop loving you."

"What are we going to do?"

Harrison laughed. "We're going to get married. We've lost enough time. I have a woman I want to spend a lifetime loving, and a son I want to watch grow to be a man. I have a house I want to fill with other children so the Marquess of Lathamton doesn't grow up alone."

"Oh, Harrison. I love you."

"But only half as much as I love you," he said then pulled her into his arms and kissed her again.

"Wait until Elly hears," Harrison said when he stopped kissing Cassie to hold her in his arms. "Do you think she's the one who invited you to the party?"

"Yes, but that isn't the reason I came."

Her words confused him. "What do you mean?"

"I'm sure Elly sent me the invitation, but the real reason I came was because of the letter I received after the invitation."

"What letter?"

Cassie walked to the writing desk and opened a secret drawer. She returned and handed him the letter. "Someone blackmailed me."

Harrison opened it slowly and read.

Lady Lathamton,

In one week the Marquess of Fellingsdown will host a summer party. You will attend this event. Refusal to make an appearance will have disastrous consequences.

We know your secret. If you don't want us to share your secret with the marquess, you will be there promptly for dinner, and stay until the last guest goes home.

Don't fail us.

"Aunt Gussie and Aunt Esther," he whispered with a smile on his face.

"Who?"

Harrison tipped back his head and laughed. "Aunt Gussie and Aunt Esther. They are your blackmailers."

"Are you sure?"

"Of course. This is Aunt Ester's writing. I recognized it immediately. But the words are Aunt Gussie's. The Duke of Pendelton is known for inviting guests for dinner, then retiring for the evening before the last guest leaves his home. Aunt Gussie refuses to attend any event he hosts because she considers departing before your guests the height of rudeness."

"Are you angry with them?"

"Heavens, no! Quite the opposite. I can't wait to properly thank them."

Cassie smiled. "Me, too."

They kissed again, then Harrison pulled back. "I think I hear the doctor. We need to go to Elly."

They rose and walked hand in hand across the room.

Cassie stopped before they reached the stairs. "I think it's quite possible the Earl of Charfield has some very special feelings for Elly. Don't you?"

"Yes," Harrison answered.

Except he wasn't sure whether Charfield's feelings were real or part of the act he'd been hired to play.

If the man's feelings were real, he prayed Elly never found out the reason Charfield had been invited, or the bargain they'd made.

The wounds she suffered today would heal a thousand times faster than her broken heart.

CHAPTER 21

Brent paced back and forth in front of the bedroom door and wondered what could be taking the doctor so long.

A maid rushed in and out three times carrying basins of water and bundles of fresh towels. He'd tried to ask the girl what was happening but she ran past him in such a hurry he couldn't get the question out.

Twice he'd heard a low moan come from behind the door and it was nearly more than he could do to remain in the hall without rushing to her side. If he could just see her for a moment he'd feel much better. Not knowing was the worst part. And the waiting.

He paced the length of the hall once more. Just when he decided he could wait no longer, the door opened.

He walked up to the doctor. "How is she?"

"On the positive side, she woke up long enough to inform me I was being too rough."

The doctor smiled and Brent felt part of the weight lift from his chest.

"Her head will ache for a day or more, but I told Nanny Graybrim to keep the drapes closed. I left some drops to put in her tea when the pain gets too bad. She's a strong girl. Always has been. She shouldn't need it for more than a day or two."

"And on the negative side?" The knot in Brent's stomach grew.

"What happened to her didn't do her foot any good. It's swollen and bruised worse than I've ever seen it. The drops will help with the pain, but..."

"But, what?" Brent knew whatever the doctor said, it wasn't going to be good.

"We won't know how badly Lady Elyssa's foot is injured until the swelling is down."

"If it's bad?"

"There's a chance she won't be able to walk." He said his grim prognosis so there was no chance Elly could hear.

"Is there anything we can do to make sure that doesn't happen?"

The doctor shook his head. "Pray. That's all that will help now."

Brent nodded. He wasn't an expert when it came to praying, but for Elly he'd learn to be.

"Don't let her out of bed for at least a week. Maybe longer. Then after I give her permission to get up, I don't want her walking on that leg. She'll have to be carried if she goes anywhere. And keep her leg elevated. That will help more than anything."

Brent nodded.

"I'll check back in the morning," the doctor said. "It won't hurt to give her a little brandy if she's in too much pain. But not too much. Her head's going to ache enough the way it is. No sense making it worse."

"All right." Brent walked to the door and the doctor headed to the stairs. Lady Lathamton and Harrison waited at the bottom. He knew the doctor would give them the same information when they asked about Elly and they would see him out.

He walked to her room and opened the door.

The drapes were drawn and the room was dark, as the doctor said it should be. There was a potent odor from the medicine and salve he'd used and the smell brought home how serious Elly's injuries were.

Nanny Graybrim stood beside the bed and placed a fresh cold cloth on Elly's forehead.

"Is she asleep?" He pulled up a chair on the opposite side of the bed and held Elly's hand.

"She wakes every few minutes," Nanny said, "but mostly she sleeps. That's good, considering all she went through."

Brent swiped his hand down his face. He could still see the look on her face when Waverley pushed her and she lost her balance. He could still see her eyes close when her head hit the wall. And he could still feel the fragile weight of her limp body in his arms.

He moved his gaze to the foot of the bed. A thin blanket covered her foot, but Brent knew the extent of her injuries. He'd seen her red, swollen ankle.

He slowly reached until he touched her hand, then twined his fingers with hers. Nanny Graybrim worked around him but he hardly noticed. He was too intent on watching her. It wasn't until the door opened behind him that he realized he wasn't alone with her.

Brent lifted his gaze to the open doorway. Fellingsdown and Lady Lathamton crossed the room, then stopped at the bed.

"Is she asleep?"

"Yes. The doctor said she probably wouldn't wake for a while."

Fellingsdown and Lady Lathamton sat in chairs someone had placed close to the bed. Fellingsdown kept his gaze on Elly's foot. "Has she told you what happened to her?" he asked. "Why she's like she is?"

"No."

The corners of Fellingsdown's mouth lifted upward and a sad smile crossed his lips.

"I should have known she hadn't. She's never told a soul the truth of what happened that day. Not even Mother or Father."

Lady Lathamton rose, then took the cloth from Nanny Graybrim, and with a silent nod, the nurse left the room.

"I was thirteen years old when it happened. Elly and George were eleven. Spence nine, Jules seven. Poor Elly had the misfortune of being the only girl sandwiched between four brothers. She constantly tagged along after the four of us and we constantly tried to avoid her.

"I remember complaining to Mother once because we couldn't leave the house without Elly following us. I couldn't understand why she couldn't stay at home and play with the twins. They were girls. Mother explained that there weren't too many things Elly could do with two three-year-olds."

Fellingsdown leaned forward in his chair and rested his elbows on his knees. "One day the boys and I were playing down by the stream. We found a tunnel burrowed into the bank. It was the biggest tunnel we'd ever seen and we were sure it was dug by a sea monster. We waited all day hoping our monster would appear but it didn't. When it turned dark, we went home, but we couldn't wait to go back.

"The next day, we each took a weapon to slay the monster when he appeared and walked to the stream. I took a wooden sword I'd spent hours sharpening, and George had a bow and arrow. I can't remember what Spence and Jules brought but it doesn't matter. As we left the house, Elly ran across the yard after us. She had a club in her hand.

"We told her we didn't want her to come with us but she followed anyway. She stayed far enough behind she didn't think we knew she was there, but we did. And we didn't want her with us. We were going to slay our monster. It was *our* monster and we didn't want a girl tagging along. So we decided to lose her. And we did."

Fellingsdown rose to his feet. He walked to the window in the pretext of looking outside even though the drapes were drawn. There was nothing to see.

"We waited all day for our monster to show up but he didn't. Finally when it started to get dark, we gave up and went home. It was dinnertime, after all, and we hadn't thought to bring along anything to eat.

"We washed up then went down for dinner, but Elly didn't come down.

"Mother sent a servant up to get her. The maid returned and informed Mother Elly wasn't in her room; that it didn't look like she'd been there all day.

"I remember being so pleased with myself," Fellingsdown said walking back to the foot of the bed and leaning against one of the bed posters. "Our plan to lose Elly had worked very well. Mother suggested that she might be lost, but George told her Elly was probably playing a trick on us because we wouldn't let her come along. We were all certain she pretended being lost to get us into trouble."

Brent gave Elly's hand a gentle squeeze.

"Thankfully, Mother and Father didn't believe for a moment that Elly would stay out this late intentionally. Within moments, Father called all the servants together and organized a search.

"Mother kept Jules and Spence with her because they were too young to help in the dark, but Father took George and me with him. We retraced our steps from the afternoon, but couldn't find Elly anywhere."

Fellingsdown was silent for several long seconds. Lady Lathamton stepped to where he stood and reached for his hand. He smiled down on her, but his smile didn't contain happiness.

"The next day, Father sent a message to the neighboring estates asking for help. Our neighbors came with every servant they could spare. Even people from the village came to assist in the search."

"When did you find her?" Brent asked.

"Two days later. Elly had fallen through some rotten boards covering an abandoned well. She mangled her foot when she fell. When they pulled her up, I remember looking at it and thinking that she'd somehow managed to put her foot on backwards. Her right foot was ten times larger than her left and purple and black in color."

Fellingsdown closed his eyes. "I can still hear her screams as the doctor tried to straighten her leg. George and Spence and Jules and I huddled together in Father's study and covered our ears to try to shut out her cries, but nothing helped. In the end, the doctors prepared to amputate her foot, but Mother wouldn't let him. Elly was so exhausted and weak, Mother was certain she'd die. And she nearly did."

Fellingsdown raked his fingers through his hair as if reliving every painful memory, then sat back in his chair and propped his elbows on his knees.

"Elly's foot became infected and she developed a fever from the two nights she spent in the cold. Thankfully, she survived. But we all have scars from what happened."

"She doesn't blame you, Harrison," Lady Lathamton said. "She doesn't blame any of you."

"But she should." Harrison swallowed hard. "Elly is like she is because of us. Because of *me*."

Brent understood now why her brothers were so protective of their sister. It wasn't just because they felt responsible for her injury. They felt responsible for *her*. But there was an error in their thinking.

They thought her limp made her weak. It didn't. Elly was stronger because of her limp.

She was the most gifted woman he'd ever met. She was braver than any of the simpering females to whom he'd been introduced, more intelligent than any person he knew, and a more accomplished horsewoman than anyone - male or female - he'd ever met.

Why couldn't her brothers see that? Why did they allow their guilt to blind them to her strengths?

Brent wanted to list Elly's strengths, but her low, pained moan stopped him.

"It's all right, Elly," he whispered, trying to keep her from moving too much. "Lie still."

She quieted, then slowly lifted her eyelids.

"Lie still, sweetheart," he whispered again.

"Brent?"

"I'm right here. You're safe now."

"Is Waverley...?"

Her voice was weak but she seemed remarkably alert.

"He's gone," Brent said, intending to keep the details from her.

"Dead?"

He wanted to laugh. This was a perfect example of her understanding. Her perceptiveness was far more than anyone, including her brothers, gave her credit.

"Yes. He's dead."

"He wanted to kill...Andrew. I tried to—"

"I know. You are the bravest person I've ever seen."

"Rest a little while longer, Elly," her brother said leaning toward her. "Parkridge and Berkingham went to get the twins. You know how much rest you'll get once they arrive."

Everyone laughed. Even Elly tried to smile, but Brent saw the pain it caused her.

The chatter of voices came from the hallway and Brent knew he'd lost any chance to be alone with her.

The door opened and Lady Parkridge and Lady Berkingham took control as if their mission was to remove them from Elly's presence. They hustled Fellingsdown and him from the room.

Brent knew it would be days before he could be alone with Elly – several long, empty days and nights.

He wasn't sure he'd survive.

CHAPTER 22

It was two weeks and four days before the doctor finally declared Elly fit enough to travel. Brent carried her to the waiting carriage and handed her up to Fellingsdown. They'd placed a cushion on the floor between the seats and added a dozen pillows so her leg would ride in comfort.

"Are you comfortable?" he asked when she was situated.

"Yes, very. It's not wise to pamper me this much."

"It's not?"

"No. I could get used to it."

"And that would be bad?"

She smiled. Oh, he loved it when she smiled.

"Yes, I'd become a spoiled brat."

"It can't happen. Being a spoiled brat isn't in your nature." Brent took the cover Lady Lathamton handed him and placed it over Elly's legs. "Are you ready to go?"

"Yes."

Brent stepped outside and joined Fellingsdown and Lady

Lathamton. "Thank you for allowing me to remain after everyone left," he said.

"I enjoyed your company," Lady Lathamton said. "And so did Elly. I think your presence is the reason she healed so fast. You were good for her."

"Thank you." Brent hoped that were true.

"If you'll excuse me, I want to say good-bye to Elly and assure her we'll be over soon."

Lady Lathamton stepped to the carriage to speak with Elly.

"I think Cassie's correct," Fellingsdown said. "You deserve the credit for Elly's fast recovery. Perhaps it's best to find out what your intentions are toward my sister."

Brent faced Elly's brother. "I intend to ask her to marry me."

Fellingsdown's eyebrows shot upward. "Have you asked her yet?"

"No. I want to speak with your father first. I want to assure him that I will be a good husband to Elly."

"What about the bargain we made?"

"I consider any bargain we struck null and void."

"You don't want the breeding rights to El Solidar?"

"No. The bargain was made before I met Elly. The bargain was made before—" He stopped, then proudly stated what he wanted the whole world to know. "Before I realized how much I loved her."

Fellingsdown smiled. "I know exactly what I intend to give you for a wedding present."

"Your Arabians have nothing to do with my wanting to marry your sister."

Fellingsdown laughed. "I know. That's what makes my gift so perfect."

Brent felt an elation he'd never experienced in his life but it had nothing to do with the gift Elly's brother promised. It was because Fellingsdown approved of his request to marry Elly.

Brent walked back to the carriage feeling as if he walked on air.

"Are you sure you don't need us to accompany you," Fellingsdown asked Elly after Brent was seated.

"No, I'll be fine. Lord Charfield will make sure I get to The Down safely."

"We won't be long," Fellingsdown added. "A week perhaps. Two at the outside. Just long enough to study the last of the estate books and make sure the new steward doesn't have any more questions."

"Settle things here first, Harrison. This is more important."

"Take good care of her," Fellingsdown said, then closed the door and gave the driver the command to leave.

Brent sat back against the cushion while the carriage took off.

Elly waved a final time, then settled back against the seat and looked at him. "Will you be leaving The Down right away?" she asked.

"Only if you want me to."

Her cheeks flushed a delightful shade of pink and she shook her head. "No, I'm glad to have your company. The house will be quiet now that everyone's gone back to London. Although I have to say it was none too soon to have the twins stop hovering over me."

"They were very attentive."

"Attentive? They nearly smothered me with their concern."

Brent laughed. It had been more than amusing to watch Elly's two sisters compete with each other over which one of them could take better care of her.

"Then I'll stay for a while longer, if you don't mind."

"I'd enjoy that. Perhaps until Harrison and Cassie come. They said they'd stop by for a few weeks before they went to London to talk with the Lathamton solicitor. But I don't think that's the only reason Harrison wants to take Cassie to London."

"You don't?" He folded his arms over his chest as the carriage made its way down the road. "Just what ulterior motive do you think your brother has?"

"I think he wants Society to see him in Lady Lathamton's company so when they announce their betrothal it won't be such a shock."

"You're sure your brother and Lady Lathamton will marry?"

"Of course. Anyone can see how much they love each other."

"They can?"

"Stop teasing." She wrinkled her pert little nose and frowned at him. "You can't tell me you haven't noticed."

Hell, but she was a beauty. His heart did a somersault every time she looked at him with her dark smiling eyes.

"All right. I've noticed. There does seem to be an attraction."

"More than an attraction," she contradicted. "The two are madly in—"

The carriage hit a rut in the road that nearly unseated her.

Brent bolted from his seat and reached for her. He sat on the cushion next her and wrapped her in his arms.

"Are you all right?"

"Yes, fine. More surprised than anything."

"So sorry, Sir," the driver said from above. "I didn't see the rut."

"No one hurt," Brent answered, holding Elly securely in his arms.

"Oh, good, Sir," the driver answered, and Brent noticed that the speed of the carriage slowed a bit.

"It will be better soon, Elly. We're nearly home.

She laid her head against his chest.

They sat in silence while the carriage rocked on its way. His first thought was that he should be a better companion and keep a conversation going, then realized there were times when silence was preferable. This was one of those times.

After a few minutes, he felt a change in her and looked down. "What?" he asked when he noticed the smile on her face.

"I was just thinking what a wonderful time I had this summer."

"Wonderful? How can you say you had a wonderful summer?"

"Oh, Waverley is not what I'll remember when I think back."

"What will you remember?"

Her smile broadened. "I'll remember our races every morning. And my first croquet match. How special you made every day for me when you didn't have to." She paused. "And my first waltz."

His heart swelled in his chest. He'd never forget the first time he saw her race across the meadow. Or the gleam in her eyes when she challenged him. He'd never forget the first time she trusted him enough to hand over her cane and let him be her support. Or the first time he held her in his arms and danced with her. Each one would be a memory he'd always cherish.

But something about her statement disturbed him. "You talk as if you assume there won't be any more memories to remember. Is that what you think?"

She lifted her gaze and met his. "I'm simply stating a fact. Our summer party is coming to an end and I'm so glad you were invited. You were the most gracious companion any girl ever dreamed of having. As well as the most attentive. And the most handsome. Both Patience and Lilly warned me you would be before they realized I'd met you."

"*Warned* you?" he asked. "What exactly did they warn you about?"

"They warned me to beware because you were the most sought-after man in London. They said your name was at the top of every debutante's list of eligible husbands. That you were not only wealthy beyond description, but one of the most charming and intelligent men in London. And you have the distinction of being known as a rake of the worst kind."

His eyes opened wide. "I see I've acquired quite a reputation. I'm not sure I'm capable of living up to such high standards."

She laughed. "I doubt I'm telling you anything new. For years you've no doubt realized what people said about you. And enjoyed every scandalous word."

Brent couldn't help but laugh. He had been aware of his reputation and even been proud of it at times. But he didn't want Elly to think of him in those terms.

"I'm not sure what this has to do with the time we spent together."

Elly's cheeks darkened and she lowered her gaze to a spot on the other side of the carriage. "Everyone knows you can have any woman you want."

"Which you assume eliminates you?"

"Please, Brent. Don't insult me."

She clenched her hands together in her lap but when he moved to place his hand over hers she pulled them out of his reach.

"When Harrison first told me his plans for a summer party I tried to think where I could go for two weeks. But when I mentioned that I wanted to leave, he was adamant that I stay. He said that each of my brothers had invited a young lady who was special to them and he wanted my opinion of their choices.

"At first I thought Harrison had invented the story." She smiled. "I didn't even know any of my brothers were acquainted with someone. But now I'm not so sure. George seems quite taken with Lady Brianna and Jules with Miss Hastings. And Spence...well, I have no doubt he and Lady Hannah are an excellent match."

"Why would you think Harrison invented a reason to invite guests to The Down?"

"I thought perhaps he'd found out—" She stopped.

"What did you think he'd discovered?"

"That I— I—"

"What?"

"For more than a year I've corresponded with a certain gentleman. He writes the most charming letters and keeps me informed of all the latest happenings in London. I dearly look forward to receiving his letters."

"Do you know his name?"

"Who he calls himself? Or who he really is?"

"You think your secret admirer is a fraud?"

Elly giggled. "My secret *admirers* are my sisters."

He couldn't hide his surprise. Fortunately, she didn't realize he knew about her admirer, but thought his reaction was out of shock that her sisters would do something so underhanded.

"I know, Lord Charfield. You find it hard to believe that my two innocent-acting sisters would pretend to be my admirer. But it's true."

"How did you discover this?"

"I'm embarrassed to admit I didn't realize it immediately. It wasn't until the second or third letter. That's when my charming suitor used the same quaint saying for which my sister Lilly has a fondness. After that, it was a matter of taking note of all the details to which my admirer knew the answers. For instance: my favorite color, my favorite food, my favorite flower. There wasn't one single thing on which my admirer and I didn't agree. Can you imagine anyone more boring?"

Brent laughed. Oh, she had her whole family fooled. "And you think I have been patronizing you, that I was tricked into partnering you?"

"Not tricked, exactly. Perhaps coerced would be a better term. Let me explain. I want you to know that I enjoyed your company more than any person's I've ever spent time with and I wouldn't give up one moment of our time together. But I'm afraid you were deceived."

"How is that?"

"Surely you noticed that every guest invited to the party had a companion. Every guest except you. And me. You were an intended victim, Lord Charfield."

"I hardly feel like a victim."

"Thank you," she said with a smile. "But that doesn't change matters. Even though you were brought here under false pretenses, I will forever be grateful to whichever of my siblings thought of having this party. You made me feel very special and I'll always cherish that."

"You don't believe I was sincere?"

She smiled again, but this time her smile held a hint of sadness. "Of course not. You are very gallant. You've had years to practice such chivalry. But I haven't taken anything that's happened this summer seriously."

"What if I asked you to?"

Her smile faded. "I couldn't."

"Why not?"

"Have you forgotten why I avoid London and prefer to stay here? Have you forgotten that you've had to carry me wherever I need to go?"

"Actually, I had. And I've only had to carry you because you were injured, and that hasn't been an imposition at all. I enjoyed having you in my arms too much to think about the reason you were there."

She blushed again. "Please, don't. I'm trying very hard to keep these last weeks in perspective."

"So am I."

"No, you're being charming and heroic and wonderfully endearing. But your efforts are only making matters more difficult."

He turned so he could face her more directly. "I'm trying to show you what I see when I look at you. I've grown very fond of you during the past several weeks."

She shook her head and Brent knew no amount of words would convince her. She needed proof.

He knew of only one kind of proof she might believe. Before she could turn away from him, he lowered his head and kissed her.

CHAPTER 23

Elly knew nothing could come of the emotions running rampant through her. She knew the dreams of a future with the Earl of Charfield would only end up shattered the same as so many others had. Yet every time he kissed her she lost all sense of what was real and what was fantasy.

Somehow he made kissing him in a moving carriage the most remarkable experience ever.

He braced his elbows on either side of her and cradled her head in the palms of his hands. Then moved his mouth over hers.

She couldn't get enough of him. She wrapped her arms around his neck, then opened her mouth beneath his to allow him to kiss her more deeply.

She wasn't sure why she thought it was important to remember every sensation she felt when kissing him, wasn't sure why she thought it was important to memorize the feel of his touch. Perhaps because she knew she'd never experience such wonder again. Perhaps because she knew when he left their paths would never cross again. Perhaps because her mind knew for a fact what her heart refused to accept.

"Does this give you an idea of how fond I am of you?"

She didn't answer him. She couldn't. She didn't want to consider for a moment that he might be serious. He couldn't be. He was the Earl of Charfield, the most sought-after bachelor in London.

He was nearing thirty, yet he'd never been married. Why? Because even the most perfect of the debutantes hadn't been what he was looking for in a wife. She wouldn't be foolish enough to believe that he'd found what he was searching for in her. And yet...

He brought his mouth down on hers again and kissed her with a passion raw with desire. She wouldn't let herself believe she could mean something to him. But that didn't mean she could stop herself from developing feelings for him. Deep feelings.

Feelings so intense she ached from them.

But she didn't love him.

She wouldn't allow herself to fall completely in love with him. That would be disastrous. She would love him just a little. Like she loved the special quiet at dawn or the vibrant colors of a perfect sunset. Like she loved the freedom of riding at full gallop over the fields and meadows, or the fresh smell after a spring rain. That's how she would love him. Like something special. Like something she would yearn for until she experienced it again. Except this was the only time she would ever know what loving him was like.

He turned his head and deepened his kiss.

She raked her fingers through his thick hair, enjoying the

feel of it as it curled around her fingers, and she pressed him against her.

Her breaths came in sharp, jagged gasps, as if he were taking the lifeless air from her body and replacing it with a charged substance that could explode at any moment. She held onto him and let him take her to that magical place they always aimed to reach.

Suddenly, his mouth lifted from hers and he pulled away with a loud, agonized gasp.

She wasn't ready for this to be over and tried to pull him back.

"We're home."

"At The Down?"

"Yes."

Before they were ready, the carriage door opened and a footman lowered the steps.

"Is your mistress's room ready?" Brent asked as he lifted her from the carriage.

"Yes, my lord. Lord Fellingsdown sent word earlier that Lady Elyssa would be returning."

Brent nodded then carried her up the walk and through the open front doors. She knew he'd take her to her room and Genny would be there to take care of her. She wouldn't see him again unless she sent for him. Or perhaps he'd send word that he was leaving The Down. All the other guests were already gone so there would be no reason for him to stay.

She couldn't let him go. Not yet. Not before…

"Make love to me," she whispered.

There was no doubt he heard her. They were nearly a third the way to the top of the stairs and he stopped. One foot halted as he took a step upward and the muscles in his arms jerked.

He lowered his gaze.

"Love me," she repeated.

He took in several shallow gasps and his breathing turned heavy. He opened his mouth, then closed it, as if he couldn't find the words he needed. He took the stairs with greater determination and walked past her maid.

"Genny," she heard herself say, "I won't need your help. You may leave."

"Y...yes, Miss."

Genny's cheeks turned scarlet and her gaze dropped to the floor and didn't lift.

"Thank you, Genny," Elly said, refusing to let her maid's reaction affect her. "I'll call you when I need you."

"Yes, Miss." Genny bobbed nervously then rushed from the room.

"She knows," Brent said when the door closed behind the maid.

"I don't care." And she didn't. She didn't care about anything except being in Brent's arms and being kissed by him, and touched by him, and being loved by him.

"Kiss me," she said as she raised her head to meet his lips.

She didn't know how they reached the bed but when he lifted his mouth from hers she realized she was lying on the mattress with a pillow beneath her head.

"Are you sure, Elly?"

"Yes. I'm sure. Would you mind?"

He laughed. The sound was different from any laugh she'd heard from him before. This one was hoarse and throaty, and filled with passion.

"That's not exactly a question a woman usually asks a man before...well, before."

"I know, but I haven't had much experience with this sort of thing."

"Much?"

She felt her cheeks warm. "Any."

"You know what's going to happen, don't you?"

Elly breathed a sigh. "I know. Except it won't if you don't stop talking."

He laughed and she studied his high, arched cheek bones and grew warm all over. She looked at the strong angle of his jaw and noticed the faint shadow across his face like Harrison got when he visited and took the luxury of not shaving twice during the day. She wanted to touch his face.

She reached out her hand and cupped her palm to his cheek. A quivering ribbon snaked down her arm, through her chest, then down further to that hidden place between her thighs.

Some primitive need exploded inside her and forced her to admit she was desperate to have him touch her.

"Brent? Please."

He ground out a deep growl that shook of emotion then lowered his head and kissed her again.

Elly wasn't sure how it happened or when, but one piece of clothing after another came off between his kisses until she was naked. She knew she should be embarrassed but she wasn't. Nor was she worried that he'd see her foot because the doctor had wrapped it several times to keep it from being jostled while they traveled.

He came over her slowly, taking care not to touch her ankle, then lowered his body onto hers until his warm flesh pressed against hers. A thousand starbursts exploded inside her.

"Do you know how often I've dreamed of having you?"

"Have you?" she asked, not caring that his words weren't true.

She'd dreamt of having him, too, and was about to realize her dreams. She lifted her hands and brought his head down to kiss him. Fiery flames ignited with each kiss and touch of his hands caressing her.

Their lovemaking was magical and she trembled as he led her to a place she'd never imagined existed.

There was pain but she'd expected it and knew it wouldn't last. He held still inside her until she relaxed again, then moved in a slow, steady rhythm that carried her to someplace high above the clouds.

She clasped her fingers around his shoulders and held on with an all-consuming fierceness until she could hold on no longer. She gave in to the emotions raging within her and fell from the high cliff she'd climbed.

Before her rampaging heart could slow, she heard his voice call her name. Nothing had ever sounded sweeter, more perfect.

She clasped him to her and cradled him in her arms. This was what she would always remember. His rough stubble pressed against her tender flesh. His heart thundering with such ferocity she could feel it beating against her breasts. His heavy body resting blessedly atop her, his fit perfect.

For a long while she simply held him. She let her hands move over his corded shoulders and down his sinewy arms. She touched every part of him she could reach, trying desperately to memorize every inch of him. The day would come when he wasn't here to see or touch or kiss. She would have to draw upon her memories of this one time he'd made love to her.

Eventually, he pushed himself up on his elbows and looked at her. She knew her magical time was over but refused to have any regrets. Brent had given her a memory she would always cherish.

She tried to smile at him, but his unbelievably handsome face blurred from the tears that filled her eyes.

"Are you all right?"

His voice was filled with concern and Elly swiped at the tears that rolled from the corner of her eyes then put a smile on her face.

"Has anyone ever told you that you're beautiful?" she said, struggling to get the words out.

His smile broadened and he slid to her side and pulled her to him. "I hear it all the time, sweetheart. You'll have to come up with something more ingenious."

Elly laughed and laid her head against his shoulder. "What if I told you that you were amazing?"

"Just amazing?" He sounded disappointed.

"Remarkable?"

"That's better, but I'm sure you can find a more fitting word."

"I can," she said cupping his cheek with her hand. "But I'm not sure it's wise for me to say it."

"Why not?"

"Because you're already a very confident person. My complimentary opinion of you will only build on your exalted estimation of your abilities."

"Tell me," he said, leaning over her. He kissed her on the mouth then moved his kisses down her throat and lower yet. "Tell me."

His kisses set her skin on fire and she knew if she didn't

stop him now they'd repeat what they'd just done. And they couldn't. For as much as she wanted to make love to him again and again, she knew each time would only increase her chances of being with child.

And, for as much as she wanted to have a child—

No, for as much as she wanted to have *Brent's* child, she didn't want the child they'd created to grow up with the stigma of being illegitimate.

"Tell me," he demanded again, and this time Elly stopped his teasing by cupping his face between her palms.

"You are perfect. Absolutely, remarkably, undoubtedly perfect. I wouldn't have wanted the man to whom I'd chosen to give myself to be anyone but you."

"I'm going to hold you to that, Lady Elyssa. I'm going to make sure I'm the only man to whom you *ever* give yourself."

Elly brushed the hair back from his forehead. Then she traced a finger over one eyebrow and down the side of his face to where the sharp line of his jaw angled to his chin. He had remarkable features, features that guaranteed very handsome children, were she foolish enough to risk having them.

"And I'll leave you so satisfied every time we make love," he continued, "that you'll tell me I'm remarkably perfect even when we're old and gray."

Elly's heart skipped a beat.

As if he felt her hesitation, he rolled away from her to sit on the side of the bed.

"What?" he asked, looking at her.

"We can't do this again." She kept her gaze locked with his to make sure he understood. "I can't risk bringing a child into the world who has no father."

"Every child has a father."

"You know what I mean."

He stood and Elly pulled the covers beneath her chin when he looked down on her.

"Do you think I'd make love to you without already having decided to make you mine?"

He reached for his shirt and pulled it over his head. "Do you think I don't realize there's the possibility that I've already planted a child inside you?"

Elly heard the anger in his voice and knew that anger was directed at her.

He sat on the chair beside her bed and pulled on his boots. "Do you think I would make love to you then leave you, knowing I'd spoiled your chances to marry another man?"

He thrust his arms into the sleeves of his jacket. "Do you think I'm so indiscriminate about the women I take to bed that I'd sleep with you if I hadn't already decided to marry you?"

A feeling of dread washed over her. He didn't understand why marrying him was impossible. She couldn't let him think it was. "We can't marry, Brent. It's not possible."

"Are you saying that because you're the daughter of a duke and I'm only an earl, you won't marry someone beneath you?"

"Don't be ridiculous! That has no bearing on my reasons and you know it."

"Oh." He dropped his hands to his sides and assumed a battle-ready stance. "It's my reputation, isn't it? You're afraid you can't trust me."

"It's not you! It's—"

"I promise you," he said, interrupting her before she could get that last word out, "I will never be unfaithful to you. If you want my pledge in writing, you may have it."

"It's not you," she repeated. "It's—"

He stopped her last word by interrupting again. "Knowing what I've told you of my parents' marriage, and my reason for not marrying before now, do you think I'd be foolish enough to repeat their mistake if I truly didn't believe our marriage would be different?"

He paced the floor at the foot of the bed. "I'll be a good husband, Elly. I love you. I'll take care of you and provide whatever you need. There's nothing I won't do for you. All you need do is ask."

The blood drained from her head and she was lightheaded. He was serious. He actually thought she would consider marrying him. He actually thought she would fit into his world. That she'd find the courage to go to London. That she'd be successful in playing the role of a Society wife. That she'd be brave enough to lumber clumsily on the arm of one of the most handsome men in Europe and not die of mortification. That she could ignore the stares and comments. That she could overlook Society's speculation as to how a man so perfect could marry someone so flawed.

She swallowed past the lump in her throat.

Perfect.

That's the word that described him best. Brent was *perfect.* And she was...

Not.

"What are you thinking? I don't like it when you have that look in your eyes."

"I was thinking that I'd like to wash now." She pulled the crumpled sheets closer beneath her chin. "I'd like to get dressed."

"Why don't I believe you?"

"Because you're a skeptic?"

He propped his fists on his hips and narrowed his gaze. "I've put my stamp on you, Elly. Whether you like it or not, you're mine."

She broke out in a cold sweat. She couldn't let him leave the room thinking she would marry him. But she couldn't have the serious discussion she had to have without any clothes.

"Please, give me time to dress, then we'll talk. I can't let you think I'll—"

There was a loud knock and the door flew open. Elly stopped mid-sentence.

"Mistress! Oh!" Genny spun around to face Brent. "My Lord, you have to leave!"

"What is it, Genny?"

Elly thought of ducking beneath the covers but Genny was so excited Elly doubted if she'd notice if Elly got out of bed and stood naked in the middle of the room.

"They're here!"

"Who's here?"

"His Grace! Her Grace!"

"Father? Mother?"

Elly jerked her gaze to where Brent stood on the other side of the room. If the situation weren't so tragic she might be able to find some humor in the way his face lost every hint of color.

"Brent?" she said because she couldn't think of anything else to say.

"Yes, my lady. If you'll excuse me. It might be best if my first meeting with your parents weren't in your bedroom."

Elly clutched the sheet to her breasts as she watched him leave the room.

"Genny, help me dress! Then ask one of the footmen to come up to help me downstairs."

"You can't be on your foot, Miss."

Elly kept a sheet around her as she slid to the edge of the bed, "What I can't allow is for Lord Charfield to face my parents alone."

CHAPTER 24

Brent walked down the hall at a clip he hoped wouldn't seem like a run if anyone saw him. He took the stairs even faster. He'd have a bloody hard time explaining what he was doing in the wing opposite where his room was located.

He breathed a sigh of relief when he reached the bottom. He stepped across the marble-tiled foyer and willed his thundering heart to slow.

"Oh, there you are, Charfield."

He turned as Fellingsdown walked toward him.

"I just sent a footman to your room to get you."

"I...uh...was—"

"It doesn't matter. Mother and Father have arrived."

Brent tried to look pleasantly surprised and felt like the worst actor to ever attempt a part.

"Come, meet them."

"It would be my pleasure." Brent followed Fellingsdown across the foyer and down the hallway to a more private area of the manor home.

"A servant came with a message not an hour after you'd left with Elly. Mother and Father wanted us to know they were on their way. I came as soon as I could. Cassie will follow tomorrow. With Andrew."

As they neared the study, Brent instinctively straightened his jacket and tried to appear as presentable as possible. He wanted to seem as if he were composed and perfectly in control, but his conscience refused to allow any sense of calm to settle inside him.

When they reached the room, Fellingsdown opened the door and Brent entered behind him. His gaze found Elly's parents immediately.

Elly's mother was seated on a rose-colored velvet settee, her poise the picture of a duchess.

Her coloring wasn't at all like Elly's, but the same as Elly's twin sisters. Her hair was a golden blonde and her eyes a warm shade of blue. There was a glimmer in her eyes that indicated her intelligence and keen sense of humor. This she'd passed on to her oldest daughter, for Elly had that same sharpness about her.

She smiled and the room lit up the same as it did every time Elly smiled.

His Grace stood beside the fireplace, the massive stone hearth a perfect backdrop to his tall, muscular frame. He was as impressive a figure as Brent had imagined him to be.

He straightened to greet his guest.

"Father. Mother. May I present the Earl of Charfield? Charfield, my father and mother, the Duke and Duchess of Sheridan."

"Your Grace," Brent said, bowing low over the Duchess

of Sheridan's proffered hand. "Your Grace," he said, bowing again to Elly's father.

"Charfield, I can't tell you what a pleasure it is to meet you," the duchess said. "Harrison informed us of the travesty that endangered Elly and the risks you took to save her. Her father and I want to personally thank you."

"Yes, thank you," His Grace offered. "I'm not sure how the duchess and I would have handled it if anything had happened to Elly."

Brent became serious. "No one would have found it easy to cope with the idea of Lady Elyssa being injured. Everyone is very fond of your daughter."

The Duke and Duchess of Sheridan shared a look and a smile.

His Grace pointed to a circle of chairs. "Why don't we sit down? Harrison, would you get us each a glass of brandy and a glass of wine for your mother?"

"Of course." Fellingsdown went to a small cupboard and opened a levered door. He took the stopper from one of the crystal decanters and filled three glasses, then placed a deep red liquid from another decanter into a fourth glass.

The duke motioned for Brent to take a chair opposite the duchess, then sat on the settee next to his wife. After Fellingsdown handed them each a glass, he sat in a chair next to Brent.

"Now, Harrison," the duchess said, "why don't you explain what prompted you to host a party at The Down."

"I'm not sure why you think it so odd for us to want to have a party here. It is, after all, the perfect place to—"

The duchess raised her hand and Fellingsdown stopped his explanation.

"You can dispense with your attempts to camouflage whatever it is you're trying to hide. You forget, your father and I know you better than anyone."

The duke set his glass on the table next to his wife's and leaned back against the cushions. "You might as well tell your mother the entire tale," he said crossing his arms over his chest. "She won't give up until she knows every detail."

Fellingsdown took another sip of his brandy then sat back in his chair. "Several months ago the twins—"

"I might have known the girls would be the cause of this," the duchess said, rolling her eyes heavenward.

"What have those two done this time?" the duke asked.

"They were only trying to do Elly a kindness," Fellingsdown began when the duchess sat forward on the settee.

"What have they done to Elly? They know how—"

"Nothing, Mother," Fellingsdown said. "Elly's fine. She doesn't have a clue as to what they did."

Brent couldn't help but smile. He tried to bring his glass up to his lips before anyone noticed, but he wasn't sure he was successful. The Duke of Sheridan gave him a look that said he might not have been quick enough. His words confirmed it.

"You know how impossible it is to get anything past Elly," the duke said. "Isn't that true, Charfield?"

"Um...Yes. Quite."

"Go on though, Harrison. What mischief have the twins caused now?"

"Well, to make a long story short—"

"That will be the day," His Grace said beneath his voice.

"...the twins decided Elly needed a romance."

"A romance!" The Duke and Duchess of Sheridan spoke at the same time. From the surprise in their voices it was obvious they found the idea as preposterous as her other siblings had.

"Yes. A romance. So they made up a fictitious suitor."

"Who?"

"It doesn't matter, Father. Elly's fictitious suitor didn't have to make an appearance."

"Then what was your reason for having a party?"

"Because Elly asked to see her secret admirer. She wanted to meet him. And there was no one for her to meet."

"But you understood her real motive for asking to meet him, didn't you?" the duchess asked.

"Of course I did, Mother. It meant that Elly had formed a serious attraction to this fictitious person."

There was a short silence before the duchess answered. "No, Harrison. That's not what it meant."

"What did it mean then?" Fellingsdown asked, obviously confused.

"Oh, men," Her Grace sighed. "They understand us so little."

Fellingsdown shifted his gaze to his father, obviously hoping he'd enlighten him. His Grace just shrugged his shoulders.

"It means, *son*," the duchess said with a sigh of frustration, "that your sister saw through the twins' scheme. She knew there was no secret admirer. Isn't that right, Lord Charfield?"

Brent couldn't hide this smile beneath his glass any longer and faced the duchess. "I believe Lady Elyssa did mention that she thought her sisters might have invented some scheme to give her an adventure."

"What a nice way of saying that she saw through what they'd done," the duchess said. "Go on, Harrison. What did you do?"

"Well, the six of us planned this party. We thought if Elly discovered what Patience and Lilly had done she'd be terribly hurt and we didn't want that. So I came up with the idea to host a party and include several guests, plus, of course, Aunt Gussie and Aunt Esther."

"Your aunts were in on this?" Her Grace asked.

"No, they didn't know anything about it. We invited them to make sure there wouldn't be any improper rumors that might circulate after our party was over."

"Well," the duke said, "that was at least one wise decision you made."

"All we wanted to do was give Elly a grand time. And maybe the twins were correct. Maybe Elly did need a romance."

The frown on Her Grace's forehead deepened. "Playing matchmaker is a very dangerous game, Harrison. It can backfire on you as easily as it can be a success."

Fellingsdown smiled for the first time. "I think I can assure you that my first attempt at playing matchmaker has been quite successful. Do you remember how you always told us that the wish you made every year on your birthday was that at least one of your sons would give you a daughter-in-law that year?"

"Yes." The duchess sat forward with a bright expression on her face.

"I think you might receive several years' wishes quite soon."

"Oh!" The duchess clasped her hands over her mouth. "Who? Which one? Did you say several? More than one of you? Who?"

"I'm not sure, of course. But perhaps all of us."

"All!" both parents exclaimed in unison.

Tears of joy ran down the Duchess of Sheridan's cheeks

and a broad smile covered the Duke of Sheridan's face.

"Who have the boys chosen?" Her Grace asked. "Will they make them happy?"

Brent sat back in his chair and listened while Fellingsdown revealed the choices each one of his brothers had made. The duke and duchess were acquainted with the girls and seemed enormously pleased with their sons' choices for wives. Especially their eldest son's choice when Fellingsdown explained Lady Lathamton's situation and what had happened four years ago to destroy their dream of happiness.

What Brent noticed, however, was that not once did the Duke or Duchess of Sheridan mention Elly, or inquire if she might have developed a fondness for anyone. It was as if the idea of her falling in love – or anyone falling in love with her – was beyond the realm of possibility.

"What part did you play in my children's scheme, Charfield?" the Duke of Sheridan asked.

His question pulled Brent out of his wool-gathering. He thought back to the meeting he'd had when Fellingsdown offered him the prize he'd always wanted if he'd attend a summer party and play escort to his sister. He thought how all he'd ever wanted was a colt sired by the magnificent El Solidar.

Now he'd pass up a thousand colts from every magnificent Arabian Fellingsdown had at The Down if acquiring them meant giving up Elly. He realized how lucky he was to have met the woman of his dreams, how he'd finally been given a gift more precious than anything he could imagine.

"I—"

"Charfield did us a favor," Fellingsdown began before Brent could finish his sentence.

"Why do I think I'm not going to like this?" the duchess

said with a skeptical look on her face.

"Don't worry, Mother. I made a bargain with Lord Charfield that would benefit everyone."

"Even Elly?"

"*Especially* Elly. We hired Charfield to attend our party and play escort to Elly. We wanted someone to shift Elly's affection away from her secret admirer."

"You *hired* Lord Charfield?" Her Grace asked. There was a tone of concern in the Duchess of Sheridan's voice as well as a look of horror on her face. "Tell me that's not what you said."

"Are you saying that you paid Charfield money to pretend to be fond of your sister?" the duke said in a voice that sounded close to an angry growl.

Brent tried to interrupt. He tried to explain that it wasn't like that at all. The bargain was how their plan started, but not the way it ended.

He needed to tell them that he loved Elly. That he wanted to marry her.

He knew he should talk to Elly first, but this whole conversation was getting out of hand. They made it sound as if their initial bargain was something vulgar and ill-mannered. As if they'd deliberately played a malicious joke on Elly.

He couldn't allow her parents to think he'd intentionally done something cruel to her.

Or, worse yet, that her siblings had given her a romance because they pitied her.

It was important that they understood his intentions before they thought the worst of him. He needed to assure them that he wasn't ashamed to be seen with their daughter; that he loved her; that he couldn't live the rest of his life without her; that he intended to marry her and he wouldn't take no for an answer.

"Have you lost your mind?" His Grace bellowed at Harrison. "Do you know what it will do to your sister if she ever discovers what you did?"

"She won't. And it's not how you make it sound. It's not as if we paid Charfield *money* to escort Elly."

There was a noise at the door and everyone turned.

Brent's heart plummeted to the floor, where it shattered to pieces.

Elly stood there, a cane in each hand to support herself.

It was obvious she'd struggled to manage the stairs as well as the long hallway. Her face was void of color, her features pulled tight. But it wasn't exhaustion he recognized on her face, or pain from walking on her leg the doctor ordered her to stay off of, but the devastation in her eyes that concerned him most.

He struggled to put a term to the expression on her face so when he needed to remind himself of what he'd done, there would be a specific word that would come to mind. But he couldn't find just one. There were so many: hurt, anger, disappointment, devastation.

Except he hadn't touched on the term that most accurately described what she felt. Nor was there any way he could come close to describing the raw, ugly pain he saw on her face.

She was hurting – and he was the cause of her pain.

"What did you offer him if it wasn't money?"

"Elly, it wasn't like that at all." Brent rose to his feet then stepped toward her.

"What did they offer you? I can't imagine anything Harrison has that you need. What could you possibly want that was so important you would agree to be seen with a cripple for two weeks?"

"Elly, no. That's not how it was."

"What? How much was I worth?"

Brent didn't want to answer. He knew once he did, there was nothing he could say to undo the harm he'd done.

"What?" she repeated.

One lone tear streamed down her cheek and his heart shattered.

"A colt from El Solidar."

She sucked in a breath that seemed to affect her balance. "Of course," she whispered.

She hesitated as if she had a hard time accepting the fact that the bargain had been over a horse.

"Elly, please, let me explain. That may have been how it started out, but that's not how—"

He took one step toward him but she stopped him with a sharp lift of her hand. "Don't come near me. Don't you ever come near me again."

"Elly, come sit down," Harrison pleaded. "Let us explain. We didn't mean to hurt you."

"I know, Harrison. No one ever does."

She turned and took a few steps. When she reached the door she stopped.

"Father," she said without turning around, "Lord Charfield will be leaving shortly. Will you send someone to assist him?"

Her statement required no answer.

CHAPTER 25

Brent sat in a leather wing chair in his London townhouse study and stared at the dying embers in the massive fireplace. Their glow faded with each passing hour, turning first to white-hot ashes that eventually shifted to darkened soot with only a few red-hot spots peeking through.

Fall had arrived and the nights were chilly, although Brent hardly noticed. He noticed very little these days.

It had been six months, three weeks, five days, and – the mantle clock chimed twelve times – eight hours since his world ended. Not even six full months of an anguish more agonizing than he thought he'd survive, and he had a whole lifetime of agony ahead of him.

He reached for the glass he never allowed to become empty and took a long sip. The day would come when he wouldn't be entitled to dull his pain with the effects of alcohol, but that day hadn't arrived yet. The hurt was too new, the loss too great to survive without anything to numb it.

He lifted the decanter from the floor beside his chair when

a knock came from the front door.

Even though the chance was nonexistent that Brent's late-night visitor was the one person he was most anxious to see, he couldn't stop his body from reacting. He held his breath and listened, hoping to hear her voice.

A low, male voice echoed from the foyer beyond his door and he lowered his head to the back of the chair and closed his eyes. Each disappointment was more difficult to take.

He waited for the visitor to leave, but instead, there was a knock, and his butler, Markham, opened his door.

"You have a visitor, my lord. The Marquess of Fellingsdown."

Brent's heart raced in his chest. "Show him in."

Something must be wrong with Elly. That's the only reason Fellingsdown would come to see him at this hour.

"Is Elly unwell?" he asked the second Fellingsdown walked through the door.

"And a good evening to you, too." Fellingsdown walked into the room and scanned the area. "Do you always sit in such gloomy surroundings, Charfield?"

The muscles in his body relaxed the same time his temper rose. Obviously Elly was well or her brother would have told him when he arrived.

"I prefer it this way. The darkness seems to match my mood."

"My, how we've changed. I remember when—"

"I'm not interested in what you remember." Brent sat back in his chair and took a drink from his glass.

"Do you mind if I join you?"

"Suit yourself." Brent lifted the crystal decanter from the floor and held it out. There was a glass on a tray the servants had placed on the corner of the table and Brent handed it to his guest.

"I know we didn't part on the best of terms," Fellingsdown said as he filled his glass, "but I'd like to remedy that if possible." He placed the decanter on the table, then sat in the chair opposite Brent and took a drink of his liquor.

"I've had all the help I care to ever have from you."

"I know why you think that way," Fellingsdown said, his voice quiet and the tone filled with regret, "but I didn't think there was a chance the two of you would fall in love."

Brent's temper flared. "Why? Do you honestly think your sister's that impossible to love?"

Fellingsdown looked shocked. "No! We've all known Elly would make the most wonderful wife and mother in the world. It's you."

"Me!" Brent sat forward and clenched his empty hand around the arm of the chair. "You pompous ass. If you were worth the powder it would take to shoot you, I'd call you out."

"Hold your temper, Charfield. I only meant I didn't think you were the sort of man Elly would look at once, let alone twice. I definitely didn't think you were someone with whom she'd fall in love."

"Obviously, I wasn't. She didn't hesitate longer than the blink of an eye before she ordered me to leave The Down."

"She was hurt."

"Nor did she give a second thought as to whether or not she wanted to see me the twenty or so times I begged to be admitted."

"Maybe you weren't persistent enough."

"Bloody hell, man! I nearly broke down the door. When I finally made it as far as the foyer, your father told me very plainly that my presence was not welcome."

"Yes, Father said he's never seen anyone so tenacious."

"A bloody lot of good it did me." Brent threw the remainder of liquor in his glass to the back of his throat. "Your father was no more agreeable than that butler of yours."

"Perhaps you simply didn't use the right approach." Fellingsdown stretched his legs out in front of him as if he were settling in for the night.

That was all Brent could take. He wanted Fellingsdown gone. "You're the last person I need advice from, Fellingsdown. I wouldn't be in this predicament if it weren't for you. You and your lame idea."

"If I remember correctly, you were more than eager to jump at the possibility of getting a colt from El Solidar."

"That was before I met your sister. That was before I knew I'd fall in love with her!"

"Yes, that *does* change the way we look at things." Fellingsdown lifted his glass and took another swallow. "Love can do that to a man."

"A lot you know about it. You won back the woman you loved."

"But the time I lost cost me more than I can live with at times."

Brent knew what Fellingsdown meant. He was talking about the son he could never acknowledge as his own. The son who had Prescott blood running through his veins, yet carried the Waverley name. The son who should in truth be the future Duke of Sheridan, yet would always bear the Marquess of Lathamton title. Yes, he knew what time had cost Fellingsdown.

"Why are you here?" Brent felt his loss more tonight than he had since the day his dreams were shattered.

"I'm here because I don't want you to go through what Cassie and I did."

"Do you think *I* do?"

"No, which is why I need to ask you a question."

"I don't want to answer any of your questions."

"You will if you want my help."

Brent hesitated. This was the first glimmer of hope he'd had since he'd lost Elly. "What's your question?"

"Do you love her?"

"I've already told you I do."

"How much?"

"That's none of your business."

"It is if you want me to help you get her back. How much do you love her?"

Brent raked his fingers through his hair then leaned forward in his chair with his elbows propped on his knees. He looked down at the dark pattern on the carpet at his feet and took a deep breath. "Enough that I don't think I'll survive another day if I don't get her back. Enough that I think my heart's dead and I can't figure out how it can still go on beating."

Brent closed his eyes and swallowed hard. "Enough that I don't *want* to be alive if Elly's not here with me."

For a long time the only sound was the occasional crackle of dying embers in the grate. Finally, Fellingsdown spoke in a soft voice that commanded Brent to listen.

"I've come to see you because I'm concerned about Elly. We all are."

"I thought you said Elly was well."

"Elly's not ill, which I believe is what you think I'm implying."

"You know bloody well what I'm *implying*. What's wrong

with her?"

"The same thing that's wrong with you, from the look of it."

Brent sat straighter and waited for Fellingsdown to continue.

"I promised Mother and Father I wouldn't interfere, and I intend to keep my word, but I can't sit by and watch the two of you go through what Cassie and I did. Especially if there's something I can do to prevent it."

"What do you intend to do?"

"Nothing."

"But I thought you said—"

"I said I wasn't going to interfere. And I'm not. If anyone does anything, it will be you, Charfield."

Brent stared in confusion as Fellingsdown rose from his chair and walked to the door. He stopped before he stepped out into the hall.

"Did you hear," he said looking over his shoulder, "that the Earl and Countess of Dunlevy are hosting a ball tomorrow night to announce the betrothal of their daughter, Lady Brianna, to my brother, George?"

Brent was too irritated to answer. He didn't care about the Earl of Dunlevy, or his daughter, or even Elly's brother, George, for that matter.

"It should be quite an affair," Fellingsdown continued. "My *entire* family will be there, of course."

It took a moment for Fellingsdown's intent to sink through Brent's brandy-muddled brain. When it did, his heart shifted in his chest.

"Elly's in London?" Brent bolted from his chair. "Why the hell didn't you tell me that when you came?"

Fellingsdown turned serious. "I don't remember mentioning

that Elly would be there."

"But you said—"

Fellingsdown raised his hand. "I promised my parents I wouldn't interfere, Charfield. And I'm a man of my word. If you recall, I only mentioned that the Earl of Dunlevy was hosting a ball tomorrow night to announce his daughter's betrothal to my brother. And that my family would be in attendance."

With that, the Marquess of Fellingsdown turned and left.

And for the first time since Brent's dream of a life with Elly had been shattered, he realized a glimmer of hope.

———

London was the same now as it had been ten years earlier when she was a young naïve girl glimpsing its glamour for the first time. And she was just as disappointed as she'd been then.

Although she was older, and not nearly as sensitive as she'd been then, it still hurt to see people stare at her when she walked down the street. The whispered comments people made behind her back no longer offended her, yet it was uncomfortable to know they talked about her.

"Oh, look at this," Lilly said, pointing to an elegant peach silk fabric she'd found in the dressmaker's shop. "Don't you think it would make the most divine evening gown?"

"Yes, it would," Patience agreed. "But by the time I'm able to fit back into anything made this season, I'm afraid it will be out of style."

It took a moment for Patience's announcement to take hold, but when it did, the Duchess of Sheridan and her two other daughters came to the same conclusion at exactly the same time. They all squealed with delight and one by one gave

Patience a hug of congratulations.

Luckily, there were only two other ladies in the shop at the time because their undignified behavior drew immediate attention.

"How long have you known," Lilly asked her twin as soon as the duchess was able to usher them out of the store.

"Not long. I just told Ellery last week."

"Oh, wait until your father hears he's going to be a grandfather," the duchess said.

"What about you, Mother?" Elly put one hand through her mother's arm and kept her cane in the other. "Will you mind being a grandmother?"

"Heavens, no! I've anxiously awaited the day since the twins married more than a year ago. Your father and I didn't have seven children because we didn't like babies, you know."

The duchess's last statement elicited a hidden laugh from each of her daughters. They knew how much their parents loved each other and had often remarked in private that perhaps the duke and duchess didn't like children half as much as they enjoyed the act that created them.

Elly had always thought the same thing. But until she made love with Brent, she didn't realized how special it was to give your body to a man you loved.

The nagging ache that gnawed inside her chest clawed at her again. How long would it be before she didn't hurt each time she thought of him?

How long would it be before she didn't think of him every minute of every day?

Her mother and sisters were still laughing gaily but Elly looked to the other side of the street so they wouldn't see the sadness that refused to leave her. Her heart stopped in her breast.

Brent walked toward her as if thinking about him could make him appear.

Lilly and Patience noticed him soon after Elly did and their laughter faded. Elly's mother noticed him last and a deafening silence blanketed the quartet of Prescott women.

"Good day, Your Grace," Brent said when he came close enough to speak. "Lady Parkridge. Lady Berkingham. Lady Elyssa."

Elly's heart thundered in her breast. Why could he still do this to her? Hadn't she been hurt enough by him? Was she so weak that all he had to do was speak and she was drawn to him all over again?

Elly hated to admit it, but she was. She loved him that much.

"Good day, Lord Charfield," the duchess answered in her most regal voice as she pried Elly's fingers from digging into her arm.

Neither Elly's mother, nor Lilly or Patience, was overly friendly in their greeting, which didn't surprise her. If Brent noticed the chill in their voices, he didn't show it.

"And Lady Elyssa. How have you been?"

"Well, thank you," she said, thankful her voice sounded more in control than she felt. "We were shopping and are on our way home." She turned a desperate glance to her mother. "Mother, are you ready? I'd like to go."

"Of course," her mother answered. "If you'll excuse us. Lord Charfield."

"May I escort you back to your—"

"No," Elly answered with such force it took her mother and sisters by surprise. The only one who didn't seem embarrassed was Charfield. He seemed to expect her reaction. And accept it.

"Very well," he said with a most flattering bow. "I will bid you good day, then."

"Good day," her sisters and mother answered.

He walked down the street in one direction and they walked in another.

"Are you all right, Elly?" the duchess asked when they were out of hearing.

"Of course," she lied.

She was anything but all right.

CHAPTER 26

The inside and outside of the Earl of Dunlevy's London townhouse was so brightly lit the guests could see their destination for blocks before they arrived. Elly looked around from her seat against the far wall of the ballroom and took in the festive décor. This was truly a night to celebrate. And an occasion worthy of the elaborate lengths to which Dunlevy had gone to show the *ton* his daughter was equal to the task of being the Duke of Sheridan's second son's wife.

Unfortunately for Elly, this was only the first of four such evenings.

Each of her four brothers were about to become engaged to the female they'd invited to the summer party at The Down: George, to Lady Brianna Donnelly, daughter of the Earl of Dunlevy; Jules, to Miss Amelia Hastings, daughter of Viscount Kimball; Spence, to Lady Hannah Brammwell, daughter of the Marquess of Crestonridge; and finally, the ball her parents would host two weeks from tonight to announce the engagement of their eldest son, Harrison, to Lady Lathamton.

Elly couldn't be happier for each of them, but she wasn't looking forward to the next two weeks. Attending such public functions would put her more in the spotlight than she wanted to be.

"They look happy, don't they?" Patience said, taking the chair beside Elly. "I remember how happy I was the night of our engagement ball."

"They look very happy," Elly agreed. "Brianna is a perfect match for George. I was alone with her the other day while we waited for George to finish his conversation with Father and I was impressed by how intelligent she is. George said she keeps him on his toes and I can see why. She knows as much about what is going on in the world as George."

"I knew George would never pick someone with a shallow mind. Next to Harrison, he is the most serious of the four of them."

Elly laughed. "And Spence the least serious. Which means Lady Hannah—"

"Will give Spence a run for it. I've not met anyone who enjoys life like she does."

"No wonder Spence chose her."

"And Jules?"

"No need to worry there, either. I think I'm glad I'll have a head start on them. I wouldn't be surprised if Jules and Amelia give Mother a new grandchild within the year."

"What makes you say that?" Elly asked looking over to where Jules and Amelia were talking to some friends.

"Oh, Elly. Take note of the way they look at each other. It's the same as you and Charfield looked at each other last sum—"

Patience clasped her hands over her mouth, then reached out to place a hand over Elly's clutched fingers.

"Oh, Elly, I'm so sorry. I don't know how I could have been so insensitive. It's usually Lilly who—"

"That's all right, Patience. I was quite the fool."

"The cad," Patience said in anger.

"I hope you aren't talking about me," a deep, velvety voice said from behind them.

Elly knew the voice belonged to Brent. She'd heard it so often in her dreams she could bring it up with little effort. But she didn't expect him to be here. She'd even checked the guest list to make sure his name wasn't on it.

"Actually," Patience said with an impolite lift of her chin, "we were."

"Well, don't stop simply because I've arrived. I find it's always more enlightening to hear insults from people firsthand rather than second or third."

He stepped around the empty chair next to Elly and held out one of the two glasses of punch he had in his hand. He offered the first glass to Patience. "May I offer you something to drink?"

"I don't care for anything you have to offer," Patience said in a tone Elly didn't know Patience was capable of using.

Brent smiled as if he hadn't noticed her rudeness. "Lady Elyssa?"

"Please leave." She looked around Brent in hope of catching one of her brothers' attention. Harrison was the only one who noticed her and Elly wasn't sure she wanted him to come to her aid.

"I want you to leave." Elly couldn't lift her gaze. She didn't want to focus on his face or look into his eyes.

"I'm sure you do." He still held the glass in his hand. "But I desperately want to see you."

"Lord Charfield—" Patience started, but Harrison reached them in time to interrupt what Elly knew would be a scathing remark.

"Is everything all right, Elly?"

"No, Harrison. It's not."

"I thought you might need some assistance." Harrison turned to Patience and offered her his arm. "Patience, would you accompany me to the refreshment table? I believe Elly has several things she'd like to say to Charfield. None of which are fit for your delicate hearing."

Patience's expression turned to shock.

Elly was filled with a mixture of panic and dread.

Patience blinked. "I don't think that's what Elly meant, Harrison."

"Of course it is. After what he did to her last summer she deserves the opportunity to express every contemptuous thought she's kept bottled inside for the last six months. Isn't that right, Elly?"

Elly wanted to cry out that being left alone with Brent was the last thing she wanted but before she could say anything, Harrison helped Patience to her feet and escorted her to the other side of the room.

Elly's heart filled with dread as they walked away, leaving her alone with Brent.

"Was this another scheme you and Harrison planned to humiliate me?" she whispered without turning her gaze. "What did you offer him to allow you the opportunity to annoy me? I hope not much. You won't be here that long."

She couldn't look at him. She didn't dare. She hurt more

every time she did.

"I want to explain about last summer, Elly."

"There's nothing to explain. You were offered the gift of one of Harrison's magnificent Arabians and couldn't pass it up."

"That's only how it started. But it wasn't how it ended. Your family was worried about you and—"

"There was no need for anyone to worry."

"They didn't know that. They were afraid you might have formed an attachment to the secret admirer your sisters had created."

"I don't want to talk about this." Elly swiped her trembling hands across her skirt as if straightening some annoying wrinkles.

"We have to. You have to understand what—"

"I don't have to understand anything!"

Tears welled in her eyes but she refused to weep in front of him. "I want you to leave. Several of the guests have noticed you sitting here. If you're not careful, rumors will circulate about you."

"They aren't rumors if they're true."

"Stop this, Brent. There's no need to pretend any longer. You successfully completed your part of the bargain and deserve the prize you and Harrison agreed on. I cannot even remember my fictitious suitor's name. And by spring you should have a colt from El Solidar in your stables."

"I refused Harrison's offer."

"Then you're a fool."

"I was a fool to *agree* to Harrison's offer. I'd never seen you. I didn't know you. I thought I could spend two weeks with you and walk away without a second thought. Until I met you."

"Stop, Brent. People are staring at us."

"Let them. I want them to watch us together for the rest of our lives."

"Don't, Brent."

"Look at me, Elly. I want you to look at me when I tell you I love you."

Elly thought this must be what it was like when your heart broke. She wanted to flee, but she couldn't. She needed to escape but the only place to which she wanted to run was into Brent's arms.

"The day I met you I realized I could never walk away from you. I realized I didn't *want* to walk away from you. Ever."

"Do you think I can believe that? Look around you, Brent. Take note of all the females in the room ogling you."

"I don't care about any other female."

"Then look at the confused looks on every matchmaking mama's face. They're trying to figure out what you could possibly have to talk to the cripple about."

"Don't you *ever* say that again." Brent took her hands and held them. "Look at me."

Elly tried to pull her fingers from his grasp but he wouldn't release her.

"I love you, Elly."

"No." She jerked her hands hard enough he was forced to let her go. "You got what you want. Now leave me alone."

"Dance with me."

Elly's heart leaped to her throat. "No!"

"Then walk with me."

"No."

"Walk out onto the terrace with me. We'll take in some fresh air then come right back in. I promise I won't even try to kiss you. Unless you want me to." He had a twinkle in his eyes.

"Why are you doing this?" She turned her head to look at him. "You don't have to prove anything. It's too late."

"It can't be too late. If it's too late that means I've lost you. And I won't live the rest of my life without you. I love you too much."

Elly swallowed hard. A small part of her wanted to believe him. A small corner of her heart wanted to trust that he really did love her. She loved him so much she would grasp at anything to believe his words were true.

Another part of her knew he couldn't love her. No one in the ballroom would ever believe someone so perfect could have feelings for the Duke of Sheridan's crippled daughter. She could see it on their faces. Everyone was staring.

"Please, Elly. Walk with me. For tonight that will have to be enough."

A battle raged inside her and she knew she'd lost the fight. On one side were Brent's smooth words and vows of affection. On the other were his lies and the cruel reminder of how easy it had been for him to deceive her.

If only she didn't love him so much.

Just when she thought she wasn't strong enough to hold up, her Mother and Father walked toward her. They'd come to rescue her and yet...

How was it possible to feel such relief and regret at the same time?

"Your Grace," Brent said, standing to bow over her mother's hand. "Your Grace," he said, greeting her father.

"Charfield. I have to admit I'm a little surprised to see you here." Elly's father's tone was none too friendly.

"I've been a friend of Dunlevy's for years."

"Business or personal?"

"Both," Brent admitted.

"I've heard he has some valuable silver mines in which he's allowed a few select friends to invest. I didn't realize you were one of them."

"Nor I, you," Brent said.

She listened as the two discussed several other matters and knew from the expression on her father's face that with each comment and opinion, Brent impressed her father more.

Why did that surprise her? Brent was one of the most intelligent, versatile men she'd ever met. Growing up, she'd never thought it was possible to meet a man who held a candle to her father, or who could compete with any of her brothers. But Brent did. He was as wonderful as any of them. As admirable. As...

Brent's handsome face and commendable qualities swam before her eyes and the room shifted around her. She reached out for her mother's hand.

"Elly? Are you all right?" Her mother tightened her hold.

She lifted her gaze as Brent and her father rushed to her side.

"Are you ill, Elly?" Brent sat in the chair to her right.

"I'm fine. I just..."

Elly lowered her gaze to her lap, where Brent's hands were covering hers. "People are staring, Brent."

"Let them. Are you all right?"

"Yes." She looked up. "I'd like to leave. Father, would you call the carriage. I'll send it back when I get home."

"Of course." Her father held his arm for Elly to take.

"I'd be more than happy to see you home, Lady Elyssa."

"Thank you, Lord Charfield. But that won't be necessary."

"Are you sure?"

Elly didn't answer him, but placed her hand on her father's forearm and pulled herself up. With one hand hooked into her father's elbow and the other clutched around the handle of her cane, she took her first step across the ballroom.

Her ungainly limp seemed more pronounced tonight. The rhythm she usually found when walking with her father was impossible to find. Her right hip dipped with each step, forcing her skirt to swing more noticeably than usual. Each clunk of her cane thundered like a rifle shot. And the hand she'd placed on her father's sleeve pulled his arm in an ungainly jerk.

She didn't want to see what she looked like as she walked away from the staring crowd. She'd never felt so ugly. Never felt so revolting. So repulsive.

She hoped Brent was watching. If he was, he had to be as disgusted by her unsightly lumbering as everyone else in the ballroom. And she knew they were because...

...every pair of eyes in the room watched her.

———

Brent watched her walk across the floor. So did everyone else in the room.

This is what Elly meant. These were the ugly stares she'd endured her whole life – at least from the more polite members of Society. The not-so-polite ones turned their heads or lowered their gazes so they wouldn't have to look at her.

He clenched his hands into tight fists. He wanted to shout at each of them. He wanted to chastise them for their crude ignorance. He wanted to tell them what a remarkable person Elly was – which they'd know if they got to know her. But no one did. No one had ventured near enough to discover her intelligence and courage and remarkable personality. Instead, they avoided her as if she had the plague.

He spun away from the still-gaping crowd and found the Duchess of Sheridan still standing beside him.

"I beg your pardon, Your Grace. I was distracted."

"I see that."

The duchess gathered the white, lace handkerchief Elly forgot on the chair and tucked it into a pocket in her skirt. "This is what Elly had to endure when she was a young girl. Her father and I have always been able to see her as the extraordinary person she is. Unfortunately, very few of Society can get past her injury.

"If we had known she was going to receive such an impolite reception all those years ago, we wouldn't have demanded she come for a Season. We didn't make that same mistake this time. We gave her the option of staying in the country, but she chose to come. She said celebrating with her brothers was too important."

Brent turned his attention to the duchess. There was a point to what she was revealing but he wasn't sure he knew what it was just yet.

"I learned something important about myself the last time Elly came to London. I think it's a reaction only a mother can have..."

She stopped and narrowed her gaze.

"...or perhaps someone deeply in love. It's a protective instinct that demands we do everything in our power to safeguard those we love. For a moment, I thought I recognized that same intense protectiveness when you watched the crowd's reaction to Elly."

"If you did?" Brent asked.

The Duchess of Sheridan breathed a deep breath. "If you are pursuing Elly to ease your conscience, then heed my warning. I won't rest until I make sure Elly is safe from any harm you might inflict on her."

"If I'm not?"

She paused as if uncertain whether or not to continue. "If you truly love her—"

She turned her gaze to where the Duke of Sheridan escorted Elly from the ballroom.

"If you have serious intentions toward Elly, you will call on my husband tomorrow at your earliest convenience. If, however, you aren't serious about my daughter, you would be very wise to stay as far away from my family as possible."

Brent gave Her Grace his most elegant bow. "Your meaning is quite clear."

The Duchess of Sheridan nodded, then turned away from him.

Brent responded before she took her first step. "Tell His Grace he can expect me at his earliest convenience."

The duchess halted, then continued across the ballroom floor.

CHAPTER 27

The two-week round of balls was finally at an end. Tonight was Harrison's engagement ball, the last of the four events to announce her brothers' engagements. Then she could return to The Down with her memories.

Elly watched the couples swirl around the dance floor and remembered the magical time she'd spent in Brent's arms. For a few exquisite moments he'd allowed her to feel whole, complete. With his arms supporting her she could pretend she was the same as any other female dancing in the arms of a handsome man. The same as she'd felt when he'd held her and taught her to play croquet. When she was in his arms, she didn't feel different from any other woman.

If only she'd never discovered the reason he'd made such an effort to give her two perfect weeks. If only he hadn't destroyed the memories he'd given her.

The four walls of the ballroom closed in around her and she rose from where she'd been since the ball to announce

Harrison's engagement to Cassie started. Thankfully, after tonight she could go home where she wouldn't be an oddity and no one would stare at her wherever she went. After tonight she could begin her plans to expand the stable area as she and Harrison had wanted to do for some time. Somehow she'd find a way to put her heart into it.

She made her way to the nearest exit and walked down the hallway to her father's study. She needed to be by herself. Her family had redoubled their efforts to include her in Harrison and Cassie's celebration. Her mother, father, or one of her sisters or brothers had stopped by at regular intervals all evening. They brought her something to eat or drink as an excuse to check on her, or just stopped to share a bit of gossip they'd heard while mingling. Even Aunt Gussie and Aunt Esther made a point to spend time with her. The pretense of convincing her family she was enjoying herself was exhausting. Even humiliating. Above all, depressing. Their attention made her feel like an emotional invalid as well as a physical one.

She opened the door and stepped into her father's study. Somehow, she'd survived George's betrothal ball, and Jules's, and Spencer's. She'd survive Harrison's, too. Then, she could go home, which should make her happy.

But going home meant she'd never see Brent again. She suddenly realized she'd miss him. He'd been to every engagement ball. He'd spent the majority of every evening trying to ease his way back into her life, trying to make her laugh. Trying to convince her he wasn't embarrassed being with her, that they made the perfect couple. She had to admit she enjoyed his humor and even looked forward to the way he teasingly tried to make her believe he loved her.

She smiled as she remembered his humorous remarks

from last night. She only had to withstand his attempt to win her over this one last night.

She walked to the fireplace and stared into the brightly burning flames in the grate. Last week at the Marquess of Crestonridge's ball she'd almost given in. His jovial personality and teasing banter were wearing her down. For a moment she'd forgotten how uncomfortable it would be to spend months every year enduring Society's critical comments and cruel remarks.

"They told me I'd find you in here."

Elly stiffened. She usually sensed his presence, but she'd been so lost in thought he'd surprised her. She readied her emotions for the jolt of seeing him, then turned around.

She thought she was prepared, but she wasn't. Her heart did a somersault.

He was as magnificently handsome as ever, and the expression in his eyes when he looked at her caused every nerve in her body to tingle. But tonight there was something serious in his expression. A look she'd only seen once before, and that had been when Waverley held her at the top of the stairs.

She swallowed hard.

It was the same look he'd had when he thought he might lose her.

"Your brother tells me you're leaving London in a few days."

"Yes. I'm going to The Down. I like it much better in the country."

"So do I. In fact, my staff is packing right now."

Elly couldn't hide her surprise. "You can't."

"Really?" He arched his brows. "Why ever not? I enjoy the country better than London, too. There are no matchmaking mamas there to try to trap me into relieving them of their daughter."

Elly smiled.

"My horses are there."

The smile stayed on her face.

"And no one is there to watch me nurse my broken heart."

Her smile died.

He crossed the room as if he weren't in any hurry and came to a halt at the other end of the fireplace. He propped one elbow on the mantel and faced her. "I came in search of you because there's something I need to tell you."

"Brent, plea—"

"Hear me out, Elly, and please, just this once, let me have my say."

Her stomach churned with unrelenting nervousness and she gripped the handle of her cane tighter.

"For the past several weeks, I've tried to cajole you into forgiving me. I thought if I used the charm I'd perfected since I was a green lad, I could make you forget how much I'd hurt you and how angry you were with me. But I was wrong." He slid one of the miniatures on the mantel from one spot to another, "You've left me no choice but to bare my soul."

He dropped his hands to his side and faced her. "I love you Elly. I'll never love anyone but you. I always dreamed I'd find the perfect woman – a woman to love, to have children with, and grow old with. But that was in my dreams. I never expected to find her in real life."

He pushed back his open jacket and eased his hands in his pockets. "Then I met you." He smiled a hollow grin. "It was as if you walked out of my dreams and appeared before me in real life.

"Oh, there was that silly agreement I made with your brother, but I didn't once consider you'd take exception to it. There wasn't a reason for you to find out what I'd agreed to, and if you did, I assumed you'd love me so much you'd brush it aside the same as I had." He paused. "But you didn't."

Elly took his moment of silence to gain control of her emotions. She couldn't do this. Refusing him was so much easier when he teased her and tried to make her see the humor in what had happened. Hearing him seriously admit he loved her and was afraid he'd lose her tore her heart in two.

"I've done everything I know to do to convince you that I love you. That I want to spend my life with you. That I want you to be the mother of my children. There's nothing more I can say or do." He laughed. "I certainly can't force you to marry me. So, I have decided there is only one option left me."

A stabbing of fear raced through her.

Brent paced the floor from the fireplace to her father's massive oak desk, then back again. "This is your brother's night. I will stay until his engagement is announced. Then, before I leave, I will ask you one final time to marry me. Whatever your answer, I will accept it."

Elly wanted to say something. She opened her mouth but couldn't find the words. Even if she found them, they wouldn't have done any good. Brent held out his hand to stop her from speaking.

"Please, don't give me your answer yet. I want to enjoy the evening with you. I want to walk with you through the crowded room and show you and everyone here how proud I am to have you at my side. I want to keep you close to me all night long so if this is the—"

He paused. "Well," he said, "I just want to have this one

night with you."

Tears filled her eyes. When she blinked away the wetness, she realized with clarity the *real* reason she rejected him. It wasn't because of the agreement he'd made with Harrison. Oh, it had hurt when she'd first discovered what they'd done, but eventually the pain wore off enough to admit that Harrison had formed his plan to save her from being hurt. And Brent had agreed to play his part because of the prize at the end. After all, he'd never met her. He had no idea they were going to fall in love.

Her breath caught in her throat. Yes, Brent loved her. Somewhere deep inside her she'd known it for a long, long time. Perhaps since the first day she challenged him to race. If not then, soon after.

She was the problem. *She* was the one who was afraid to let herself accept his love. *She* was the one who couldn't trust that anyone could love her because of her limp. *She* was the one who was at fault but she couldn't change what she knew would happen if she accepted his marriage proposal. As his wife, she'd be expected to attend functions like this and she'd be an embarrassment to him. Because of her, people would wonder why the magnificently perfect Earl of Charfield chose such a flawed wife. And eventually he'd hate her because of her imperfection.

Elly looked up at him as the first tear spilled over her lashes.

He stepped up to her and brushed the tears from her cheeks. "Don't cry, sweetheart. I know I haven't given you much to love." He leaned down and kissed her on the cheek. "I'm sorry."

He took her in his arms and held her.

She didn't have the courage to step away from him.

She wrapped her arms around him and for the first time, wondered if she could be brave enough to face her life with him. Wondered if she could overcome her fears and doubts and find the joy and happiness she knew she'd find as his wife. Wondered if—

But if she couldn't and this was their last night together, she wanted it to be a night she would always remember.

"Will you give me this one night, Elly?"

A myriad of doubts and fears raced through her. She wasn't sure she was brave enough to expose herself to the crowd of onlookers. And yet...to be held in his arms this one night. To have this one last gathering of memories to cherish forever. To know that for one perfect night she'd been loved.

She hesitated.

Just this one night.

Then held out her hand for him to take.

The broad smile on Brent's face was blinding.

He reached for her and tucked her close. "Thank you, sweetheart."

Together, they walked across the room. His gait matched hers perfectly, as if they were two halves of a whole, as if he was the support she needed to be perfect.

He wrapped his arm around her waist to be her anchor and kept her close to him.

The din of conversation grew louder as they reached the entrance to the ballroom. Her heart beat faster, blood thundered in her head. They would see her now. The crowd of onlookers would watch her enter the room on the arm of the Earl of Charfield. Everyone would focus on them as they walked toward them and—

She looked upward and met Brent's gaze. She wasn't

sure what she expected to see, but the overflowing love and adoration she saw stole her breath.

"Smile, sweetheart. I want everyone here to know how perfect we are for each other."

She gave him a smile she prayed indicated the depth of her love.

His smile broadened and he lifted her hand to his mouth. "Come, my love. I want the world to know you're mine."

Elly searched for an emotion to describe how she felt and the only word that came to mind was...perfect. For the first time in her adult life, she felt perfect. And Brent was the reason.

Because of his love and support, she was whole again.

She was loved.

———

The atmosphere in the ballroom was the same as every other social function but tonight was like nothing he'd ever experienced before. Tonight Elly was at his side.

Brent smiled at everyone they met and wanted to laugh out loud at the confused expressions on their faces. Elly had been right. She told him no one would believe he could love her and he could see they didn't. How blind they were. He could tell they didn't see Elly's strengths. They didn't realize how deserving she was of his love and how undeserving he was of hers.

He wanted to stand on the dais the Duke of Sheridan had erected to make the announcement of Harrison's engagement and shout to the world that he'd finally found the woman of his dreams. That he'd finally discovered the woman with whom he wanted to spend the rest of his life. But most of all, he wanted to tell everyone how much he loved her.

He looked at Elly as they made their way around the room. Her family was the first to make their way to her side to greet her. Brent could see by the excitement in their gazes they were overjoyed that Elly was part of the gathering instead of sitting in the shadows against the wall.

"You look beautiful," Cassie said, giving Elly a gentle hug. "So beautiful, in fact, that Lord Charfield pales in comparison."

Brent laughed. "Your assessment is perfect, my lady. Lady Elyssa far outshines me."

Brent gathered Elly closer. This was where she belonged – on his arm, at his side. As his wife.

They visited with her family a little longer, then made their way through the crowd. He knew the stares and whispers made her nervous. Her grip on his arm tightened each time someone new came up to them. When they reached the open doors that led outside, he stepped with her onto the cool terrace.

"Are you getting tired?" he asked when they were alone.

"Not really. I'm just..."

"Overwhelmed?" he asked, finishing her sentence for her.

"Perhaps a little."

She smiled, but there was a hint of unease in her eyes. A flash of terror identical to the fear he'd seen that first night when her brother suggested Brent escort her in to dinner. She wasn't comfortable with so much attention. "You're doing marvelously, sweetheart."

"That's because I haven't made a spectacle of myself - yet."

"You won't. And if you do, we'll shrug it off tonight and laugh about it in the morning."

Her eyes opened wide as if what he suggested was impossible. "Come here," he said and tucked her near. He took the cane from her arm and leaned it against the railing, then wrapped his arms around her. "I love you, Elly.

"You—"

He pressed his finger to her lips to silence her.

"Nothing is important but you and me. Anything else can be ignored."

"But it can't, Brent. It's only a matter of time until something happens. You've seen the look in people's eyes when they look at me – the pity. You've seen them stare at my clumsiness when I walk through the room."

"That's because they don't know you. They don't love you like I do."

She smiled. "And I love you. But love isn't enough. My brothers love me, but every time I attempt something and fail, I see the pity in their eyes, the guilt and regret on their faces. The day will come when you'll wear that same look and I can't bear to see it."

"So what's the alternative? We both live our lives alone and lonely because you aren't brave enough to take the risk that I won't fail you? Are you really willing to throw away the thousands of ways we can prove the love we have for each other because of the few moments of embarrassment?"

He brushed his fingers down her cheek. "Elly, those few times will be insignificant. Our love is all that's important. Living our lives together is all that's important. Loving each other and the children we will have together is all that's important."

He stopped and cupped his hands on each side of her face. "Please, trust me. Do you think I'm not afraid you might come to resent me when I ask you to take risks you aren't willing to take?"

He pressed a gentle kiss to her forehead. "There are risks for both of us but I'm willing to take them. And I hope you are too because I can't continue like this. I love you. I want to spend my life with you. But I need you to want the same thing." He took a deep breath and prepared to issue the ultimatum that might destroy a future with her.

"I told you I'd stay until Harrison's engagement is announced. After your father announces Harrison's engagement, I will ask you one final time to marry me. Whatever your answer, I will accept it. If you say no, I'll walk out of your life and never come back."

He pulled her into his arms and held her. "But please think long and hard about what you'll force both of us to give up if your answer is no."

"Brent, I—"

"Shh," he whispered. He kissed her once more, then lifted his head. "Listen. They're playing a waltz."

She shook her head. "No, Brent. I can't. Not here. People will see us."

"You can, Elly. You have me to rely on."

He saw the question in her eye, the doubts, the fear. But he'd issued a challenge, now he prayed her pride wouldn't allow her to back down. "No one will see us." He held out his hand and waited.

She looked to the open doorway. "My brothers are watching right now."

"George?"

She smiled. "Spence."

"Good. I want him to see what a remarkable feat you've

accomplished."

She looked into his eyes, then lifted her trembling hands, slid them up the front of his jacket and wound them around his neck.

He pulled her close to allow her to anchor herself like she'd done before and wrapped his arms around her waist.

He held her scandalously close, then slowly moved to the music.

She turned her gaze to where her brother stood. "Jules is watching, too."

"Don't look at them," he whispered. "No one matters except you and me."

She lifted her chin and locked her gaze with his.

He held her close and moved to the music.

"Are they still there?" she asked after a few turns.

He smiled. "Yes, and so are your parents and the twins."

She looked to where her family stood.

Perhaps if he had realized that the awe-filled looks of amazement on her siblings' faces would have such an affect on her he might have tightened his grip. Perhaps if he hadn't been so lost in the deep richness of her eyes, he would have anticipated that the sight of her mother swiping tears from her eyes would break her concentration. But he'd been so consumed with emotions he couldn't explain, he didn't realize what was about to happen until it was too late. Elly lost her footing and stumbled forward.

He caught her, but not before she'd nearly fallen to the ground.

Her arms flailed in desperation as she struggled to regain her balance, but her lame foot was no good to her.

Brent reached for her and lifted her into his arms. "Are you all right?" he asked, tucking her close to him.

She looked to the open doorway. Her entire family stood there as well as a large gathering of guests. The expressions on their faces could only be described as embarrassment. The expression on Elly's was mortification. Her cheeks turned a deep red as she struggled to hide her shame.

She stood before him. "Are you satisfied, Brent? Is this the performance our guests will come to expect when invited to our home? The Countess of Charfield stumbling clumsily from one room to another?"

"Elly, no. That's not at all—"

Before he could explain, Harrison and George were at her side. Jules and Spence were close behind. They flanked her two on a side and eased her onto the nearest chair.

Brent waited until her family was assured she was all right, then stepped near her. "Elly?"

She looked at him, the hurt and embarrassment visible on her face. "I can't be what you want me to be. Please don't ask me to be."

He stepped near enough to her so she had to look up. "What is that? What do you think I want you to be?"

"Perfect." She swiped her hand through the air. "I thought suffering through a Season was the most humiliating time of my life." She laughed. "Now I know it wasn't. Pretending I'm as normal as everyone else is a thousand times more embarrassing."

"You are embarrassed?" he said loud enough that her family looked at him. "How can being the bravest, most courageous, most desirable woman in the world be embarrassing? How can determination and resolve be humiliating? The person who learned to walk when the doctors said she wouldn't, and rode when the doctors said she couldn't, wouldn't be embarrassed because of a misstep.

"The woman who trusted me to keep her from falling when she learned to swing a croquet mallet, and relied on me to be her anchor so she could waltz, that woman wouldn't have allowed something as insignificant as a near fall to affect her. That woman would have laughed in the face of defeat and risen to try again."

Elly stared at him with the same shocked expression as her family. Finally, she whispered, "Perhaps I'm not that woman any longer."

He looked deep into her eyes. He'd pushed her too far. He'd expected too much from her. But, didn't she know that with him at her side, there was nothing she couldn't do. "That would be a shame, my love."

She shook her head, then gave her father a frantic look. "Help me inside, Father. Please."

Brent watched her father assist her in rising, then followed behind her family as they surrounded her and took her away. He stopped when he reached the doorway, not sure he could endure the rest of the evening.

He'd promised to wait until the announcement of Harrison's engagement, but he wasn't sure his heart could survive that long.

———

Elly clutched her father's arm as they walked through the ballroom. Her family had rushed to her side as they always did when she stumbled, but tonight the gesture of kindness made her feel more like a cripple than ever.

"The twins told me you've learned to play croquet," her father said when they reached the far side of the dais. It was time to announce Harrison's engagement. "They said you are nearly as accomplished as Harrison." Her father laughed. "Remind me to challenge you next time we're at The Down."

"Father—"

Her father lifted his finger to halt her words and walked with her to the corner where they were hidden from full view of the guests. He let her steady herself with her cane, then stood in font of her. He crossed his hands over his chest and leveled her with a most regal look. "How much do you love Lord Charfield?"

She lowered her gaze and looked to a spot on the floor to her right.

"I asked you a question, Elyssa. Is refusing his offer worth the pain and loneliness you will both suffer for the rest of your lives?"

Elly shook her head. "What if I become such an embarrassment that Brent eventually hates me?"

"Oh, Elyssa. The person you've always been wouldn't even have entertained that thought. She would have grabbed hold of the gift Charfield offered her with both hands and lived life to the fullest. She would have done everything in her power to make the man she loved the happiest man alive. Instead of running from the challenges he placed in front of her, she would have embraced them and issued challenges of her own."

Her father placed a finger beneath her chin and tipped her head back so she had to look into his eyes. "You've always been someone I've been proud to call my daughter. What you thought of as embarrassing clumsiness was only that in your eyes. Never in your mother's eyes. Never in mine. Never in the eyes of anyone who loved you."

Elly swallowed hard. "Oh, Papa. What am I to do?"

"Whatever you can live with, Elly."

CHAPTER 27

Brent stood at the side of the ballroom nursing the drink a footman had offered him. This wasn't the time to drink himself senseless. That would come later. When Elly walked out of his life forever.

He watched her family gather on the opposite side of the room. Elly stood beside her father, no doubt explaining that Brent had embarrassed her once too often. That she didn't trust him enough to believe he could love her.

Then her father placed his hands on her shoulders and leaned in to say something. She turned her head, her eyes finding him in the crowded room. She shook her head, then stepped into her father's arms.

His broken heart lay shattered at his feet. It was all he could do to remain until Harrison's engagement was announced.

If it weren't for the fact that this was the last time he'd see Elly, he'd leave. But he couldn't force himself to give up even one minute of this last night with her.

He focused his gaze to where she stood on the dais at the opposite end of the ballroom. The Duke and Duchess of Sheridan took center stage with their children and their fiancées and husbands surrounding them. The Marquess of Fellingsdown stood to the right of the stage with his future bride, Lady Lathamton, at his side.

But none of Elly's siblings or their partners held his attention. Only Elly.

She'd never looked as beautiful as she did tonight.

She wore a dark green gown that accented her mahogany hair. The strings of tiny pearls wound through her silken tresses made him want to gather her curls in his hand and hold them.

She leaned on her cane like she always did, but it was such a part of her she wouldn't look natural without it.

She wouldn't be his Elly.

Her gaze hadn't found him once since she'd taken her place on the platform, but he hadn't expected her to look at him. She'd made her feelings known when she'd left on her father's arm.

He knew then that she'd made her choice.

Now if he could live with her decision.

The ache inside his chest made him doubt he could. Perhaps in ten years or twenty the discomfort wouldn't be so bad. But that was unlikely. What he feared most was that the hurt would grow stronger. He wasn't sure he was courageous enough to live with that much pain.

He sucked in a deep breath and held it.

The Duke of Sheridan stepped to the front of the platform. In a moment he would announce the betrothal of his son, then everyone would gather to congratulate the happy couple.

There would be no reason for Elly to stay longer. No reason for him to stay either.

He braced his shoulders and pretended to be as happy as the rest of the guests in the room.

The Duke of Sheridan took his place. "Welcome, friends." He held up his hands to quiet the crowd. "Thank you for attending this most special night."

There was a robust round of applause.

"It's not often parents get to see their family nearly double in a matter of a few short months like Her Grace and I have."

A chorus of laughter as well as a spattering of applause echoed from the ballroom and the duke tucked his wife's hand in his.

"Tonight, though, is a most extraordinary culmination to what has, without a doubt, been the most exciting round of events anyone could imagine."

There was another round of applause.

"All of you think you know why you were invited. And you're correct."

The crowd cheered.

"But that announcement is only part of the reason we are celebrating. I have another disclosure to make that is equally, if not even *more* exciting."

A hush fell over the crowd and everyone seemed to move closer to the dais to make sure they caught the duke's surprising announcement.

"Before I divulge this special secret, let me preface my announcement by making a statement only one of you in this room will understand."

The duke paused, then turned his gaze to where Brent stood.

Brent's heart raced.

"The answer," he said, prolonging the rest of his sentence an agonizingly long length of time, "is...yes."

Brent's heart skipped one beat, then a second. His gaze darted to Elly and his heart threatened to burst. There was a smile on her face as well as an unmistakable look of love and affection.

It took him a moment to move. Then, on legs that trembled beneath him, he made his way through the crowd toward the dais.

When Brent reached the platform, the duke continued.

"It's not every father and mother who have the honor of announcing the betrothal of not one, but two of their children the same evening. The duchess and I have been given that honor."

The duke stopped and Brent was glad he waited until the crowd realized what his presence on the dais meant.

"It gives me the greatest pleasure to announce the engagement of my daughter, Lady Elyssa, to Brentan Montgomery, Earl of Charfield. And my son, Harrison Prescott, Marquess of Fellingsdown, to Lady Lathamton."

Squeals of shock and a rousing applause followed the announcement, but he didn't pay any attention to it. He was too focused on holding Elly in his arms and kissing her.

"You'll never be sorry, Elly," he said over the shouts of well-wishers and the thunderous applause that seemed to grow louder with each passing second.

"How could I be?" She touched his cheek with the fingers of one hand and wrapped the other arm around his neck. "I have your love."

Brent gathered her into his arms. He wasn't sure where her

cane was, but it no longer mattered.

From now on, she had him to lean on.